WinterKill

Joyce K. Walsh

Spinsters Ink
2009

Spinsters Ink
P.O. Box 242
Midway, Florida 32343

Printed in the United States of America on acid-free paper
First Edition

Editor: Katherine V. Forrest
Cover designer: LA Callaghan

ISBN-10: 1-935226-00-2
ISBN-13: 978-1-935226-00-0

For John

With special thanks
to Peg Holzemer for producing my play Gooseberry Tarts, and
to David Porter for suggesting it could be a novel.

About the Author

Joyce Walsh is the author of three mystery novels (Juckets, Swamp Yankees, Bog Men) in "The Pittsley County Chronicles" series. She is also the recipient of a Massachusetts Artist's Grant in Playwriting as well as a fellowship from the Artists Foundation of Massachusetts and an American Regional Theatre Award; her plays have been performed in Boston and New York. Joyce lives in Lakeville, Massachusetts with her husband, two dogs who run the household, and assorted woodland creatures—including four generations of red-shouldered hawks who expect to be fed several times a day. (International animal protectionist, John Walsh, it may be known, has rescued the greatest number of animals since Noah.) Additional information about the author may be found on her website at www.joycewalsh.com.

win-ter-kill

1. *to kill by or die from exposure to the cold of winter, as wheat.*
2. *an act or instance of winterkilling.*
3. *death resulting from winterkilling.*

VERMONT

NEW HAMPSHIRE

Preston
Weekes

RALEIGH, NH

SQUANTUM
LAKE

Madeline
Abbott

Celia
Eastman

WICKESSETT, VT

Chester
Weekes

Muskataqua

N

W E

S

Illustrated by Sarah Bender

CHAPTER ONE

"Thou know'st 'tis common; all that lives must die,
Passing through nature onto eternity."

The afternoon sun bounced off the lake ice like a bullet, sending shafts of frigid light deep into the woods and, along its trajectory, illuminating the bronze statue of an Indian woman just above the shoreline. Set on a marble base, she stood erect in fringed deerskin and boots, with arms stretched out over the lake toward the west. The plaque at the base was inscribed:

Muskataqua
b. (?) - d. 1887
The last of her kind.

There were sizable footprints emerging from the woods to and around the statue, then back through the trees. The snow had been brushed from Muskataqua's upturned face and the icicles that had hung from her arms like stalactites had been knocked away.

A Model-B Touring Car careened twelve miles per hour downhill around the frozen lake, the snow piled high as hedgerows along the sides of the narrow road. As the young driver chattered amiably away at his silent passenger, the elderly woman had a stricken look on her face. Not only was she apprehensive about the driver's cavalier attention to his driving, the redoubtable Madeline Abbott was even more dismayed that someone of his station in life was attempting to converse with her.

Finally arriving at their destination, Madeline paid the driver from her coin purse, closed her navy leather pocketbook with a dismissive snap, and walked briskly up the path to the green house. She knocked three times with the brass doorknocker monogrammed with an *E*, waited briefly, then continued to knock steadily until the door was opened.

"My goodness, Georgie, what took you so long? I could freeze to death waiting on the doorstep!"

Georgie Skates looked at a loss for words, his eyes downcast in a face whose features resembled those of the bronze statue. Madeline, at sixty-five, twenty years his senior, was still a striking woman— tall, spare, quick, and as upright and unyielding as a white ash. His shoulders hunched, Georgie mutely stepped aside.

It was slightly later that same afternoon when David McKay drove his blue Plymouth coupé the five miles from town toward Celia Eastman's house. His tire chains crunched and rattled over the packed snow atop the dirt and gravel beneath.

It was early spring 1932, five months after he first arrived in Raleigh, New Hampshire, to research his new novel. He had weathered his first New England winter, made a dear friend with a useful library, and fallen in love, as yet unrequited. Because of the latter, his eagerness today to share good news with Celia was overshadowed by his impatience to see her companion again. David's eyes brightened as he contrived how this time he might manage to be alone with Mira, no matter how briefly. Mira, the embodiment of the woman he had conjured in fiction who was as real and as beautiful as he had ever imagined her. Mira, his Maria. A smile played on his lips as he thought of her raven hair, her gentian eyes . . .

An insistent whirring of a radial engine intruded on his fancy. David frowned and pushed away a forelock of blond hair as he peered upward into the cloudless sky. A yellow bi-wing Stearman skimmed high above the tall snowcapped pines. The pilot was leaning out of the open cockpit, the icy air whipping across his face, holding onto the struts of the plane to get a better view of the hilly countryside.

At the lofty height of two hundred feet, the airman would take in both New Hampshire and Vermont at a single glance, encompassing all four homes on Squantum Lake. There were two small cedar-shake cottages, one at the north end of the lake and its mirror image at the south; opposite and alike, even the smoke from their brick chimneys puffed up in parallel plumes. The other two houses at the east and west, one green and the other white, were larger and more formal. They stood facing each other like queens on a chessboard. The green house belonged to Celia Eastman and, along with both cottages, was on the New Hampshire side.

The white house on the Vermont side was perched throne-like on higher ground above a series of steps and landings leading down to a dock at the lake's edge. Next to the dock, a wooden Old Town canoe was stored upside down on cement blocks. The canoe and the wooden stairs were layered with crusted undisturbed snow. The house, and indeed it seemed the very air surrounding it, belonged to Madeline Abbott. He'd heard of her through Celia but had not yet met the eccentric friend of his friend. Nor had he met the Weekes brothers who seemed to keep only their own company and not each other's.

David clutched and braked then shifted into neutral to watch as the pilot, braving the cold air aloft and the radiant cold from the still-frozen water below, swooped down to nearly treetop level. It could only be Matthias Carson. Anyone that bold, David reluctantly concluded, had a willful determination that was quite above the ordinary. Such scope of ambition. So like Matthias Carson, he admitted, so unlike me. His grip on the steering wheel tightened.

From the breakfast discussion at David's boardinghouse, he knew Carson's purpose that day had been not merely the pleasure of being airborne and viewing the lakeside geography. The lawyer was returning from a neighboring county where he had expected to get an overview of inaccessible land involved in a boundary dispute. He represented the complainant in the lawsuit and he carried both land and aerial maps of the territory in question, and a camera in his flight bag. He intended to win the case for his client. And of course he would. Carson was a man bred for detail. He made his living at it. Those who knew him said he could count your fillings as you smiled. From Yankees, this was a commendation. Only David thought otherwise.

The plane circled, turned, and dropped down to buzz his car in a provocative gesture that David interpreted as a taunt.

"I know you see me," David muttered under his breath.

His frown deepening, he ground the gears as he shifted back into third and continued on to Celia's.

Madeline swept into the living room ahead of the lumbering Georgie. He followed aimlessly as though intending to announce her if only she would let him.

"Celia, darling, what a ride! What a ride! That driver! Lord, they can't keep four wheels on the ground in this state of yours. I felt like the Russian wolves were snapping at our heels."

From her wheelchair Celia Eastman held out her hands in greeting. "It's so good to see you, too, Maddie, after such a long winter."

Madeline unceremoniously draped her navy woolen coat over Georgie's arm and tossed her purse onto the sofa next to a dark-haired young woman sitting with a notebook in her lap.

"Long and dismal." Madeline took Celia's hands and bent to kiss her on the cheek. "How have you been, my dear?"

"As usual." Celia smiled engagingly. "I hibernate through winter like a bear." Her white hair was framed in light from behind by the bay window overlooking the lake.

"And who is this?" Madeline inquired.

Without seeming to have noticed and not looking in her direction, Madeline observed that the maroon velvet sofa seemed to enhance the color of the young woman's eyes. She wore a simple white middy blouse with its sailor-collar neatly pressed, and a navy skirt flared just below the knees. Quite common, Madeline thought.

"Do you still need me, Miz Eastman?" Georgie asked rocking back and forth.

"Oh, I'm sorry, Georgie, I didn't realize you were still here. Certainly you may go." As he turned to leave, Celia added, "Mira will fix supper tonight. So if there's anything you'd like to do, you're free to do it." At his baffled look, she explained, "Mira's going to prepare a special diet. Not that there's anything wrong with what you fix, Georgie. But this is supposed to do some special something for my innards."

"Increase red blood cells," the young woman offered.

"Increase red blood cells," Celia repeated to Madeline with a sly smile.

Georgie muttered a glum "Yes, ma'am" and left with Madeline's coat to prepare their tea.

Madeline arched her eyebrows. "What's wrong with your cells, Celia?"

"My doctor says they're low. That's why I've been so weak."

Madeline assessed the dark circles under her friend's eyes and her bluish lips. "Who is this doctor who talks about cells?"

"Roland Niles. Do you know him?"

"No," Madeline said dismissively and gestured toward the young woman. "And this is . . . ?"

"Oh, my goodness, I'm sorry. I'm getting so forgetful. Madeline, may I present Miss Mira Webster? Mira, this is Miss Abbott who lives across the lake."

"Vermont side," Madeline asserted with a sharp look at the young woman's bare collarbone.

"How do you do, Miss Abbott." Mira folded her hands in her lap.

Madeline fixed her gaze on Celia. "And who *is* she?"

"Mira is my nurse, amanuensis, cook, everything."

"Where is she from?"

"Oss-ippee," Mira answered.

Madeline pursed her lips. Was there a slightly disrespectful edge to that voice? She wasn't quite certain.

"And I'm lucky to have her," Celia quickly affirmed. "Mira dear, you don't mind if Miss Abbott and I have a little visit together, do you?"

"Oh no, Miss Eastman." She placed the ledger on the coffee table. "Will you have your tea now, Miss Abbott?"

"Of course I'll have tea." Madeline turned to Celia. "English, is it?"

Celia nodded and Madeline shook her head. "One of my ancestors dumped it in Boston Harbor. One of yours too, probably."

As Celia chuckled in response, Mira hastily retreated to the kitchen.

Madeline moved about the room, taking inventory. Not an item had changed since her last visit. Nor in the years she'd known Celia. Nor, she suspected, in all of Celia's life. The furniture was still the same Victorian furniture with faded maroon upholstery, not out of frugality but simply that the owner paid little attention to such things. Madeline pointed to the ledger.

"What is she writing there, Celia?"

"Oh, that's mine. I'm compiling the town history for our centennial next year. Mira's helping me."

"Really."

Madeline picked up the notebook and scanned it perfunctorily. In truth, she paid scant attention to the history of Vermont, much less that of New Hampshire, even though her library was stocked with reference books that had been her father's. She had lived most of her life in Massachusetts, whose history she felt she knew well enough.

She dropped the ledger back on the sofa. "Anything noteworthy?"

"In some ways, I suppose, Muskataqua was our most noteworthy resident," Celia answered. "She was an Indian princess, after all."

"Indeed." Madeline blinked her eyes slowly in evident doubt.

"Well, I found something regal about her. Even in poverty. She just seemed so . . . dispossessed."

"You actually knew her?" Madeline asked in surprise. "You never mentioned it."

With effort, Celia wheeled herself closer. "She was living here when Father and Mother bought this land seventy-five years ago—before I was born—so they let her stay. Her little shack was in the clearing where the statue is now. When I was little, Mother would make up food baskets for Father and me to deliver to her every week. And when I got older, I made them up and brought them to her myself. Sometimes she would come out of her shack, and sometimes she wouldn't. And sometimes we'd just talk through the window—her on the inside, me on the outside. She'd tell me stories about the things as they used to be. I think now, that she must have been quite lonely."

"Well, if that is the highlight of your town pamphlet, it's not exactly *The Pickwick Papers*, is it?"

"Hardly," Celia said with a wry smile.

"I used to do some writing, you know. Years ago, I kept a journal. That was when I had something worth recording. Now I give myself over to knitting and reading French cookbooks. Imagine! Life has become very tedious."

"Then you must find a way to make it less so."

"I scold. That is my amusement now. Don't I do it well?"

"Flawlessly," Celia answered as she struggled to wheel herself nearer the coffee table.

Madeline studied her friend closely. "You look very tired and pale, dear. Do you feel all right?"

"I'm fine. Please sit down, Madeline. It would make us both more comfortable."

Madeline complied, sitting on the sofa where Mira had sat, smoothing her navy blue gabardine dress fastidiously over her knees so the hem draped down past her black-stockinged ankles to her black-laced shoes.

"So tell me, dear, what tasty morsels has Georgie prepared for us today?"

"Gooseberry tarts."

"Oooh, that's nice, I love gooseberries."

"I told him he must not make almond tarts because Miss Abbott says almonds are only for holidays."

Madeline ignored this gentle jibe. "You are so lucky to have Georgie. I've had that stupid girl—Alva, Elva—whatever she calls herself. Hopeless. Couldn't boil water without a recipe. I had to let her go."

Georgie reentered with an antique silver tea service. On the filigreed tray were delicate pink bone-china cups and saucers and a platter of hot pastries, perfectly golden tarts with seams of bubbling syrup. As he set the tray on the coffee table, Madeline unceremoniously plucked a tart from the platter as though it were not impolite.

"Just on the perfect stroke. I'm famished."

Georgie lifted the teapot by the handle wrapped in a pink napkin. "Should I pour it, ma'am?" he asked Celia.

"Yes, quickly, Georgie," Celia said dramatically, "Miss Abbott is famished."

As he poured, Madeline relished her tart silently. After Georgie left, she dabbed at her mouth with her napkin, then folded it in her lap before leveling her gaze at Celia.

"So tell me the truth, Celia, what's going on here? Why are you doctoring?"

"Well . . ." Celia shrugged, sipping her tea. "Right after Christmas I started feeling poorly. I mentioned it to Mr. Carson and he—"

"Who is Mr. Carson?"

"Matthias Carson. My lawyer."

"Since when?"

"Recently. Anyway he recommended Dr. Niles—"

"The cell doctor."

"—and Dr. Niles felt I needed a nurse—"

"Is she an actual nurse?"

"—and Mira's been very helpful. But I don't seem to be getting better."

"What's wrong with you?" Madeline added milk to her tea and took a sip.

"He hasn't said exactly."

Madeline lowered her teacup in astonishment. "Surely he must tell you if you ask."

"I don't ask."

"Why not?"

"I don't really care to know the particulars."

"But Celia!"

"It's not important. I have plenty of medicine and there will be no more talk of doctors."

Madeline scowled her concession. "In that case, tell me about this lawyer you've found."

Celia sipped the last of her tea. "Matthias? He's only been here a year but he's already made quite a name for himself."

"Where's he from? Oss-ippee?" She mimicked Mira's rural inflection.

"Boston, originally."

"A Brahmin?"

"I don't believe he's a Brahmin, Madeline." Celia refilled her teacup but still did not touch a pastry.

"Then what's so marvelous about him?"

"Well, he has a lot of clients. And he's on the town board of selectmen."

"A lawyer-politician?" Madeline sniffed. "Those are secondhand goods."

"You are most wonderfully opinionated, Miss Abbott."

"Of course. I think tolerance is greatly overrated."

Celia laughed softly. "Dear Maddie, without you, there would be no condiments in my life whatsoever."

Madeline reached for her second tart just as the door knocker sounded.

Celia registered surprise. "It must be David. I completely forgot he was coming today."

"Who?"

"My Californian. He arrived in Raleigh last December. You remember, I wrote to you about him in my Christmas card."

"Oh, yes, the dime-novelist." Madeline wiped her lips on the pink linen napkin as though the very words were distasteful. "What in the world do you want with him?"

"He uses my library and I enjoy his company. You'll like him, too. You'll see."

"A Californian?" Madeline said, as though liking such an individual were unimaginable.

A skeptical expression lingered on Madeline's face as the young man bounded into the room, his blond hair disheveled, his eyes feverishly blue.

"Guess what, Celia! I got it!" he announced enthusiastically. But seeing the forbidding-looking visitor, he brought himself up short. "I'm sorry, I'm interrupting you."

"Not at all. Come in, come in." Celia waved him forward. "Congratulations, David, good for you!" She patted the arm of the sofa. "Come and sit with us and have some tea."

"No, thank you. I won't stay today. But I wanted to tell you the good news about the advance."

"Advance?" Madeline asked Celia.

"From his publisher," she explained. "Madeline, may I present Mr. David McKay? David, this is my dear friend, Miss Madeline Abbott who lives across the lake. In Hill House."

"Vermont side," Madeline said imperiously.

He extended his hand. "How do you do? I live in the Kingdom of New Hampshire myself."

She offered a limp hand in return, which she felt he persisted in holding longer than well-bred. "I thought you were a Californian." Madeline pointedly withdrew her hand.

"One migration only. My parents were from Bismarck, North Dakota."

"I suppose everyone in California is from somewhere else."

"Aren't we all? Us non-Indians?"

As Madeline rolled her eyes to Celia, the other woman quickly added, "David is writing a book about the Abenaki Indians who once lived in this area."

"Oh. Is that sort of thing publishable?"

"My editor tells me it is," David answered.

"Have you written other . . . books?"

"I wrote a fictionalized account of the Bickford murder. She came from Vermont, too, you may recall."

"No."

"Well, my book is called *The Descent of Maria Danforth*. I changed the name from Bickford to Danforth. Perhaps you read it?"

"I don't read those kind of novels. Was it popular?"

"Well—" he faltered.

"Well, I certainly enjoyed it," Celia said. "David's new book is about a young Abenaki brave whose father is a tribal chief. His uncle kills his father in order to take his wife and become the new chief."

David sat down on the arm of the sofa. "Then Nawasta pretends to be the ghost of his father and accuses his uncle of murdering him, and the uncle runs off, never to be seen again."

"Sounds like *Hamlet*," Madeline said brusquely as she reached for the largest pastry on the tray.

David hesitated. "I suppose it does, in a way."

Madeline pondered between bites of her gooseberry tart. "That ghost business with the uncle. That wasn't proof positive though, was it?"

"Well, no. But Nawasta knew his uncle was guilty. At least for the purpose of the tale."

"Whereas in real life," Celia said somewhat wistfully, "things are seldom that simple."

"But that's the beauty of a novel," David replied. "You can make things happen the way you want them to."

Celia chuckled. "I'm afraid I don't have that liberty with my stories for the Historical Society."

"Then you should try a novel," David suggested.

"I'm afraid I don't have the imagination for it."

"Don't be silly, darling," Madeline said, "how much imagination does it take to change a name here and there?"

David grimaced.

"I think there's a little more to it than that, Maddie," Celia said. "And David is a very talented writer. Some day, he'll be famous in his own right."

"Doubtless," Madeline replied.

David grinned painfully and stood up. "Well, I don't want to interrupt your visit and I've got to be getting back home to work. I'll come by tomorrow, Celia, if that's all right."

"Of course, David. But stop in the kitchen before you leave and get some tarts to take with you. Georgie just made them. Tell Mira I asked her to make up a package up for you."

"Thank you, I will. I'd never pass up a chance to have Georgie's desserts. Miss Abbott, a pleasure to meet you. Good-bye, Celia."

After he left, Celia's voice dropped conspiratorially as she leaned closer to Madeline. "I'm trying to make a match between him and Mira," she confided.

"Oh, for heaven's sake, Celie, really."

"Why not? He's a sweet young man, don't you think?"

"Charming."

"I don't believe you mean that, Madeline Abbott, you're being very naughty."

"I just wonder what he wants."

"What do you mean?"

Madeline sipped her tea noncommittally.

"Madeline Elizabeth Abbott," Celia said sternly.

Madeline yielded with a shrug. "There's a look about him. Underneath all that boyish charm."

"He's young, Maddie. That's what it's like. Don't you remember?"

"Darling," Madeline replied eyeing another pastry, "I can barely remember menopause."

As the afternoon progressed, their conversation continued onto topics social and political, in particular the upcoming United States presidential election. Madeline lamented that after Mr. Herbert Hoover trounced that Irish Catholic, Alfred E. Smith—from New York, no less—in the last election, now he was faced with the "damn Democrat" Roosevelt, who was rumored to be Jewish. In fact, neither Catholic nor Jewish was as repugnant to Madeline as Democrat. The whole idea of a Depression was nothing but party propaganda.

"Mr. Hoover says we have a slight recession, but prosperity is just around the corner," Madeline concluded.

"Then Mr. Hoover hasn't looked at the breadlines outside the White House windows."

And so it went for the next hour, with Madeline decrying the usurpation of the social order by the lower classes with Celia contrapuntal at every turn. Suddenly, in the midst of conversation, Celia bent over holding her sides.

"Celia? What's the matter? What's wrong? Celia?"

But Celia did not respond and her breathing became irregular.

Madeline rose swiftly and rushed to the door of the living room. "Girl! Girl! Come quick! Miss Eastman's ill!"

Within seconds, Mira entered. Celia had slumped over the side of her wheelchair. Mira moved quickly and efficiently to Celia's side, motioning Madeline out of the way. She knelt down next to her charge.

"It's all right, Miss Eastman, it's Mira. I have your medicine."

She deftly set Celia upright but her head lolled back and her eyes were still closed. Mira laid the medicine bottle and spoon on the table and extracted another smaller bottle from her pocket.

Madeline watched anxiously as the girl removed the stopper from the smaller bottle and passed the smelling salts under Celia's nose. The pale woman inhaled the acrid odor and sputtered to semiconsciousness. Mira put the small bottle back into her pocket and immediately uncorked the medicine bottle. She poured a portion of the brown liquid into the spoon and placed it between Celia's lips.

"Swallow now, Miss Eastman."

She gently held Celia's head back and the patient swallowed involuntarily. After a short while, Celia finally sat up and began to take deep breaths.

"That's better," Mira said.

"Are you all right, Celie?" Madeline said, although she did not know what she might do for her friend if she wasn't all right. To her relief, Celia nodded, albeit weakly.

Mira rose to her feet. "I think you should lie down for a while, Miss Eastman."

Celia nodded and then turned to Madeline. "Forgive me, Maddie," she said in a quaking voice.

"Don't be silly, dear, you just rest and regain your strength."

"I'll put her to bed," Mira informed Madeline perfunctorily. She then wheeled Celia out of the room.

Madeline stood watching. She could use some smelling salts herself. She hadn't known her friend was so very sick. She did not like the way this girl had pushed her out of the way. Or the manner in which she took command. This whole thing was very disturbing.

Her eyes fell upon the open medicine bottle still on the table where Mira had left it. It was a narrow, rectangular glass bottle without any markings. Madeline picked it up for a closer inspection. Half empty. She sniffed at the contents. Unpleasant smell. Familiar but unidentifiable. What did it remind her of?

She was sniffing it a second time when Georgie appeared at the doorway. Instinctively, she put down the bottle like a guilty child and then admonished herself for her reaction.

Georgie entered tentatively, his broad shoulders slumped in worry. "Is Miz Eastman all right?"

Madeline debated how to answer him and finally said, "Miss Eastman had some sort of pain in her stomach, but it passed."

His round eyes were serious and unblinking. His face sagged.

"Do you think it was my suppers?"

She was about to scoff but saw the look of alarm on his face. "I shouldn't think so, Georgie."

"I worried that might be the cause of it. She didn't want my cooking no more. Just hers." His reference to Mira was tinged with resentment.

"This girl, Georgie, what's her name? Mira? Is she good to Miss Eastman?"

Georgie shuffled his feet. "I guess she is. She don't let me stay around long."

"Does anyone know her, Georgie?"

"No, only the doctor."

"And does anyone know the doctor?"

"No, only Mr. Carson."

"And I don't know him either. A world of strangers."

"Yes, ma'am, they don't talk to me."

"Used to be, one would know all the professional people. Most likely, you knew three generations of their family as well."

As Mira reentered the room, Madeline heard the sound of a car stopping outside. Perhaps her ride had come.

"If that's my driver," she instructed Georgie, "tell him to wait. I'm not ready yet."

"Yes, ma'am," Georgie replied, heading for the door.

Madeline turned toward Mira, resenting having to ask this upstart about her friend.

"How is she?"

"Better. She'll sleep for a while now."

Mira recorked the medicine bottle and put it and the spoon into her pocket.

"I want to know what's really going on with Miss Eastman."

"The doctor says it's just taking a long time to recover from her illness." Mira did not look directly at her.

"Will she recover?"

"Yes, of course."

"You know that for a fact?"

"Well . . . yes."

"Are you a certified nurse, Miss Webster?"

Mira jerked her head up. "I don't have a certificate. But I have experience."

"And you work for this Dr. Niles?"

"Yes."

"And does he have a certificate? Or just experience?"

Mira squared her shoulders. "Dr. Niles has a medical degree from a university."

Madeline was about to say more, but stopped abruptly as a darkly attractive man in his thirties appeared at the doorway. Under his dark gray woolen coat and fedora, he wore clothes more befitting a safari than for formal calling, but he carried a black leather folder.

He walked across the room with the proprietary ease of a resident cat. He glanced at Madeline without registering any expression and then spoke directly to Mira. "I just got back from the airport. How is she?"

"She's come around. But I've called Roland anyway. He'll be here as soon as he can. I've put her to bed."

He nodded. Then his gaze settled on Madeline.

"How do you do? I'm Matthias Carson. Miss Eastman's attorney." It was less of an introduction than a pronouncement and he did not extend his hand.

"Madeline Abbott. Miss Eastman's friend."

"Ah, yes, the neighbor across the lake." He looked toward Mira for an explanation.

"Miss Abbott was visiting when Miss Eastman took sick. I called Dr. Niles."

"I see. I expect the stimulation may have been too much for her."

Madeline stiffened. "Are you suggesting that I'm the cause of Celia's collapse?"

"Certainly not purposely."

"How very comforting." Madeline glared at him.

"I'm sure this has been a trying afternoon for you, Miss Abbott.

My car is outside. I'd be glad to drive you home if you like."

"Thank you, but I will stay until Miss Eastman recovers."

"As you wish. But it's not advisable." Matthias seated himself comfortably in the armchair. "She's had these spells before and it usually takes her a long time to rally. Sometimes several days."

Madeline remained standing. "What exactly are these spells, Mr. Carson?"

"What has she told you they are?"

Typical lawyer, Madeline thought, a question for a question. Well, she was not to be outdone by this one.

"Some nameless illness," she replied. "Can you be more specific?"

"I'm afraid I can't."

"Can't, Mr. Carson?"

"I assume that if Celia wanted to be more specific, she would be." He exchanged glances with Mira.

Just then, Madeline heard another car motor and assumed it was Master Hingham for her return ride. There would be little purpose, she decided, in staying any longer.

"I have reconsidered. You may indeed be correct, Mr. Carson. There is little I can do for Celia tonight. That will be my driver and I shall leave with him. I'll be back tomorrow. Good day."

Without waiting for a reply, she strode out of the room certain that their eyes were upon her back. Yet, she did not walk to the front door but rather lingered in the foyer out of sight. She didn't care if eavesdropping was improper, not when it concerned her friend.

"You wouldn't believe what I've been through with that old witch," she heard Mira complain.

"Yes, I would," her companion responded, "I know the breed. All too well."

That was as much as Madeline cared to hear and she was about to leave when she recalled leaving her purse on the sofa. As she came back to the doorway, she stopped dead in her tracks as she observed Mira walk over to Matthias and ease onto his lap, pressing her body up against his. He kissed her bare neck, unbuttoned her blouse, and then slipped it off her shoulders. She smiled seductively when he slid his hand inside the top of her white satin slip and cupped her breast. Mira arched her back.

Madeline entered the room with a flourish.

Startled, Matthias withdrew his hand and Mira clutched at her blouse.

"I forgot my purse."

With a withering look, Madeline marched over to the sofa, retrieved her bag, and left.

She heard them laughing behind her.

A freak ice storm prevented Madeline from returning to visit Celia the following day. Although it was not unusual for a winter storm to arrive so late in the spring, this one hovered over the lake, pinned between the mountains, lingering there like an unwanted relative until it had completely spent itself, covering everything with layers of glassy ice. Tree limbs snapped under the weight, the sounds echoing through the woods like firecrackers. The lake road would be impassable again until the freeze was over and the melting rains began.

Although Celia had a telephone, Madeline did not, nor ever would own one. She could not tolerate the idea that someone on a party-line, or even an operator, could listen in on her private conversation. Thus her communication with Celia in between visits had always been by letter. But not even the mail came through after the storm. So as the days passed, Madeline watched her friend's house across the lake and felt like a forlorn child pressing her nose against a store window. She saw the ghostly lights go on in one room and off in another during the evening and, at times, during the night—for Madeline slept fitfully and would waken two or three times in the hours after midnight. During these interludes, she would arise and walk from her bedroom to the enclosed porch and sit, bundled in her robe and blanket, rocking in the moonlight.

On the fifth and sixth nights, Celia's house was aglow with lights in every room, causing Madeline some concern. But on subsequent nights, the house settled back into a normal diurnal pattern.

It wasn't until ten days later, on April 26th, that the ice melted, the road was open again and mail delivery resumed. On that morning, Madeline found a long white envelope in her mailbox at the end of the driveway. It had Matthias Carson's name and office address printed in the left corner. Her own name and address were typed, signifying business. What possible business could he have with her?

She did not open the letter until she was seated back on her porch. She used a knitting needle to slit it open, and drew out a sheet of white bond paper, watermarked in the middle. The letter was dated April 23rd.

Dear Miss Abbott,
This is to inform you that Celia Eastman passed away on April 17th from a lingering illness. The deceased will be cremated in North Conway. A funeral service will be held at St. Mark's Church in Raleigh, New Hampshire, on April 26th, immediately after which her friends will assemble at the dock of the Eastman residence. The ashes of the deceased will be scattered on Squantum Lake according to her wishes.

She could not read his signature, but Matthias Carson, L.L.D. was typed under the small tight scrawl of his name.

"April twenty-sixth?" she repeated aloud. "That's today."

Madeline sat in her rocker, with the woodstove blazing, and stared across the lake at Celia's house with the letter in her lap. It was impossible for her to attend the funeral service. She had no car, no telephone, no way to arrange to get there. Surely Matthias Carson would have known that, she thought bitterly.

After an hour had passed, a group of people began gathering at Celia's dock. She could see Matthias Carson, David McKay, and "the girl," along with a number of other people she did not know. Georgie stood off to one side. Even the Weekes brothers were there, standing like doppelgangers as far away from each other as possible. The assemblage was being led in prayer by a tall man who appeared to be a minister.

She watched, horrified, as Matthias Carson, holding a shiny urn, climbed into a rowboat with the cleric.

Matthias paddled away from the dock, breaking the now-thin skim of ice with strong strokes. He stopped in the center of the lake and bowed his head. The Reverend prayed over the urn, and then the lawyer stood up and cast the ashes upon the water.

"Oh, Celie," Madeline said softly, "please forgive me for not being there."

As she watched the glassy surface of the water grow mottled with ashes, she reflected on her meeting with Celia over twenty years ago when Madeline and her father first came to Squantum Lake.

Her family had vacationed in northern Vermont as far back as she could remember, in elegant hotels and well-appointed lodges. She and her father continued to do so even after her mother and brother died. Then, one summer, her father discovered Hill House and bought it. He was at that time, in 1910, the same age she was now, but still vigorous, still managing his prosperous fleet of merchant vessels out of Boston and New York, as well as serving on the Board of Trustees of Harvard College (his alma mater) and the Board of Directors of the Boston Athenaeum.

The day after they took up their first summer residence in the house, Madeline had walked down to the lake's edge to admire the beauty of the gently lapping water reflecting the cloudless blue sky. There was no activity on either end of the lake in the two look-alike cottages but suddenly a woman appeared across from her on the dock in back of the green house. She wore a white dress and appeared to be plump and middle-aged with sun-bright hair. The woman waved to her and Madeline waved back. Within seconds, the woman startled Madeline by stepping into a canoe and paddling vigorously toward her.

From the beginning, Madeline admired Celia's spontaneity and natural generosity of spirit. Although political and social opposites, they became instant and unwavering friends, bonded together by geography, intellect and spinsterhood—both of them in their forties and beyond the niggling competitiveness of younger women. Each laughed at the other's foibles and Celia had always been charitable toward Madeline's verbal transgressions and attitude of *noblesse oblige*.

After Madeline's father died three years ago, she'd sold the entire business and moved permanently to the house that held so many happy memories. But principally she came back because of her long-time friendship with Celia and the notable absence of any other such relationships at home. Madeline had never had that particular camaraderie with anyone else—and if she hadn't met Celia, she would never have known the grief of its absence.

Tears spilled down her cheeks as she mourned the death of her only friend.

That she and Celia were both on the downslope of age was undeniable. But surely, Madeline thought, this illness and death had come in a sudden and untimely fashion. And there was that cluster of new people that had surrounded Celia at the end—including that wanton young woman and the lascivious lawyer. Madeline's eyes hardened and she brushed away the tears.

"Something is wrong here," she said aloud. "Something is dreadfully wrong."

CHAPTER TWO

*"But in the gross and scope of opinion
This bodes some strange eruption to our state."*

Young Thomas Hingham, the sole livery driver in the town of Raleigh, New Hampshire, never reneged on a commitment. Although he might be delayed by inclement weather, he would not shirk his duty. Accordingly, he and his automobile appeared at Madeline's door, as promised when he last drove her home from Celia's. There stood Master Hingham, the day after the funeral, cap in hand with his light brown hair loose in the wind, freshly shaven for the occasion, and properly respectful.

"I haven't forgotten, ma'am. You engaged me two weeks ago before the storm, to drive you back to Miss Eastman's. I wasn't able to get here before now. But Miss Eastman being gone and all, do you still want my services?"

"If only you had come yesterday," she lamented.

"Couldn't, you know. Impassible from our side. Only the mail truck could make it up this far from the Wickessett side. Is there somewhere you might be wanting to go?"

There was indeed.

During the ride around the lake, young Tom resumed his amiable discourse about the effects of the storm, the worsening economy, and the plans he had to buy a truck himself, and establish an interstate livery business. He intended, one day, to own a fleet of trucks.

Madeline could see his smiling brown eyes become intense as they were reflected in the rearview mirror. It quite amazed her that, at the age of nineteen, he had goals. She wondered if he were typical of his generation and upbringing.

Thus, in the space of one hour, Madeline somewhat modified her opinion of her driver as she was whisked from Wickessett, Vermont, to downtown Raleigh, New Hampshire. It was the nearest village to the houses on either side of the lake.

"On whose say so was she cremated?" Madeline demanded of Police Chief Ellsworth Tanner.

"Her own, Miss Abbott," he replied, interlocking his chubby fingers on his desk and looking earnestly across at her. "Miss Eastman's lawyer," he explained, "had the instructions in her will."

Chief Tanner had a reputation for being patient with the funny old venerables who invariably called on him for every imaginable offense to God and Nature, be it this one's son who ate the apples from that one's orchard, or a calico cat in distress up a tree or down a well. He was patient with them because they were women, because they were old, and because they were the backbone of the community. They did the Good Works. Sewed the quilts for the orphanage, baked every month for the volunteer fire department's supper, made crafts for the disabled veterans' Christmas party. And while the woman who was reminiscent of his stern third-grade teacher, Miss Steinholtz, was not from Raleigh, he was polite by custom and conviction.

"I don't suppose you ordered an autopsy, either," Madeline said.

"We would have to have authorization for the medical examiner to perform a *post mortem*. Or the death would have to be . . . unnatural."

He lowered his head and Madeline could see the bald spot in the center. "And," she asked pointedly, "what constitutes 'authorization'?"

"A request from the attending physician, or the next of kin, or when the medical examiner deems something warrants further examination."

Madeline gripped her purse. "She had no next of kin. And I believe the circumstances of her death were ambiguous, to say the least."

The only indication that Chief Tanner's good humor was being tested was the slight whitening of his folded knuckles.

"Rest assured, Miss Abbott, if there had been any reason to do an autopsy, it would have been done. But there wasn't. It's all in order."

Madeline stood up, tight-lipped, and tucked her wedge-shaped purse under her arm. "Thank you for your time," she said coldly.

Instead of returning immediately home, Madeline had Master Hingham stop at Celia's house on the way.

Uncertain who might come to the door when she knocked, Madeline was relieved it was Georgie. She followed him into the living room. Celia's empty wheelchair was still at her desk.

She recalled all too well the progress of the rheumatism that condemned Celia to that wooden chair. By fifty, she was walking with a cane; by fifty-five, she used a roller; and by sixty she could not walk at all. The disease had robbed Celia of her mobility but never her spirit. It was that winsome spirit that Madeline could almost feel as she caressed the back of the chair.

"You're sure the girl isn't here, Georgie."

"Yes, ma'am. I've been cleaning out the closets and drawers and putting them in boxes. Mr. Carson says we must give them to the charity."

"Are all Miss Eastman's things gone, Georgie?"

"Except for her family Bible. I kept it out of the box. Do you think that's the right thing?"

"Yes, I'm sure she would want you to have it," Madeline replied, preoccupied. "But what about Miss Eastman's medication?" She tried to recall the exact smell. "Do you know where her medicine bottle is?"

Georgie thought for a moment and then shook his head. "No, ma'am. We got rid of that after. Went to the dump with the rubbish."

All she knew about what happened was in Matthias Carson's letter—that Celia had grown increasingly ill and then in a weakened state, simply died. In answer to her questions, Georgie told Madeline that he did not see Celia during that time, other than from the doorway of the bedroom. She had been awake once and looked at him, but could not speak. The doctor had come every day and Mira stayed with her day and night. He could provide no other details.

Madeline did take advantage that day of inviting Georgie to come to work for her once his obligations there were finished. But he merely shook his head as though he could not consider it. "Think it over," Madeline told him.

Two weeks later, another assembly was convened by Matthias Carson, this time in Celia Eastman's living room. And this time, Madeline was included—along with David McKay, Georgie, "the girl," and a sixth person whom she had seen on the dock the day of the funeral. Dr. Roland Niles was a short, balding man in his fifties, with a milky look to him, soft and pudgy, almost baby-like. Eyes like soft-boiled eggs.

Matthias Carson stood in the center of the room and read the will with appropriate gravity. This time, he was dressed in a dark blue suit. Acceptable, Madeline assessed, but definitely not Savile Row. At the conclusion of the bequeathing, Madeline, Georgie and

David McKay were to receive tokens of Celia's gratitude, but "the girl" inherited the house. Even more astonishing, this insolent lawyer received the entire bulk of Celia's financial estate, almost three hundred thousand dollars.

Madeline was stunned not only by the amount of Celia's money and its disposition, but that Mr. Carson could read such unnerving things so implacably. And what was Dr. Niles doing here? There was no mention of him in the will.

"Are there any questions?" Still holding the parchment in hand, Matthias Carson looked at each of the legatees until he came to Madeline.

"What is the date of that document?" she asked.

"April sixteenth."

Right after her last visit to Celia, Madeline calculated. "And do you maintain," she said, "that Celia was of sound mind when she signed this? As sick as she was?"

"Yes, of course." Carson then turned to the balding man on his right in a way that seemed rehearsed. "But I defer to the medical profession to make that diagnosis. Dr. Niles?"

"Oh, yes." The doctor's voice oozed like treacle. "In my medical judgment, Celia Eastman's mind was perfectly sound. Her health may have been impaired, but not her reasoning."

Madeline ignored the doctor and stared at Carson. "And is it legal for you, as a beneficiary, to execute her will?"

"Perfectly legal."

She waited a beat, then said, "I see," in a way that clearly indicated that she did not.

"Are you satisfied, Miss Abbott?"

"I have no more questions."

"Does anyone else have a question?" When there was no further discussion, he concluded with, "Then, if the rest of you don't mind, I'd like to have a word with Miss Abbott privately."

Madeline had a sudden apprehension about that declaration. It was delivered with the same tone her principal might have used in giving detention to Horace Viggers.

As the others moved into the kitchen for the dessert buffet that Georgie had prepared, Carson addressed Dr. Niles.

"Ro, I'd like you to stay too, please." He turned again to Madeline as the doctor joined them. "I understand, Miss Abbott, you made inquiries to the chief of police about an autopsy on Miss Eastman. May I ask why?"

However this information had reached Matthias Carson, Madeline knew the line between them had now been drawn. As he regarded her unwaveringly, she thought his eyes were like New Hampshire granite, gray and hard.

"To ascertain the cause of death," she answered as expressionlessly as possible.

"There was no mystery about Miss Eastman's death. Dr. Niles has listed the cause on the death certificate. Celia died of pneumonia."

"Something other than pneumonia was wrong with Celia," Madeline blurted. "She as much as said so."

Carson glanced at Niles, who nodded back to him. Then Niles addressed Madeline with slow deliberation.

"Miss Eastman was in my care for many months—"

"She wasn't ailing before Christmas," Madeline interrupted. "And she wasn't in your care then."

The doctor resumed, as though speaking to a child. "Her disease was silent for a long time before the symptoms became apparent. And by then, it was too late. Miss Eastman suffered from leukemia."

Madeline gasped in disbelief. "That's not what you told her."

"No, because I wasn't certain she cared to know. I left enough clues for her if she wanted to learn the truth or ask questions. She didn't." Then his tone became paternal. "I know she was your friend and her death is painful for you. But believe me, Miss Abbott, we did everything we could."

She took a deep breath and remained silent. It had been many years since she had been swimming, but her ears felt plugged as though she were submerged. Her head felt as though the weight of the water was upon her.

"Is there anything else we can do for you, Miss Abbott?" Dr. Niles's brow was furrowed and he opened his hands in a benign gesture.

"No," she managed to say, as though coming up for air. "Thank you."

The doctor looked at Carson for acknowledgment and then excused himself.

"You should have known Chief Tanner would call Dr. Niles," Matthias said. "You've offended Roland, you know, grievously."

Madeline cared not in the least whether that so-called doctor was offended. But she was infuriated at the victory she sensed in this snake of a lawyer.

The lingering silence between them was breached by a Georgie-knock at the open door.

"Come in," Matthias said.

Madeline bristled to think this man assumed that he had the right to order someone in or out of her presence.

"Miz Abbott?" Georgie planted his feet several inches apart and began swaying slightly from side to side.

"Yes, Georgie?"

He looked down at his scuffed brown boots. "Miz Webster just talked to me about staying on here now that the house belongs to her."

"And?"

"I thank you for offering me to come to work for you, Miz Abbott, but I reckon that this is the place I ought to be. I spent most of my life right here in this house. I'm a New Hampshireman not a Vermonter."

"It's only the other side of the lake, Georgie."

"Yes, ma'am. But it's Vermont."

"Yes," Madeline sighed wearily, "it's Vermont."

She saw that Mr. Carson took all this in with a certain satisfaction.

"Has Dr. Niles left yet, Georgie?" Matthias asked.

"No, sir. He's talking with Miz Webster still."

"If you'll excuse me, Miss Abbott, I must try to catch him."

He did not wait for her to reply before leaving the room. She could see that he was already thinking about something else by the time he reached the door.

Georgie was about to depart as well when Madeline called him back. He inched back to her like a puppy caught chewing the carpet.

"Georgie, tell me, did Miss Eastman ever talk about Mr. Carson?"

"Not to me, ma'am."

"You know, Miss Eastman had a great deal of money, Georgie. Did she ever say what she was going to do with it?"

"Oh sure."

"What did she say she was going to do with it, Georgie?"

"Buy a new coalstove in summer, when prices go down."

"I see. Thank you, Georgie."

He took this as permission to go, leaving Madeline in thought. After a few moments, she marched to the library door.

"Mr. McKay? Mr. McKay, may I speak with you?"

David entered as though summoned to an audience at Court. The Queen was pacing. This did not bode well. He had a full cigarette case in his jacket and was tempted to take one out. A cig right now would be just the thing, but he knew that it would offend her and she looked as though she were already skirting the edges of her temper.

"Could you please tell me, Mr. McKay, when you last saw Miss Eastman?"

"The same day you did, Miss Abbott. The day before the ice storm. Why do you ask?"

"Just curious, Mr. McKay."

"I got the impression in there that you were more than just curious. Suspicious, I'd say."

Madeline stopped pacing for a moment to face him. He read her expression as something between embarrassment and regret, and it momentarily softened him.

"I don't mean to give that appearance," she said. "It's just my nature."

"But you were obviously troubled by the will."

"It is a rather peculiar document, don't you think?"

He sat down again on the arm of the sofa and crossed his ankle over his knee. "You don't question the provision allowing me to use her library, do you?" He permitted just a hint of teasing in his voice, but she paid no heed.

"I don't know why Celia didn't leave you the books outright instead of just giving you library privileges. But I suppose she had her reasons."

He could only think of one—to legitimize his continued visits to what would now be Mira's house. He thought he'd successfully concealed his feelings about her from Celia, but perhaps not. No need, however, to discuss it with Madeline Abbott.

"Are you disturbed," he asked instead, "because she only left you a statue?"

"I find it odd that she didn't leave the statue of that Indian woman to Georgie. After all, it's his mother."

"Georgie's mother?"

"Out of wedlock, of course. Didn't Celia tell you?"

"No." But of course that would explain his Indian features, he thought.

"She died in childbirth in her cabin. They didn't find Georgie until several days after. God only knows how he stayed alive. Of course, it took its toll." She let that trail off and then continued. "Celia was most particularly fond of that statue. Perhaps that's why she wanted me to have it. And speaking practically, my owning it secures it for Georgie, too."

"Well, then, if that doesn't concern you, what does? Mira inheriting the house?"

Madeline shook her head. "It goes against my grain but, knowing Celia, I suppose it is plausible. Her heartstrings were easily plucked."

David smiled crookedly. "So then we come to what really bothers you—Matthias Carson inheriting three hundred thousand dollars."

Madeline began pacing again. "Doesn't that seem at all strange to you?" she asked.

Not so much strange, he thought, as misplaced. Hadn't Celia known *him* just as long as she'd known that self-important lawyer? In truth, it was galling. But he answered calmly, "I don't know. I gather she didn't have any family."

"No, but I can think of so many other ways she might have used that money. She might have given some to charity. Or Georgie. I can't believe she didn't leave anything to Georgie."

"But she did."

"What he gets is a stipend," Madeline snapped, "not an inheritance."

"Perhaps she felt he wouldn't benefit from a lot of money. Who knows what was in her mind?"

"I knew Celia well enough. And I do not believe she would have made such bizarre bequests on her own."

"Frankly, even if the will is a fraud, do you think a man like Carson would leave any loose ends? If it's a swindle, you can bet it's a damn good one."

Once again she stopped pacing and faced him. Her motion brought her to the empty wheelchair at Celia's desk.

"Just look at the constellation of events. Celia was in fine health until January. Then, suddenly she gets sick and dies—"

"Over the course of months," David corrected.

"Sudden enough! And suddenly it's leukemia—"

"Leukemia? Celia had never mentioned such a thing."

"—and suddenly she's left all her money to her lawyer, her lawyer, mind you! And then conveniently she's cremated."

"Who told you it was leukemia?"

"That quack of a doctor." Madeline shook her head in disgust. "It's all too easy. Cremated with her ashes scattered on the lake. Total invisibility. It just isn't logical. The one thing Celie believed in was history. She would never obliterate herself that way."

"What exactly are you saying?"

"Just that this all seems very wrong."

"Can you prove it?"

"I don't know how."

"Well, then?"

"I thought . . . perhaps you might help me."

"Me? Why me?"

"Because," she answered, "Georgie only rides half a horse. Because I don't know who else to ask. Because you admired her. And I believe that Matthias Carson conspired with Dr. Roland Niles to get Celia's money. I'm not sure about the girl. I found them in a compromising position the first day I met him."

"Mira and Dr. Niles?" The idea was ludicrous.

"No. Mr. Carson. I saw her disrobing for him."

Shocked, David rose from his chair. His nails dug into the palm of his clenched fist as he fought to maintain control. "Forgive me, Miss Abbott, I'm going to have to withdraw now."

"You may not want to hear it," she said sternly, "but the fact is, Celia should not be dead. She did not become sick until she became involved with these people. They never had her best interests at heart. They are capable of anything. You must know what I'm saying is all very plausible."

Was it? No, it couldn't be. The old biddy was surely crazy. "I think," he said, trying to sound calm, "you'd better have very good evidence to go down that path."

"It's all gone," she answered enigmatically. "But surely you can see that none of this is right. There is malevolency here."

"I have no reason to think that." And yet . . . could he really put anything past Matthias Carson? Even seduction?

"The alternative is to think I'm a harebrained old woman. Have you reason to think *that*?"

"I don't know," he answered candidly. "Hobson's choice."

She gave a short laugh. "Well, at least you're direct. That's a quality I find congenial. I'm rather direct myself."

Then her tone became lighter, almost charming, almost the way, he imagined, she might have sounded had life taken her down a different path.

"Perhaps you're right. Perhaps I'm seeing shadows. I know you were Celia's friend, too, and we have that in common. You know, I also have some rare books that might interest you. Histories of New England."

"You're not going to try to co-opt me into helping you play sleuth, are you?"

"Of course not. Why don't you come to my house for tea and I'll show them to you?"

Mira silently entered the room before he could respond.

"We didn't hear you knock," Madeline said haughtily.

"I'm not required to." She lifted her chin disdainfully and moved to the center of the room, virtually in the same spot where Matthias Carson had read the will.

"Just so," Madeline acknowledged sourly. Then she turned to David. "I'll see you on Wednesday next. Two thirty, p.m."

"With pleasure."

"Good day, then."

Madeline swept past the interloper on her way out.

Mira turned and smiled beguilingly at him. "It seems Miss Abbott is anxious for her and me to be enemies."

"Why do you suppose that is?"

"I think she may need an enemy. Makes her feel good."

David tried not to stare openly at her. He had found her incomparably desirable from the first moment he saw her. Looking at her now, he was convinced she was the incarnation of Maria Danforth. Although he did not know what the real Maria looked like—the papers had merely referred to her as "the beautiful Bickford woman"—he had fashioned her into an image of the woman he was looking at now.

She wore a light-purple dress today, with a white lace collar around the scooped neck that revealed her collarbone and the rise and fall of her chest. Her skin looked soft and inviting. He wanted to touch his lips to the curve of her neck.

Mira continued, "Matt thinks she's a—"

"Matt?" David was caught off guard by the familiarity. He had been to the house on two occasions when Carson visited Celia and he had formed an instant dislike of the man's manner.

"Matthias," Mira corrected herself.

"Oh. Carson," he said snidely, wondering if it might be true about the two of them after all. "And what does he think?"

"He thinks she's a little addlepated. Do you think she's addlepated?"

"Maybe." He'd heard quite enough about Matthias Carson and changed the subject. "Are you planning to move in here now?"

Mira scanned the room shaking her head. "I still can't believe this is all mine."

"And I get library privileges, don't forget."

Mira sat on the sofa, looking up at him flirtatiously. "Miss Eastman made quite sure you and I would be seeing a great deal of each other."

He was close enough to smell her perfume. The scent of lilacs filled his nostrils and sent undulations of the fragrance into every part of his body.

"I suppose she did."

"Do you have a lot of research to do?"

David tried not to be obvious as he watched the way she reclined, resting her elbow on the back of the sofa. The split in her skirt fell open almost to the top of her pale stockings.

"Another six months, at least." Or more, he thought, much more. Was she unaware of exposing so much of her leg?

"You aren't one of those writers who don't like women, are you?"

"How did you guess?" he said impishly.

"You are?" Mira pouted.

"Why?"

"It can be very isolated here."

She lowered her eyes. Thick black lashes fluttered over her cheek. He blinked his astonishment. Was she toying with him?

Mira giggled. "Are you shocked?"

"Fascinated."

"Why? We're not Victorians anymore. It's the Thirties after all."
David chuckled.

"What's so funny?"

He leaned over her, smelling sweet purple lilacs. "I was just thinking of all the trouble Celia Eastman went to, to throw us together."

Thomas Hingham took one look at Miss Abbott's expression as she left the Eastman house and recognized that she was in no mood to converse on the drive home. She was always a little frosty, but he was usually able to get past that. Having such a sunny disposition, he was undaunted by "the dark and dour," as he called it. But this was different. Miss Abbott was as grim and wrathful as God against Pharaoh. Of course, he was dying to find out about Miss Eastman's will. Everybody knew the reading was today. Who inherited the house and who got her money? It was the talk of the town. He hoped he might be able to provide the answers. Now all he knew with certainty was that no words on the subject would pass Miss Abbott's bunched up lips on this ride.

As Madeline expected, the week after the reading of the will, David came to tea. However, he brought with him, at least from her point of view, a decidedly unexpected and unwelcome companion.

The three of them—Madeline, David and Mira Webster—sat in a semicircle on the enclosed porch facing the lake. David and Mira were opposite each other in white wicker armchairs with green sailcloth pillows, with Madeline in the center in her ladder-back rocking chair. Her black knitting bag with the red brocade rose was perched on the end table at her side. On the glass-topped wicker coffee table in the middle, in addition to the silver tea service and rose-patterned china, there was a stack of leather-bound books.

David concentrated on looking through the books one by one as Mira silently sipped her tea, intermittently eating shortbread cookies from a floral tin.

Madeline could still feel the cold wooden slats of the rocker against her spine although she had lit the woodstove an hour earlier. While it had warmed the air, the heat had not yet seeped into the floor and walls, or even the chairs. Early May in Vermont was still the outer brim of winter; the remaining lake ice had just melted.

"Thank you for loaning these to me," David said as he opened a book to the frontispiece that contained images of Indians and wigwams in a stylized fashion.

"Keep them as long as you like," Madeline replied, but her tone was as cool as the walls. She sucked in her cheeks and looked pointedly at Mira. "I'm sorry not to have any special homemade treats with our tea, but I haven't got a cook."

"I hope you don't mind my bringing Miss Webster today," David said. "I know your invitation was to me, but I thought it might be an opportunity for the two of you to become better acquainted."

"I have an ample supply of tea."

Thus rebuked, David deliberately engrossed himself in the various books in front of him while Mira turned her gaze to the bank of windows that overlooked the lake. The afternoon sun skimmed across the water like handfuls of skipping coins.

"Oh!" Mira exclaimed, "I can see my veranda from here." Then she turned back toward Madeline cheerfully. "You know I can see yours from my porch, as well. But with the screens, it's too dark inside."

How presumptuous of the girl, Madeline thought, to assume ownership of Celia's house so unceremoniously.

"I shouldn't care to have anyone peering at me while I am taking tea," she said.

Mira bit her lip and then continued. "Do you ever use your dock?"

"No. There are too many steps."

Foolish question, Madeline thought. What did the girl think she could possibly want to do on the dock? Madeline was really quite peeved that David had taken the liberty of bringing this person to her house. Especially after what she had told him about seeing the girl with Carson. Only good manners prevented her from expelling the little chippie.

"I saw your canoe down there, so I thought—"

"It belonged to the previous owners," Madeline said as she reached up to locate a stray wisp of gray hair over her ear and tuck it neatly back into her bun.

"Oh." Mira paused and then tried again. "Have you been to see your statue yet? That Miss Abbott left you?"

"No."

"Her name was Princess Muskataqua. But the children used to call her Princess Muskrat Legs."

"Do tell."

Mira turned to David. "She was the last Indian in this area. Maybe you should put her in your book."

Without taking his eyes from his treasures, he replied distractedly, "The fact is, there's a 'last Indian' buried in just about every county around here. It's common to these parts. She lived, she died. It's not particularly important."

Then, as he looked up and saw Mira's crushed expression, he added, "I'm sorry, but that's the way it is. Novelists can't concern themselves with everybody equally, you know."

"Perhaps not," Madeline interjected, "but *people* can concern themselves with whomever they please without having to satisfy art."

"Ah, you're speaking of Celia."

"That is correct."

"Miss Abbott," David explained to Mira in a stage whisper, "has some concern about Miss Eastman's will."

"What kind of concern?" Mira asked innocently.

"Carson's inheritance," he answered.

Madeline reproachfully shook her head at him.

"Don't be cross," he said to her, "Miss Webster was devoted to Celia, too. I'm sure she'd be the first to agree with you if she thought there was any wrongdoing."

"Wrongdoing?" Mira repeated. "What sort of wrongdoing?"

"Miss Abbott finds it peculiar that Celia's estate went to her lawyer."

"It's not peculiar," Mira said, "she was attracted to him."

"Unspeakable!" Madeline blurted.

"Oh, I don't mean physically," Mira hurriedly amended. "But she found him charming, attentive, smart. I think she felt young around him. She sort of flirted with him and—"

"Do not say another word. I do not care to hear it."

"But she even told me—"

"I don't want to hear it, I said!" Madeline brought her opalescent teacup down against the saucer so hard she might have cracked it.

The two women stared at each other in silence as though from their opposite verandas, beyond earshot on antipodal ground. Madeline sucked in her cheeks making her cheekbones protrude preternaturally.

"Well," David finally broke the brittle silence, "it does clear the matter up."

"How?" Madeline replied coldly.

"Because even if Carson deliberately wooed and cooed her, the will still represents Celia's last wishes."

"Perhaps. If that's all he did."

The sky had begun to turn orange, almost the color of the orange wool Madeline was using to make her afghan. Orange, turquoise and brown. A peculiar choice of colors for a New England spinster, people might think, but she did not care. She liked the bold combination.

"What do you mean?" Mira asked, in a high, quivering voice.

David smiled conspiratorially, "Miss Abbott thinks—"

"That's not for repeating," Madeline interrupted.

"—that Carson did her in."

"You can't really believe that!" Mira exclaimed to Madeline. "Matt would never do anything like that. It's unthinkable! He's a lawyer."

"Unthinkable because he's a lawyer?" David laughed derisively. "The unthinkable, good-looking Boston lawyer out here in the boondocks? 'Tupping the ewe' at Miss Eastman's lakefront. Tupping the nursie-ewe. Know what that means, cookie?"

"I can guess," Mira replied tersely. Her face was flushed as she tried to blink back tears.

"Tupping the ewe and meanwhile playing pipes to the old shepherdess. Oh, he's a real solicitor. But the question is, is he capable of murder?"

"No," Mira said emphatically.

"Why not? Under the right circumstances, anyone is. And that includes the dreary Dr. Niles."

Both Madeline and Mira stared at him in silence.

"But that doesn't prove Carson killed Celia," he continued. "Or that anyone did. And that's the issue, isn't it? Evidence. One needs proof."

"Does that mean you have a plan to find the evidence?" Madeline asked, her fingers working each other like knitting needles.

"Hell, no." David leaned back in his chair. The room glinted pink and tangerine in the western sun. "I don't think he did it."

Mira looked batted about like a ribbon in the wind. "But then what was all that talk about?"

David arranged the books neatly into two piles of five each. "I was merely demonstrating the possibility. Lest you judge Miss Abbott too harshly."

"I do not need your mediation, Mr. McKay. Nor am I interested in what the girl thinks."

"Now, Madeline," he said pleasingly, "may I call you Madeline?"

"No."

"Accusations of murder are not idle talk, Madeline. You've made charges in front of two people—"

"One person. *You* brought it up in front of the girl."

"—charges of major consequence that have to be resolved." He leaned back in the chair and crossed his legs. "As I see it, Madeline, you either have to produce some proof for your suspicions or stop the accusations."

Madeline gripped the arms of her chair as though to steady herself, but her voice was unintimidated. "Let me tell you something, young man. Celia Eastman had two people in this world who truly cared for her—Georgie Skates and Madeline Abbott. Georgie has known her almost all his life, and I have known her for over two decades. Georgie is not capable of things greatly mental, nor I of things greatly physical, but I do not intend to let this occurrence pass unresolved. You may think that because Celia was old and infirm that the loss was a small one. She was going to die sometime, what's the difference? A few months or years one way or the other? Unimportant, you think. Well, you are mistaken and God help you. I think you must be amoral."

"Could be," David answered as if indifferent to her insult.

"Well, Celia thought better of you. She never doubted anyone. Not even her," Madeline concluded with a nod toward Mira.

Mira leaned forward and spoke with a tremor in her voice. "There was no cause for her to doubt anyone. Including Matt. Including Roland Niles. Including me. I really cared for Miss Eastman, too. I wouldn't have done anything to harm her. Please believe me, Miss Abbott."

"You'll be quite surprised to learn that I do. I doubt that you have the wherewithal to carry off a plot of this magnitude."

"Thank you."

"That's not a compliment, cookie," David sneered.

Mira looked as though he'd thrown his tea in her face. Her eyes narrowed as she stood up, clenching her fists. "My name is Mira. M-I-R-A. Not cookie. Not nursie ewe." She turned to Madeline. "And not *the girl.*"

She lifted her chin, still addressing Madeline. "You say you concern yourself with whoever you please. But you don't concern yourself with the likes of me, do you? Well, Miss Eastman did. And that's why she was a better person than you are." She turned back to David. "And you, you can go 'tup' a tree!"

Mira grabbed her checkered tan-and-white spring coat and left a vortex behind her as she slammed out the door.

Madeline watched Mira from the window. As soon as she was outside, she would realize that she had no way of getting home. David had driven her there, and it was very, very far to walk. In a little while, the sun would set and the road would be dark and lonely.

She watched Mira scan the road around the lake as though steeling herself for the long walk. Perhaps she believed David would come after her. Or would she come back in the house and ask for a ride?

Madeline noticed the canoe at the bottom of the stairs at the same time Mira did. Instantly, the girl went flying down the steps to the dock. She lifted the canoe off the blocks, right side up, oars rattling in the bottom. Then she dragged the canoe to the water's edge and into the water. She tossed her patent leather shoes into the canoe, hiked up her coat and skirt and pushed off.

"Resourceful girl," Madeline said to David who had also been watching. "Now I suppose she'll tell Mr. Carson everything."

"No, I don't think so."

"What makes you so certain?"

"She's through with him. Now that she has her house."

"Yes, you're probably right." Then Madeline said, somewhat confidingly, "I want to ask you a hypothetical question, David. As a writer of mysteries. What would you do in my place if you thought Mr. Carson had committed murder?"

"Well, first I'd ask myself why he would do it."

"We know why."

"Then I'd ask how."

"Poison. I smelled something odd in her medicine." She tried to recall the aroma again, but it still eluded her. "It was a haunting smell, familiar. Behind the smell of the medicine. It could have been poison. A poison, given in small but incremental doses could have killed her."

"Do you have the medicine bottle?"

"No." She shook her head in defeat. "Dr. Niles supplied her medicine and Mr. Carson had Georgie dispose of it all." Anticipating his next question, she said, "I asked about an autopsy, but it wasn't performed. And I don't know what to do next."

"Well, don't expect a confession. Carson's not the type."

Madeline clasped her hands. "Unless someone tricked him into it." Her words came quickly. "Like your Indian brave. We could—"

"Whoa, lady! You asked me what I'd do if I were in your place. Which I am not. This is just an intellectual exercise for me. So if you think I'm going to get involved in your schemes, you can forget it."

Madeline was immediately subdued.

"You're mad at me now." He sat down next to her. "But I still want to be your friend."

She shrugged him off.

"But you'll never, never invite me back again?"

She vacillated.

"Because I'm incorrigible," David cajoled. "Much like yourself."

"Yes."

"But I speak my mind. That's what you wanted, isn't it?"

"I suppose."

"And you know, even though we don't see eye to eye, I sincerely cared for Celia."

Madeline nodded, and he took her hand.

"I'm really sorry I can't help you, Madeline. But I thank you for the books, and I'll come back to tea anytime you care to invite me. Perhaps next week?"

"Perhaps." How could she say no to him? They had the bond of Celia between them.

"With pleasure." He smiled and kissed her hand.

As he drove around the lake toward Celia's house, David saw that Mira was already nearing the shore. It had all gone awry. He had not intended to get Mira mad. Only to prove to Madeline that her suspicions were unfounded. That was important to him. His intention had been to shake both of them up a little and then pacify them. He really had not meant to go so far as to upset Mira into leaving. Why had he done that? He had given in to his need to . . . what? Show off? He had to admit, too, that he was still resentful about her former relationship with Carson. But he knew he should have behaved better, and he owed her an apology.

After David left, Madeline replayed the afternoon's visit as she resumed her knitting.

Why, she wondered, had he brought the girl to her? Was he just being kind to Mira?

No, she concluded, it must have actually been because he wanted some interaction between the two women. But why? Then she suddenly nodded in recognition. Of course. David wanted Mira to show her true feelings for Celia, so Madeline would know she wasn't involved. That was it. In such a way, he had eliminated one of the suspects.

"Oh, that clever boy," she said aloud.

She had just gone back to pearl-two on the orange-turquoise-brown stump of an afghan when she heard a knock at her door. It startled her, even though she recognized it.

Madeline opened the door and found Georgie standing there, shivering like a leaf blown up against her screen.

"I saw the Mister's car, so I waited."

"Come in, come in."

He entered carrying a black-and-white striped pillowcase-bundle in his hands. His expression, Madeline thought, was as tight as a ball of yarn.

"Is something wrong, Georgie?"

He related to her how he hid in the bushes outside for the better part of the afternoon. It had taken him two hours to walk around the lake and when he arrived, he recognized Mr. McKay's car parked in the driveway. He was cold and tired, but he had business with her that couldn't be told in front of anyone else. A long time passed as he waited. Then, suddenly, Miz Webster came streaking out of the house like a scairdy cat. He watched her stand there looking across the lake, holding the collar of her coat up around her ears. Then she went down to the dock and took the canoe. That was a strange thing to do, Georgie said. It wasn't canoeing time yet.

Still he waited for Mr. McKay to leave. And finally, he was rewarded. When the car pulled out of the driveway, Georgie came to her back door.

"I come to find out if you still want me to work for you."

"I thought you wanted to stay in Miss Eastman's house and work for Miss Webster."

"I did. But I don't no more." He clutched the pillowcase bundle close to his chest.

"Why not?"

He hesitated, then told how the morning after the will, before daybreak, he was dressed in his flannel nightshirt and, holding a kerosene lantern, he made his usual way to the basement to add coal to the stove. It would take the night chill off the house and it would be warm by breakfast.

After shoveling and stoking, he came back upstairs to go to the bathroom, as usual. But, in passing by Mira's closed bedroom door, he stopped at hearing strange sounds from inside the room. There was scuffling and then a male voice.

"The man said 'Come over here, you winch. Right this minute.'"

"Winch?" interrupted Madeline.

"Yes'm. And I didn't know what to do, but then I heard Miz Webster say 'Make me. You just make me if you can, Mr. Lawyer.'"

"Oh," said Madeline, without surprise. Wench.

"Then I went back to my room behind the kitchen and I didn't go to the bathroom until the front door closed and a car drove away."

"I see," Madeline said, imagining his discomfort.

"Then every morning, it's been the same. Sometimes it's Mr. Carson. Sometimes, it's Mr. McKay. So I come here. Because of the goin's on, ma'am. It ain't right. So is it okay to stay?"

Startled, Madeline took a deep breath. David and Mira. That was beyond what she had considered. Then she realized Georgie was waiting for her response.

"You're more than welcome to live here, Georgie."

"Thank you, ma'am."

She scanned the pitiful little bundle he carried. "Didn't you bring your things?"

He began swaying from side to side like a tethered elephant. "Haven't no things, 'cept clothes and Miz Eastman's Bible. Got those with me."

"Is that all, Georgie?"

"Yes, ma'am. That's all I need."

"Then you must be a saving-man."

"No, ma'am. I give my money to God."

Madeline raised an eyebrow. "I didn't know he worked for wages."

Georgie looked at her uncomprehendingly as her gaze drifted toward the window. She could see that the girl in the canoe was almost ashore on the other side.

"Strange how things settle out, isn't it?" Madeline mused aloud.

"Ma'am?"

Not expecting him to understand, she nevertheless answered, "I'd say you came along just when I needed you most."

"Thank you, ma'am. Was there something you wanted me to be doing?"

A delighted smile crossed Madeline's face. "We could use some sweets."

"Yes, ma'am. I'll get started now."

"Excellent. The kitchen," she pointed toward the other end of the house, "is through there, Georgie. And I'll make up a room for you."

As Georgie exited toward the kitchen, Madeline looked out over the lake again. The sky had become orange along the horizon. The sun was about to disappear.

"Thank you," Madeline said. But she wasn't sure herself to whom she speaking. Georgie, or the girl, or perhaps Celia.

Mira rowed fiercely toward her own dock as though running for home in a relentless game of tag. She got out and quickly pulled the canoe up onto the ground, leaving it like a discarded toy.

Still fuming, she strode to the back door and turned the knob.

It wouldn't open. She shook the door again and again but it was locked.

"Georgie!" she called insistently, and pounded on the door. She was exasperated at everything that had occurred. Most of all, at being locked out of her own house. "Let me in, Georgie!"

She heard footsteps through the kitchen, and the bolt slid open.

"Why did you lock—" She stopped abruptly at seeing Matthias Carson holding the door open for her.

"Where's Georgie?" She stalked past him.

"He's gone," Matthias answered calmly. He pointed to a scrap of paper on the kitchen table.

"What do you mean, gone?" Mira grabbed the note.

Mz Webster. I am gon to work for Mz Abot. I brung in wood and loked the doors. Goodby. Georgie Skates.

Mira looked angrily at Matthias. The world seemed to be conspiring against her today. "Why did he leave? Did you say something to him? What happened?"

"He was gone when I got here. What were you doing on the lake?"

"What do you think I was doing? It was the only way I could get home from that witch's house."

"Was Georgie there?"

"No. If he were there, I wouldn't be asking where he was, would I?"

She furiously unbuttoned her coat and discarded it on a chair. She crumpled up the paper and dropped it back onto the table. "I don't understand why he left."

"Maybe he doesn't like it here anymore."

"That's impossible. He loves this house."

"Then I suppose it must be you, mustn't it?" He moved closer to her, but she backed away.

"Are you sure you didn't say anything to him?" She was not prepared to take the blame for one more thing today.

Matthias shook his head.

"What are you doing here, Matt?"

"I came to visit you, of course."

"I didn't see your car."

"It's parked around the side in the trees. For propriety."

"I don't care about propriety."

"But I do."

"How did you get in? The doors were locked."

"I have a key. Obviously."

"You should have phoned first."

"My, we're getting formal, now that we're propertied." He again moved closer to her but Mira sidestepped him and walked out of the kitchen into the living room.

Matthias followed, watching Mira toss off her shoes and sit on the sofa with her feet tucked under her.

"Sorry," she said flatly. "I had an unpleasant afternoon."

"What happened?"

"It doesn't matter."

She removed the bobby pins from her updo and shook her head, letting her hair fall from its confinement. "Where did you get the key?" she demanded.

"From Celia's effects."

"I'd like it back." She held out her hand.

"Why?"

"Because it's my house now."

"Well, not exactly, darling," he responded. "You see, I'm the trustee. Technically, it's all mine until the paperwork is completed."

She withdrew her hand and clenched her fist in her lap.

"All right. Keep it then. But you can't just come and go as you please."

Matthias smiled but his hazel eyes mocked her. "In fact, I can. Yes, indeed, I can."

She glowered at him. "Then don't be surprised to walk in and find me in bed with someone else."

"Then I'll watch. Or join in. Makes no difference to me."

Mira scanned his face as Matthias casually sat down on the sofa close to her. "I can never tell," she said earnestly, "whether you're serious or not."

"If you could, I'd probably be a bad lawyer." He pushed her hair back over her ear and began tracing a circle around it.

"How do I know you're a good one?"

Matthias slid his arm around her shoulder and started to draw her toward him. Mira felt her throat pulse. He always knew just how to handle her. As much as she was angry at his presumption, she was still attracted to him. But she abruptly pulled away. She stood up, eyes flashing.

"That's all you came for, isn't it, to 'tup the ewe' again."

"'Tup the *who?*'"

"It means you came here to make love to me, that's all."

"Since when have you objected to that?"

Mira crossed her arms like a sulky child. "I'm not in the mood."

He sat silently for a moment studying her. "What's wrong? Something to do with the Lady of the Lake?" He inclined his head toward Madeline's house.

"And David McKay."

"Young Shakespeare? What about him?"

She hesitated then dropped her arms and looked at him steadily. "Tell me the truth, Matt. Before Miss Eastman knew you, who was she going to leave her money to?"

"I can't reveal that."

He seemed neither surprised nor angered by her question. His tone became lawyerly. "Why do you want to know? Does this have something to do with your visit?"

"In a way."

Mira's resolve began to fail her. She wasn't sure she really wanted this to go any further. But now he would not let it pass.

"You mean they're wondering what I did to inherit all that money?"

Mira nodded.

"There's no law against wondering. They can wonder all they want."

"I suppose nobody could prove anything?"

Matthias settled back into the pillows. "Prove what?"

"That anything was wrong."

"Nothing is wrong." His eyes narrowed. "Are you suggesting otherwise?"

"No. Of course not."

They heard a car pull up outside and Mira was glad for the reprieve.

"I suppose that would be David." Matthias rose from the sofa and picked up his dark gray cashmere coat lying neatly over a wing chair.

"You aren't leaving?"

"Why don't you let him in and we'll see."

Mira sensed that whatever decision she made now would be final. While Matthias was a little frightening, he excited her. And he was, after all, inheriting all of Celia's wealth. And what could David offer to make up for that? Besides, if it didn't work out with Matthias, David would always be there. It was an easy choice.

When she got to the door, David stood on the threshold looking contrite. His blue eyes shimmered like the lake.

"May I come in?"

Mira stepped aside as he walked past her into the living room. David halted when he saw her other guest.

"Carson," he acknowledged curtly.

"Shakespeare," Matthias returned, in an exaggerated courtly voice.

David jerked his head involuntarily at the name.

"What is it you want, David?" Mira asked.

"I came to apologize. May I speak with you alone?"

Mira looked to Matthias for an indication of what she should do.

"That's up to you, Mira," Matthias responded. "Do you want to speak with him alone?" He did not take his eyes off her.

"I'm sorry, but as you can see, Mr. McKay," she said, "I'm entertaining a guest."

David regarded Matthias resentfully then replied, "Right." He turned away. "Right."

He slammed the door as he left the house.

"Petulant, isn't he?" Matthias said as he put down his coat.

"David thinks you poisoned Miss Eastman."

She waited for the explosion, but none came. Instead, Matthias seemed entertained.

"Does he?"

Emboldened, she pressed on. "Not exactly. Miss Abbott thinks that. David merely thinks you're capable of it."

Matthias laughed with genuine amusement.

"Doesn't that bother you?"

He just shook his head.

"They why did Miss Eastman leave you all her money, Matt?"

"It was in the nature of a campaign contribution."

"What campaign?"

"Mine." He walked back to the sofa and sat. "I've just declared for the United States House of Representatives. Against the junior Republican congressman in the November election."

"Oh." She sat at the far end of the sofa. "Why?"

"Let's just say my career doesn't lie in writing wills and breaking ironclad contracts." He ran his thumb and index finger over the crease in the trousers of his dark worsted suit.

"So you decided on politics. But why here? Why not Massachusetts?"

"Because New Hampshire is Depression-poor, most of it. Because there are failing industries, and I know what to do about it. And because Boston is too bloody-blue British on the Hill."

"But I thought you were English. Isn't Carson an English name?"

"Let's just say it's an acquired name."

He said nothing further and Mira's mind was racing.

"It sounds like you've had this all planned out for a long time."

"Most of it. There's just one thing lacking."

"Which is?"

He reached for her hand. "A married candidate has a much better chance of winning than an unmarried one."

"I see," Mira responded with quick intelligence. This was not what she had expected. Not Mira Webster of Ossippee. "But I'm not the right society."

Matthias turned her hand over and kissed her palm and then ran his tongue over the center.

"With my money, you are."

He sucked lightly on her middle finger between his teeth and then took her by the wrist and pulled her against him.

"But what if you don't get elected?"

He slowly slid his hand up her skirt, past the top of her stocking onto her soft bare thigh.

"We'll still be rich."

CHAPTER THREE

*"The time is out of joint. O cursed spite
That ever I was born to set it right."*

Could it be August already? Madeline reflected. June and July seemed to have passed by very quickly, indistinguishable from more than a half-century of Junes and Julys. David had visited weekly during the early summer, but not since. The last she'd seen of him was over a month ago, right before Mira and Mr. Carson had gotten married.

When she thought of them, she could not help thinking about Celia. Still, there were so many things to do around the house to distract herself. Routines were the salvation of her life. Salvation, because without them, she would have nothing to do, no purpose except what they imposed on her. "What shall I do today?" she would ask herself upon rising. "Ah yes, I have to shake out the rugs, wash the curtains, sew the hem of my dress. Rinse my unmentionables.

Brush my hair. Brush my teeth. Make the bed. Get up, get up." There were always things to be done that began with swinging her legs out of the bed.

Perhaps tomorrow she would wash her lace curtains in the metal tub with a little starch, and stretch them to dry on the large wooden frame. She would prick her fingers several times while hooking the edges of lace over the nails that punctured the frame at half-inch intervals, so that when the lace dried, it would keep its shape. For whom to see? She would wash everything that needed washing while Georgie painted the outside of the house, repaired roof shingles, mowed the grass and cooked.

In early June, she and Georgie had planted a kitchen garden—something she did every year of her life since girlhood—that needed constant weeding, watering, nurturing. Soon, they would put up the carrots, pickle the cucumbers, stew the tomatoes, store the potatoes. Now was the time for preserving the strawberries, blueberries, gooseberries. It seemed, sometimes, that the only use for summer was in preparation for winter.

Madeline took regular trips into Raleigh in Master Tom Hingham's Model-B, sometimes with Georgie when she needed his help with the bundles. But more often than not, she went alone. The only accessible town on the Vermont side was Wickessett, but it was much farther than Raleigh. Thus, although Madeline was a legal resident of Vermont, New Hampshire was her closest source of supplies and news and she was waiting, at this moment, for Master Hingham to arrive.

On the last day of August, David went to Mira's house. He was met at the front door by her new maid. Alva was about Mira's age. Although no beauty like her mistress, she was a quick study of situations with a canny New England sensibility about human nature. She seemed to size him up in seconds and, in her large brown eyes, he read understanding.

"I'm David McKay. I've come to use the library. I have

permission."

The auburn-haired maid nodded knowingly. "Mrs. Carson said you'd be coming one day."

He nearly winced at hearing her say the name, but asked, "Is Mrs. Carson here?"

"No, sir."

Alva closed the door and led the way to the library. Walking behind her, he imagined the pitying look in her eyes.

The last David had seen of Mira was on July 4th, the day she and Carson were married. That day, he had watched across the street from the church, squinting against the bright sun so that it made the colors of the world seem like needles in his eyes. Man and wife. An entity. He imagined being in there and when the preacher asked if anyone had any objections to the marriage, he would stand up and say "I do" and Mira would realize he loved her and that she truly loved him.

Instead, he had hidden behind an elm tree, stepping out only after they had passed in their pearl white limousine with white streamers. But something must have drawn Mira to look back out of the rear window. His final glimpse of her was Mira's face framed by white lace inside the rim of the small window, staring directly at him with an unfathomable expression. She looked, he imagined, like a religious martyr.

He heard later that they had a huge reception at the Tamarack Inn in the capitol, Concord. In fact, he read about it in the *Raleigh Sentinel.* "Lavish," it was called. The social event of the season. Lavish and memorable. He saw their picture taken at the Inn amidst a table full of people whom he did not recognize. He could barely make out her features, but he could see that Mira was smiling. He imagined being there, too, standing behind a white column, watching the oblivious couple seated side by side at the head table laughing gaily. No martyr now.

After witnessing Mira driving away with Carson, he'd returned home and cried. Cried for his love of her, and for his creation, Maria Danforth, on whom he had fashioned his love. Lost to him.

What was it about that true story of the Bickford case that had intrigued him to write his first book? The essentials were simple enough. A beautiful young woman of impeccable reputation is married to an innocuous man, a laborer, who adores her. They have two children.

One day, she takes the buggy to visit her family several towns away. She never arrives at their home and never returns to her own. Just disappears without a trace of her or the horse and buggy. They scour the ditches and gullies, the side roads and fields to no avail. It is a mystery to the town and anguish to her husband.

Many months later, they find her. Murdered. Stabbed to death in the tawdry upstairs room of what was essentially a brothel miles away from home. She had arrived looking like a farmer's wife, and died in black stockings and red silk step-ins. The mystery was not so much who killed her, but how she ever came there and what had gone on during the missing months.

In David's book, Maria was a restless beauty, a rare and exquisite woman trapped by the boredom of marriage with a common man. A woman who craved excitement and sexual variety, who was stifled on the farm where she had no one to talk to, nothing to do but drudgery. He had spent three years writing about her. For three years, and ever after, he loved her until she was no longer his creation, but a reality. He dreamed about her, fantasized about her. She was all that he thought about. Until he met Mira. How alike they were. The same gleaming black hair, gentian eyes, sumptuous body. The same cravings. The same sensuality. Mira was Maria, more than any other woman he had ever known.

For days after her wedding, David never left the room he'd rented at the boardinghouse around the corner from the church. He thought about suicide. About what Mira would feel if he died. At one point, he sat on the toilet with a straight-edge razor in his hand with his wrists over the sink. For those moments, the room seemed to blacken and fade and he could only see the white enamel that beckoned him like a shroud. He wanted to open his skin and let his blood flow out onto the white surface. He would feel so calm afterward. He would just close his eyes and sleep. Nothing would ever hurt him again. And she would know that he had truly loved her. And that she was responsible for this.

But as David looked at his veins, he thought about what Carson would say to Mira about it. He would deride the act. He would tell her that David was weak. Too weak to face life. Not really a man. Carson would call him a coward. Or worse. Thus would Carson turn her from sympathy to contempt. He could not go through with it.

Finally, after days passed that seemed like weeks, he went back to his work. The piles of research notes on the maple table beckoned him. He began to believe there was something he needed to complete. He wanted to finish his book about the native Indians. It became a lifeline that pulled him from despair. Then it brought him back to Celia's library.

In the August woods, Georgie weeded his mother's gravesite, tenderly pulling up the roots and scraggles of brush, inspecting the plants almost as though his large hands would bruise them. There was a basket of ripe blueberries next to the statue, destined for pastries in the Abbott kitchen. Bent over as he cleared around the base of the statue, he looked as if he were circling in dance and prayer. A Keeper of the Spirit. Once in a while, however, Georgie would glance at the Eastman house. At those times, tears would moisten his eyes and wet the high cheekbones that looked so much like his mother's.

While Georgie was at his woodland ministrations and David sat alone in the middle of Celia's library, Madeline had been grocery shopping in Raleigh in Thomas Hingham's Model-B. Sacks of groceries were now piled in the backseat as she sat next to the driver. She was grateful, however, that young Thomas no longer attempted to make idle conversation with her. Instead, he whistled, "Daisy, daisy, give me your answer, do," and "Ah, sweet mystery of life." By this, Madeline assumed Master Hingham had a ladyfriend.

As they rode through the main street in the direction of home, she spied a magnificent silver automobile parked in front of one of the town's prettiest houses.

"Goodness," Madeline said involuntarily, "look at that!"

Thomas slowed down as he admired the car. "What would old Mr. Prentice be doing with a fancy new Phaeton?"

Just then, Dr. Roland Niles came out of the house, looking very prosperous in a well-fitting suit and bowler hat, and carrying a new black-leather doctor's bag. He was followed by Matthias Carson who walked, Madeline observed, as arrogantly as a show horse. He spotted Madeline and nodded perfunctorily as though nothing surprised him, least of all her. Dr. Niles seemed too preoccupied to notice anything as he got into the passenger side of Matthias Carson's shiny silver car. Madeline clamped her teeth together and tightened her lips as they drove away in the opposite direction.

It had been months since she had actually looked into Matthias Carson's eyes. Seeing him across the lake was maddening enough, but staring back at those storm-gray eyes focused unblinkingly at her own was like recognition from the Devil. It made her almost quake with loathing and apprehension. It took the air out of her lungs and set her heart racing. Over and over she told herself to be calm, but she was still breathing shallowly when they continued down the street.

As they rode past a store with a large sign in the window, Madeline was riveted.

"Stop! Stop the car!"

Thinking there was something in the road, Thomas stopped abruptly, sending them both forward in a jerking motion. Madeline turned her head and stared fixedly at the window of the pharmacy. Large and bold, was a sign:

ELECT MATT CARSON as U.S. CONGRESSMAN
ELECT A NEW NEW HAMPSHIRE
Rally-September 1st—North Conway

After a long silence, Madeline ordered Thomas to continue on.

As they headed for home, she silently shook her head. For too long, she had felt powerless to do anything about Celia's death, and she had allowed herself to become complacent.

"You see what complacency breeds," she admonished herself aloud. "It breeds congressmen."

Young Tom simply nodded.

Later that evening, Madeline sat on her porch, looking out at the full moon. She thought about the skein of her life that had led her to this juncture, and what was left to come. At sixty-five, she could hope, perhaps, for five or ten more good years. Few of her family had ever reached this age except for her father. Heart trouble had afflicted most of her family except for a few unfortunates afflicted with "C." No one ever pronounced the word "cancer." It was too fearful.

Five or ten years. It did not seem very much. Even sixty-five years hadn't seemed very much. Where had it all gone? And what had she accomplished? Madeline hugged her elbows and sucked in her cheeks. She wished to God she hadn't been born a woman. If she'd been a man, she would have had adventures. She would have lived her life instead of merely expending it.

She thought back to the young man she might have married so long, long ago. Harold Breton. They had kept company for three years and were planning to be engaged. Harold always called her "Maddie," the way Celia had. He had been, she knew, her only chance for a husband. Although she was from a respectable family, she was not considered a good match. She was so tall and thin that no clothes in the haberdashery fit. Her mother would select the nicest dresses and alter them. But they all looked shapeless on her, as if hung on a hanger. Madeline had been given short measure on looks, as well. Her only redeeming feature was her long dark-brown hair, which had since given way to gray. But it was small compensation and Madeline had always been self-conscious about her appearance.

Only Harold had surmounted her shyness. He was a wonderful student of mathematics and had a lighthearted nature despite a club-foot that he referred to as his "cheerful excuse." He was excused from physical training, excused from walking great distances to school, and excused from many of the chores that fell upon his brothers—but not from dying of pleurisy in 1888 when he was twenty-three. Madeline was twenty-one. Had they married, the pattern of her life would have been different. She might have had a family. Now she had nothing. No one.

She had had a much beloved brother, Nathan, younger by thirteen years. She was almost a mother to Nathan when he was growing up. What a rambunctious boy he'd been, full of energy and activity. She would mind him when he went out to play, and he delighted in tricking her by hiding or by yelling "Help, Help!" and when she ran to find him, he would pop out from behind a tree, laughing. And she'd laugh, too, because he hadn't really tricked her.

Nathan had never cared to follow their father into his merchant-vessel business, had never graduated from Harvard University. Instead, he ran away in his sophomore year despite honor grades, and went in search of his own fortune. Madeline still had the letter he sent from Amarillo, Texas, telling her all about the prairie and how it was so different from anything in Massachusetts. Then, just shy of his nineteenth birthday, Nathan enlisted in the Navy. The boy who didn't want to inherit a lucrative sea-freight company took to the sea as a petty officer. He was killed in 1898 aboard the *USS Maine*. Her father, who had opposed the Spanish-American War as Hearst yellow-journalism, never recovered from the loss of his son.

War, she was convinced, was both the vilest and the bravest of human endeavors. It was not fair that she had been taught to sit on the sidelines. Not fair that she learned it so well. She had to go into battle now, no matter what the cost. She could not, would not, come to her own end so ignobly.

Two weeks after she discovered the political poster in Raleigh, a brand new black Model-B, a replica of Tom Hingham's, was parked next to Madeline's house. She had Thomas order it for her the day after their trip to town. He tried to dissuade her from the enterprise but she would not hear of it. As soon as the car was delivered,

Madeline engaged the young man to teach her how to drive.

Tom came in the morning, prepared to spend one day at the instruction. She would not pay for more, she declared.

Madeline watched carefully as he showed her the gear positions and taught her about clutching. He went over the car from stem to stern, showing her the fuel tank, the radiator, spark plugs, mechanical brakes, and trying to acquaint her with the fact that the car would need maintenance. It wasn't like a hand pump or a woodstove or an icebox, or any other equipment she'd ever owned.

"This," he explained with a sense of proprietary pride, "is the future transportation of America."

Madeline recalled reading that in the sales brochure but did not say so. After repeatedly practicing to overcome bucking and stalling, she finally circled the house at the breakneck speed of seven miles per hour.

By the end of the day, they were both so weary they communicated only by gestures. After she paid his fee and Tom drove off in his own vehicle, Madeline sat on her porch staring at her new car. An hour passed. Her courage waxed and waned.

Finally, she thought about Celia. Celia would be disappointed in her timidity. Celia had considered Madeline the epitome of independence. She could not let her friend down.

"Georgie," she called out to the kitchen. "Come, Georgie, we are going for a ride."

With Georgie sitting stiffly next to her, hands on his knees, she tried to start the car. Instead of the motor churning over, the windshield wipers swept across the glass. Georgie peered up at the clear sky looking for signs of rain.

Madeline made a face and finally found the right switch. She clutched and gassed, and the car lurched forward and quit. After several more attempts during which Georgie closed his eyes, she managed to get the thing to run and they began circling the house.

Georgie opened his eyes, but held the seat with his one hand and the door with the other.

Madeline's shoulders ached by the third circle, so tight did she hold herself and so hard was she trying to remember to do everything at once. On the fourth circle, she took too wide a turn and veered off course.

"Brake! BRAKE!" she shouted just as they headed for the stairs to the dock.

Georgie closed his eyes again and held on.

Madeline wasn't sure what she did, but the car stopped in time. She nodded triumphantly.

David had used Celia's library every other day for the past two weeks without a single glimpse of Mira. He was feverishly anxious to see her again. He was pacing the room thinking about her as Alva entered.

"You'll have to be leaving soon, Mr. McKay. I have to lock up."

"Are you expecting Mrs. Carson back, Alva?"

"No, sir. Not till late."

He could tell she felt sorry for him. He gleaned that she didn't like Mira all that much and liked Matthias Carson even less.

"There's no use of it," she said sympathetically. "She goes out when she knows you're coming."

David didn't try to hide his disappointment. Nor was he offended by the liberty she took. She only confirmed what he already suspected.

"I'll finish up in about fifteen minutes, Alva."

"Yes sir, I'll be in the kitchen."

After she left, David stood looking at the doorway. Then, as if suddenly possessed, he left the library and crossed the living room as quietly as he could. He turned down the hallway to Mira's bedroom. In those magical nights with her, the world had flown around him like ring-around-the-rosy. Softly, he turned the doorknob and opened the door.

The bedroom was completely changed from the room he had

slept in with Mira just a few months ago. She had removed a wall, expanded the room, added a bathroom and closets, and totally changed the wallpaper, rugs, furniture, everything. The colors were ivory and shiny black, with splashes of red. There were lots of mirrors. It did not look like any bedroom he had ever seen. He knew instantly it was Carson's taste, not Mira's. It looked like the brothel, David imagined, that Maria Danforth had died in.

On the bureau was a black lacquered brush set with Chinese red coral and white mother-of-pearl flowers. He picked up the brush and saw the long dark hairs entwined in the bristles. Hers. He put it to his nostrils to catch the scent of her hair. He could almost smell her perfume. Not lilacs, but something sweeter, muskier.

His gaze fell upon their wedding picture in a matching black-lacquer frame. She's beautiful, he thought, God, she's beautiful. The train of her white wedding dress was swirled around her so that he could not see where her feet touched the floor. She looked like she was emerging from a sea of satin. But *he* was next to her in the photo, staring straight at the camera while she stared up at him. How perfectly poised he looked. And how indifferent to the bride on his arm. David wanted to rip the picture in half and take her with him.

Reluctantly, he looked over at the bed. There wasn't a ripple in the black satin quilt. No evidence of occupancy. But that was a lie and he knew it. He clenched his teeth and turned away. He hated this room.

On impulse, David decided to visit Madeline after he left Mira's house. He had neglected her over the summer and he felt guilty. She was, after all, the only person he could really talk to. She sparred with him and he appreciated her cultivated taste in books. How many times had he been tempted to tell her the truth about himself? That he had actually grown up in New York City, not Bismarck. And that his family had been wealthy, not farmers. That they had lost everything in the stock market in 1929. And that his father, a once-successful broker, had committed suicide in despair, leaving them in poverty.

That his mother refused to accept it and was now in a sanitarium. That he had assumed a pen name to conceal his relationship to the notorious stockbroker who took a dive off the Flatiron Building.

Sitting across from her now on the porch, he wanted to tell Madeline all of that but he was ashamed.

"I thought you already had a visitor," he said instead, nodding toward the car in Madeline's yard.

"No," she answered proudly. "It's mine."

"Yours?"

"That's right. I'm learning to drive."

"Good for you. That's admirable."

"Is it?"

"Yes, it is. What made you decide to do it?"

She told him about the poster she had seen in Raleigh.

"I'm sure he hasn't got a chance of being elected," David said. "But what has that got to do with your car?"

Madeline smiled enigmatically. "I'm going to his rally."

On the warm evening of September first, Madeline and Georgie drove to the Town Hall in North Conway, New Hampshire. The art of parking was still a little elusive, but she had mastered the clutch quite respectably.

As they neared the red-brick building of the Town Hall, she was surprised at the scores of people, mostly men, brandishing campaign posters for Matthias Carson.

She pulled the car snugly against the curb across the street from the throng. Georgie descended, came around to Madeline's side and helped her out. A general hush pervaded the crowd as Georgie escorted her through the sidewalk and into the hall. She was very self-conscious. Although the Nineteenth Amendment had been in effect for ten years, few women in the region voted and even fewer were to be seen at rallies.

Madeline and Georgie took seats toward the front of the noisy room. The hall held nearly five hundred people sitting on slatted wooden folding chairs. It was close and warm with body heat, and the air vibrated with low voices.

Matthias Carson sat to the right of the podium. Madeline had to concede he cut a fine figure. Dressed in a navy seersucker suit, he looked altogether comfortable, almost as though he were in a pulpit. Mira, seated onstage next to him with some other local politicians, appeared nervous. She had changed her hairstyle into a sleek short bob and was wearing a fashionable navy linen suit. But her eyes seemed wild with panic, like prey facing its predator.

A beefy politician whose thighs rubbed together in his herring-bone suit came to the podium to introduce the candidate. As Carson stood up, he smiled his acknowledgment, neither too little nor too much. The audience cheered enthusiastically.

Madeline was nonplussed. Never had she ever expected a Democrat to have such popularity in a Republican stronghold.

Carson raised his hand for silence and the audience complied. As he began to speak, he swept his eyes over everyone in the audience. She recognized the courtroom style of playing to a jury. His voice was deep and resonant.

"Prosperity died three years ago," he began, "and it cannot be resuscitated by the Republican Party. They murdered it, and cre-mated it on Black Thursday when the stock market crashed. The old Prosperity is gone forevermore." He paused to let this sink in. "The question now is what kind of future are we going to build from the ashes of the past?"

Ashes. Madeline shuddered at the reference. But she did not want to miss a word.

"Here, in New Hampshire, these prosperity-killers are in power. But the Republicans have failed the people of this state. You know that."

"We know it," shouted a man in the audience.

"You said it," echoed someone else.

And within minutes, a wave of protest and agreement passed through the crowd. Matthias waited for their attention.

"When you vote for me for representative to the United State

Congress, you are voting for change. You're voting for a party that will rescue this state and this nation from economic disaster. You're voting for a party that represents you, the everyday man who struggles to make a living in hard times."

The stirrings in the crowd were like responses to a judge's sentence. The man in front of Madeline nodded vigorously. His wispy hair covered his ears and he wore clothes that had been washed to fading, but his hands were clean.

"Government is a juggernaut. When it moves in a downward slide toward destruction, it takes a bold and mighty effort to stop it." Matthias raised his palms as though pressing back the oncoming juggernaut. "It takes the will of the people! And we are the people that can do it!"

Clapping began spontaneously and grew louder and louder until Matthias quieted the audience.

"These are perilous times. Look around you. Industries are failing. Businesses are closing. Agriculture is suffering from low prices and high costs to farmers. Government is only interested in protecting the upper classes. Who does our government represent? Only the wealthy have influence in our national Congress. Only the wealthy have influence in our state congress."

Many in the crowd nodded as he continued.

"My opponent is still the junior representative and he has been in office for seventeen years!" Matthias pointed to his chest with his thumb. "Ask yourself the question, 'What has Ed Wason done for me?'"

The man in front of Madeline pointed to his own chest and vigorously shook his head.

"That's right. *Nothing*. That's what he's done. *Nothing*. He rode the crest of good fortune and took all the credit. But now, when the going's rough, what does he say?" Matthias posed aristocratically and mimicked a patrician voice, "'Things aren't as bad as they seem.'"

He paused a beat then answered rhetorically, "Oh? Aren't they?"

"They are so!" shouted the man in front of Madeline.

Then others took up the call, with baritone responses rippling over the rows of chairs.

"Of course they are," Matthias agreed. "This country—this state—is in the worst shape it's been in since the Civil War and my opponent says things aren't as bad as they seem. Well, I say things are worse than we know, and we'd better do something about it soon!"

He pointed out into the crowd. "What do you say?"

The thin man in front of Madeline stood up and cheered and she finally glimpsed his face. It was one of the Weekes brothers; she couldn't say which one. Soon, others joined in, and only Madeline and Georgie were left seated.

What could be done to stop this terrible momentum? The audience applauded and interrupted with cheers at every turn of his speech. How easily he led them. How persuasive he was. The inevitability of Matthias Carson alarmed her.

At the end, Matthias summed up, in a pitched voice, "All of you, no matter what your party politics have been in past, all of you are here for the same reason. You're frustrated. You're worried about your families and your future. And you know something has got to change. You came here tonight to see if I'm the one who can help change things for the better.

"And I say to you, YES! I will work for you, for the working people of this state. Not the rich. Not the aristocrats. Not the patricians. Not the cronies. Not the grafters. Not the secret society of party pols. Not any of them. I'll work for you. No one else." He pointed out again at the audience. "For YOU! That's the way democracy is supposed to operate. It's time we took back our government!"

He encircled the room with both arms as if clasping them to his chest, and the audience clapped their approval over and over as though they had discovered true love. The Weekes brother—whichever one he was—whistled through his teeth. Others did likewise.

When it was done, Madeline quietly rose and waited for Matthias Carson to acknowledge her. Her legs were shaking and she steadied herself by holding onto the back of the wooden chair in front of her.

"You have something you would like to say, Miss Abbott?"

Matthias asked politely.

She was afraid her voice would betray her, but despite her trepidation, Madeline spoke clearly and calmly.

"It just occurs to me, Mr. Carson, that you don't seem to be suffering with the Depression. Lawyers seldom starve, that I know of." She pushed herself away from the chair and half-turned to the audience to make her point. "I notice that you have a costly new car. Expensive clothes. You don't seem to be economizing. How do you manage it?"

The audience murmured. Madeline could feel them wavering. She saw they wanted an answer to her question. As though he perhaps were not really one of them.

Matthias responded quickly.

"I began my life in poverty," he said softly, and the room quieted to listen. "I grew up in poverty. My family were the working poor, like many of you." He looked around slowly, commanding their full attention. "I put myself through school by my own labor. There was no free ride. I earned my law degree the hard way. I worked for it." Some began nodding. "I would have continued to practice law and make a living that way for the rest of my life if I hadn't had this extraordinary opportunity."

He paused to let them reflect on what he said and then continued. "It was only through three women who believed in me that I'm here tonight. The first was my mother, who worked double shifts in a factory to support our family. The second was an elderly friend who was kind enough to think of me in her will and give me the means to run for the Congress so that I could help others. So that I could give all of you the helping hand that she gave me. And that is my mission. Because of her, that is what I will accomplish. I will always owe Miss Celia Eastman the greatest debt of gratitude.

"The third woman to whom I am indebted is here with me tonight. It is through her continuing support that I am standing before you. I give you my wife, Mira Carson." He nodded to Mira and beckoned her to stand up. "With her by my side, I will do what I promise."

Madeline watched Mira look to her husband in a pale fever of stage fright. But Matthias walked over and took her arm, lifting her out of her seat. As Mira stood, so did the audience. Cheering him, cheering her, and drowning out the old woman's next question in applause.

Matthias waited, never taking his eyes off Madeline. When the clamor began to subside, he asked pointedly, "Now, are there any further questions."

"Yes," she answered.

Madeline and Matthias looked directly at each other. The noise in the hall diminished as everyone watched the old lady in the front row, seated next to the big Indian who came in with her. When the audience was completely hushed, Matthias spoke.

"Yes, Miss Abbott?"

Madeline cleared her throat. "You claim you understand the problems of the working poor—as you call them. Would you mind telling us, Mr. Carson, what exactly are your assets?"

Matthias broke into a smile. He put his arm around Mira's shoulder.

"You mean, in addition to my beautiful wife?"

As soon as he said it, the audience began laughing and clapping. The volume grew, filling the hall. He was Their Candidate.

Madeline continued to stand without expression and watched Matthias Carson step forward to receive their applause. Mira drifted into the background with the beefy politician. Madeline watched it all with contempt. And foreboding.

CHAPTER FOUR

" . . . to persevere
In obstinate condolement is a course
Of impious stubbornness
It shows a will most incorrect to Heaven . . . "

The October sun burned bright on the surface of the lake, bright as the fire through the screen in the woodstove on Madeline's porch. She sat once again with the afghan, which she had stopped knitting during the summer when it became too hot on her lap and the colors seemed unseasonable. But the orange of the reflected sun, of the autumn foliage, and the orange in the afghan were like the burning inside Madeline's head. She could hardly sit still from rage at Matthias Carson. He had defeated her at every turn.

No longer did she have the element of surprise on her side when she appeared at his rallies. She had been to five of them so far. It was a challenge each time to ask her questions in a different way, to try to catch him off-guard. He was always ready for her, always so gentlemanly in the way he treated her in public, so patronizing, so patient with the dotty old woman. It galled her, yet strengthened her resolve. She tried to knit, her needles clacking like a battle of antlers as she considered what to do.

There would be another rally this week. He was campaigning in Raleigh, a popular hometown appearance. She would have to think of something else to confound him. She shook her head. What did they all see in him? He made them believe he was going to work miracles. Was that what Celia had believed? Was that how he bamboozled her? Now he'd bamboozled all of them.

Perhaps she could influence a few people not to vote for him. Just enough to prevent him from a majority. She did not care if people thought she was peculiar. She did not care what anyone thought. Never had. Oh, well, that wasn't quite true. She had cared about what Harold had thought, and her brother Nathan, and her parents. And later, Celia. But that's all. Her classmates had always made fun of her. They had called her Ichabod, even though she was a girl, because she was gangly, all knees and elbows like Ichabod Crane. Then they shortened it to Icky. Icky Abbott. They said it so often, it became a name instead of a joke, and after a time she was just Icky Abbott and they forgot why. She did not become Madeline again until she graduated valedictorian.

Her classmate, Emily Standish, had been salutatorian; they had been rivals since first grade. Madeline remembered every word of every classroom competition even now.

"Does anyone know the capitol of Missouri?" the teacher had asked.

"St. Louis," answered Emily, promptly standing.

"No, it's Jefferson City," corrected Madeline who stood to face the shorter girl with the bright red Tootsie Roll curls.

"Correct, Miss Abbott. That's a minus-point, Miss Standish."

At recess, Emily had come up to her with two other girls as Madeline sat stiffly in the backbrace she wore into adolescence.

"Do you always have to be right, Icky Abbott?"

Yes, Madeline thought as they turned their backs and walked away. The three girls joined the rest of their female classmates playing double Dutch, squealing when they missed their footing in the ropes and laughing at the boys on the other side of the wire fence playing blind man's bluff.

They were so silly. She was smarter than all of them.

That was many, many years ago, she reminded herself. No point dwelling on the past.

She turned the wireless radio to the only station it received and began knitting to the music of Bach with renewed vigor. She had learned to pass years in her own company thus.

Listening to a particularly stentorian passage of Beethoven's, she never heard the car drive up to the front of the house. So when Georgie came in from the kitchen and knocked on the doorframe saying, "The lady is here, Miz Abbott. She asked to see you," Madeline had no idea who he meant.

"What lady, Georgie?"

"Missus Carson."

"Mira?" Madeline dropped her knitting to her lap. She might have expected anyone except her. Had she underestimated the girl? "Is she alone?"

"Yes'm. There's a driver in the car but he's still sitting there. She come in by herself."

"Humph," Madeline snorted. "I didn't credit her with that much gumption. But self-preservation is a strong motivator, Georgie. Show her in."

Madeline had an image of the young woman sitting on the stage with her husband, rally after rally. Each time she became a little more poised, her smile coming easier each time he turned to her. At the end of the rallies, after the rest of the audience had filed out, Madeline lingered to watch. The politicians surrounded Matthias and Mira like children around a maypole.

At first, Mira had stood next to her husband, silent and frozen. But lately, Madeline noted that Mira had become more animated, shaking this one's hand, whispering in that one's ear. Madeline recalled a cartoon she'd seen in a newspaper that showed a progression of monkeys to humans. Darwinian heresy, the caption called it. But it reminded her of Mira's transformation.

"Good afternoon, Miss Abbott." As confident as she looked upon entering, Mira's voice was almost deferential.

Madeline glanced up only briefly to notice her visitor was dressed chicly in a cherry-red woolen suit and coat to match, both with black leather trim. She wore black pumps and carried a black leather purse. Her hair was coiffed under a feathered black hat, making her look very much like a woman in the public eye. The scent of her perfume was camellias.

"Good afternoon." Madeline looked down and continued her knitting.

"Is it an afghan?" the girl said tentatively.

"Yes."

"It's a pretty design. Very . . . colorful. May I sit down?"

"As you like."

Sitting gracefully, Mira removed her black kid gloves and set her hands in her lap, her knees pressed tightly together. When Madeline said nothing to her, she took a deep breath and began.

"Matt doesn't know I'm here. I want you to understand that. I'm acting on my own."

"So you have something to say to me in secret." Madeline remained studiously indifferent, focusing on the rows of wool falling from her fingertips.

Mira frowned. "It's not a secret. I think you know why I'm here. I've come to ask you to stop disrupting my husband's campaign rallies."

"I see," Madeline said, knitting and purling, rhythmically clicking the needles. "You think I'm disrupting his rallies?" There was a note of satisfaction in her voice.

"I don't know what else you'd call it," Mira blurted. "You sit in the front row with your hand up at every chance to interrupt. Yes, I think you're disruptive."

"I only ask the salient questions."

"About his finances," Mira said accusingly.

"That's my prerogative, isn't it?"

"No. And it just makes people think there's something wrong when there isn't. You could jeopardize his election, and that isn't fair." Mira pounded her fists on her knees. "Matt will be a wonderful congressman and he deserves that chance."

"It's nice that you think so."

"You're not even a New Hampshire resident. You have no part in this election."

Madeline unraveled the last few stitches and spoke as though to a petulant child, "The announcements do not say 'residents only.'"

Mira shook her head and looked out the window over the lake. "What is it you're trying to accomplish?" Her voice took on a plaintive tone.

"You said it yourself," Madeline replied evenly. "I might jeopardize his election. I hope I can. For Celia's sake."

Mira swung around to face her. "Well just consider the fact that your friend Celia wanted Matt to be elected."

"Hardly."

Mira stood up. "You're not listening to me! I'm asking you to stop what you're doing. If you don't, we'll have to take legal action against you."

"I doubt if your husband is inclined do anything precipitous before election day."

"This isn't a game, Miss Abbott."

Madeline finally put down her knitting and appraised the young woman standing in front of her. She saw the earnestness in Mira's face. Perhaps, Mira really was here on her own.

"I know that. Actions have consequences, Mrs. Carson. That's what this is all about."

Mira began pacing. "If you're so convinced that Matt had something to do with Miss Eastman's death, why don't you just go to the police?"

"I have."

Mira stopped short with a look of amazement on her face.

"Unfortunately," Madeline continued, "there was no remaining evidence of the crime."

"There was no crime."

"So you say."

"Miss Eastman wasn't murdered. Matt had nothing to do with her death. She died from leukemia. It's all in your mind. How can you persecute him like this?"

"He took her money, didn't he?" Madeline's voice snapped closed like her purse.

"That's what it's all about, isn't it? It's a side of Miss Eastman you've never understood. You can't accept that she had feelings that you don't have. She was a believer in people. All sorts of people. She saw our best. And it was just like her to leave him the money."

"I would expect you to think so."

Mira clenched her fists and the color rose in her face. She was almost in tears.

"You are a destructive woman, Miss Abbott! You're an old spinster who hasn't got anything else to do but play out some bizarre idea about Celia Eastman's death. You're so obsessed with it, it's made you crazy."

Madeline slowly picked up her afghan and began knitting again. "Now that you've said your piece, you must be anxious to be going along."

She sensed Mira struggling to keep her composure, and it made her happy. Then the young woman turned on her heel and started to leave. But she stopped.

"Well?" Madeline said curtly.

"I don't know how to reach you, Miss Abbott. I tried to be nice and I wound up being mean, and that wasn't what I intended. I'm sorry." Then after a short pause, she added, "I don't hate you, Miss Abbott."

"I don't hate you either, Mrs. Carson. Neither do I hate your husband. But there was a wrong committed that must be righted."

"Wrongs should be righted," Mira responded with conviction.

"But I don't believe in your wrong. Nobody does." She let that lie between them a moment and then added, "Doesn't that at least make you question yourself?"

As Mira left, Madeline sat stiffly with her knitting needles poised in mid-air.

After dinner that evening, Madeline went into the living room to sit in her favorite armchair next to the mahogany side table while Georgie lit the fireplace. The nights were chilly now and only the purple-topped turnips remained in the vegetable patch. They would not be plucked until after the first frost. Everything else from the garden had been harvested and preserved. Georgie had made sweet-potato pie for dessert and they had poured a little canned, sweetened condensed milk over their pie so it became rich and creamy and delicious. Before Georgie, Madeline would simply have had the condensed milk on white bread for her treat.

Even as a child, she loved her sweets. Would rather have had dessert and nothing else. And with it all, remained skinny. But none of the desserts she had as a child were as wonderful as Georgie's pies and tarts. While he made very respectable cookies and pound cakes, she had resurrected her French cookbooks and was going to teach him to make genoise, ganache and crème brulée this winter. It would give them both something to do.

Leafing through the stack of books on her side table, Madeline read recipes by the light of the large kerosene lamp and tried not to think about Mira's visit. But the girl's words haunted her. "Doesn't that at least make you question yourself?" In actuality, Madeline had never questioned herself. And she had had no doubt whatsoever that Matthias Carson was guilty. But she had to concede the point that no one else believed it. No one.

Could she be wrong? No, she could not allow the possibility. There must be some way to prove it. Anyone with Matthias Carson's nature could never keep to the straight and narrow. He was like fancy frosting on a lopsided cake. Maybe Celia wasn't even the first person he'd duped. But she would have no way of knowing. Maybe, she pondered, Celia won't be the last, either. Her thoughts went immediately to Amos Prentice. Hadn't she watched Dr. Roland Niles and Matthias Carson coming out of his house the day she saw the election poster?

She let her fingers rest on the page that described the preparation of eclairs, and stared into the fire through the woodstove screen. The flames soothed her now.

The following day, Madeline drove to Raleigh alone. The lake, reflecting the autumn leaves, was like a vast marigold, with orange and yellow petals surrounding the center. The road around the lake was like a gorge through a canyon of bright colors. But Madeline was too deep in thought to pay attention.

As Madeline knocked at the weathered oak door and stood anxiously waiting, an elderly man finally opened it. Amos Prentice was at least as old as she was, if not older, and as tall, if not taller, but he was so hunched and twisted with rheumatism that he looked up at her from below her shoulders. Fleetingly, Madeline wondered what happened when he lay down. Did his knees straighten out? Did his back sink into the mattress? Did he have to sleep on his side like a tucked-up child?

"Good afternoon, Mr. Prentice. I am Madeline Abbott."

He peered at her through wire-rimmed glasses. "It's Miss Abbott, is it?"

"Yes. May I come in to speak with you for a moment?"

"Certainly. Always glad to have company." He gestured her inside with his black walnut cane.

The living room was dark, with navy blue drapes obscuring the windows and only a slit of white lace between them. Although there was barely enough illumination, Madeline could see the room was tidy and well-furnished. But there was a pervasive stale odor that made her want to throw aside the drapes and open the windows to allow fresh air and sunshine in.

As he invited her to sit, he apologized, "I'm afraid I can't offer you anything. My housekeeper's off today. She usually prepares my meals the day before, you know." When he smiled, his large amber teeth filled his face.

Pumpkin teeth, Madeline thought to herself, but not unkindly.

"That's quite all right, Mr. Prentice. I only wanted to ask you a question."

He sat down by placing the backs of his knees against the seat of the stuffed chair and dropping into it unceremoniously. His legs were so thin they seemed to disappear into his trousers. He adjusted himself and waited for her to continue.

"I recall," Madeline began, "seeing Dr. Niles come out of your house with Mr. Carson a few weeks ago." She searched his face for a response before he even spoke.

"Dr. Niles, yes. I was quite ill for a while this summer."

"You're recovered, then, I'm glad to see."

"Oh, yes. It took several months and I was near death's door a couple of times. But Doc Niles is a good doctor. Half the people in town are his patients. I highly recommend him, if that's what you came to ask."

Madeline was pleased this was going so well. Mr. Prentice, she felt sure, would tell her anything she wanted to know.

"And is Mr. Carson your lawyer?"

"Yes," he nodded. "Nice man. Even running for Congress, he still finds time to give me legal counsel."

"Please forgive my curiosity, but is he helping you with your will? I'm having to think about such things myself now."

"Not a youngster like you," he joked and Madeline deferentially smiled. "Oh, yes," he continued, "Mr. Carson is drawing up my will. But, as I recall, you don't live in Raleigh, do you? You're on the Vermont side, aren't you? You'd probably do better with a lawyer over there. As for a doctor, however, I think Doc Niles would come if you needed him. Are you ailing?"

"Well, I have been having some malady or another lately. Weakness and stomach pains." She felt badly about lying to this kindly old gentleman, but it was necessary.

"Goodness, that's just what I had." He tapped his stomach with crab-like hands. "I think it was some sort of summer grippe. But, thankfully, it has passed."

Amos Prentice was obviously pleased to have someone of his own age to talk with. He told her he used to have such conversations with Celia when she would come into town and stop by his house for a visit. They had gone to school together, him two grades ahead.

Indeed, in his senior year in high school, he confided, he'd invited Celia to the Independence Day Picnic, but she was so popular back then she already had a date. She was, he related, a pretty little blue-eyed blonde, so independent driving her daddy's horse-and-buggy and ice skating circles around all the other girls. She almost married the best-looking boy in school, Amos's younger brother, Justin, who had asked her out first. But Celia's daddy died when she was only nineteen and Celia had to take care of her sick mother all the rest of her life. Whoever would have believed Celia Eastman would wind up an old maid?

His brother, Amos told her, had moved to Boston and married a city girl while he stayed in Raleigh and married Celia's friend, Verna Watts. They never had any children and Verna died five years ago of pneumonia after going out of the house on a cold day without a coat to fetch the mail. Celia's father had died in a lingering way. Some rumored that it was an S-E-X disease; Mr. Daniel Eastman was a traveling man. But Amos maintained it was nobody's business but the family's. Sad thing, how Celia lost her chances. Nevertheless, she was always a good friend to Verna and helped her through the worst of it. Celia was the one who told him about Doc Niles a while back; only poor Celia got worse, and he got better. "Can't believe she's gone," he said with a little shake of his head.

"Did you have medicine for your illness?" Madeline asked, interrupting his reverie.

"Hmmm?" He took a moment to come back to the present. "Oh my, yes."

"Would you mind if I looked at the bottle?"

He registered surprise. "No, I suppose not. But you can't get it without a prescription, you know."

"I understand."

Visibly puzzled, Amos Prentice got up with effort and shuffled out of the room. When he returned, he handed Madeline a brown glass bottle half full of medicine.

"This is it. But you mustn't drink it. It might not be the right thing for you."

Madeline gingerly uncorked the bottle and smelled the contents. It didn't have the same smell she remembered. What was that smell? She couldn't recapture it. But this definitely was not it. Her face mirrored her disappointment.

"Is something wrong?"

"No, not at all, Mr. Prentice. I just wondered if this was the same medicine that I'd had once before. But I don't think it is."

Amos Prentice made his way back to the chair, saying, "I had some other medicine first. Awful stuff. But I don't take it anymore."

"Why is that?" Madeline's interest was piqued.

"Dr. Niles changed it. He said the other medicine had done its work, it was time for a new one. And he was right, because I felt lots better after that."

"How long ago did he change your medicine?" Madeline asked with particular concern.

"Let's see. A few months, anyway. Some time in August."

Around the time she saw Doctor Niles and Matthias Carson at his house, she calculated. Did they change it because they thought she might be suspicious?

"You wouldn't happen to still have that first medicine, would you?"

"Nope. Couldn't get rid of it fast enough. But all's well that ends well."

He smiled a jack-o-lantern smile and Madeline, concealing her discouragement, smiled back.

• • •

That night was a restless one for Madeline. Each time she dropped off to sleep, something seemed to awaken her. She thought she heard someone call "Maddie," and she sat bolt upright. It was a light voice, spoken quickly, and she could not be sure whether it was male or female. Nathan or Celia. But even though she strained to listen, she heard nothing more than the wind and the ticking of her clock.

The wind picked up around midnight, humming and vibrating through the cracks around the windows. Then it began to rain, pulsing rain that sounded like waves against the side of the house. Madeline imagined all the marigold-colored leaves swirling to the ground to their death.

Everything dies in its own natural time. However, it is sometimes difficult to know, Madeline speculated, when Nature is at work and when it isn't. If a storm brings on a leaf's death, is it less natural than if it drops off by itself? If Celia died of leukemia, is it less natural than if she died of old age? I don't know, she deliberated wearily. It depends on whether or not the leukemia was natural. Then she thought about Mira's visit. Around and around she went until she fell asleep at last, just before four a.m.

By six a.m., the rain stopped and Madeline awakened suddenly to footsteps in the hallway. At first, she was frozen in terror, unable to move. She felt as if she were pinned to the bed, wanting to run or scream, but somehow mute and weak. She wanted to cry out to Georgie. Then she realized it indeed was Georgie, going downstairs to the cellar to add coal to the stove and warm the house.

She sighed deeply. She was thankful to have him do these things that, for so long, she had had to do for herself. She always hated getting up to a chilly room. She shivered and pulled the covers up to her chin. Even the cylindrical kerosene heater was not enough to heat her bones. Not even the bedwarmer had been enough to warm deep into the mattress. She was becoming brittle now. The weather affected her. She fell back to sleep thinking of her cold fingers and toes as snowmen lined up in a row.

• • •

Later in the morning, as Madeline stood at the window of her porch looking out across the lake, she still had not come to a decision. How far should she pursue her suspicions? Was she obsessed and crazy as Mira had said? Was she even right in her belief?

There were dark circles under her eyes in the mirror this morning and her face looked drawn. All of her night struggles had come to nothing. What should she do?

She shook her head. She had proven nothing about Matthias Carson. No matter what she did, she had proven nothing. Was she tormenting him unfairly? Was she going to ruin Mira's life and his life on nothing but suspicion? Madeline rubbed her hands over her eyes, forehead and temples in a circular motion as if to soothe her torment.

As she pondered, Georgie entered with an armload of seasoned wood for the porch stove. Madeline barely took notice of him.

"All the pretty colors is gone now, ain't they?" Georgie said.

Madeline hadn't registered it, but indeed the leaves had all been swept to the ground by the night's storm. Nothing was left but the bare branches. Bare bones like herself.

"Yes," she replied listlessly.

"Are you all right, Miss Abbott?"

"Yes."

"Excuse me for sayin', but you look tur-moiled."

Madeline made a small attempt at a smile. "I guess I am 'tur-moiled,' Georgie."

She stood silently for a while, watching as he stacked the wood in the bin and added some to the fire. The stove crackled and sputtered as he closed the iron door.

"Tell me something, Georgie, when you go to church, does the preacher talk about Good and Evil?"

"Yes, ma'am. That's the nature of all his preaching." Georgie evened out the stack of wood in the bin like straightening books on a shelf. "The Reverend is scriptural. He says the contest of Good and Evil is our human condition since the dam-ned Fall."

Faintly amused, Madeline became serious again. Glancing back at Celia's house, she said, "I once thought I knew evil when I saw it. But now I'm no longer sure."

She watched him follow her gaze over to the Eastman house but he said nothing.

Madeline turned away and sighed. Could Celia have manipulated them all? Otherwise why would she bequeath her house to Mira? Give David access to the library? Give Carson all her money and Georgie none? Give her the statue of Georgie's mother? Was that Matthias's doing or Celia's? As much as she wanted to be convinced it was Matthias, she couldn't entirely disbelieve it was Celia.

"It seems to me," she said more to herself than Georgie, "that if Celia Eastman intended to play God, then God's intentions have gotten devilishly out of hand."

On the same morning that Madeline Abbott stood on her porch trying to decide whether to go to the rally that night, Matthias Carson was meeting with New Hampshire's senior Republican State Senator.

The new Democratic candidate stood in the marble-floored foyer of the mansion that State Senator Dalton Hargrave had named Hargrave Hall. The senator was walking down the curved staircase, dressed in his morning coat and high-top shoes. With his pork-chop whiskers, he looked, Matthias reflected, like a portrait he'd seen in the Boston Athenaeum of a Beacon Hill stalwart. He was the kind of gentry that Matthias would never be, with notable lineage in the history of the state. Matthias Carson, at this moment, was face-to-face with his envy.

"Good morning, Mr. Carson. How do you do?" The voice was mellifluous.

Of course, Matthias realized, the Republican Party officers would have been discussing him ever since he announced his candidacy. It was not so much fear of this one upstart Democrat that had put them into a frenzy. It was the fear of Franklin Delano Roosevelt and the mood of the nation. There was a mass movement taking shape before their very eyes: a storm of protest over the economy and living conditions. It would seem to them a veritable revolution, not unlike the peasants' French Revolution—not, mind you, like the patriots' American Revolution. It was a wave of discontent from the rabble, the voting rabble, and there was every possibility that a "democrat" (the worst kind of "Democrat") would take the White House.

The elder statesman's expression was patronizing, Matthias recognized, as Hargrave viewed this young opponent for the historically Republican congressional seat. After stiffly polite greetings, the senator escorted him into the drawing room and invited Matthias to sit in the brocade chair opposite his own. Hargrave fancied himself, Matthias sensed, looking like Oliver Wendell Holmes.

Most likely Hargrave knew Matthias's *curriculum vita* or at least its critical elements. Admittedly, none of it was very impressive. Second-rate schooling, second-rate career. Massachusetts-born but looking for easier pickings. And the way in which he'd inherited his new-found wealth was probably suspect. Never had the likes of him been a guest in Hargrave Hall.

But, Matthias thought, I'm a *viable* candidate, and they know that is something to be taken seriously.

The senator sat back in his leather wing chair with the confidence of a man whose bank account was in protected Swiss francs, unaffected by Depression dollars.

"You have come to our attention, Mr. Carson, in your contest for Congressman Wason's seat in the United States Legislature this term."

Matthias merely nodded in humble, seemingly grateful acknowledgment.

"We, ah," Hargrave continued, "have been observing your progress. You seem to be enjoying some local popularity."

"I hope so, sir," he replied ingenuously. "I believe in developing a constituency for my Party. I think that gives the voters the best options. Don't you?"

Hargrave didn't answer immediately. Matthias supposed he was wondering whether that was some sort of subtle jab that New

Hampshire didn't have an equal two-party system. Hargrave certainly knew the values of a two-party system and wouldn't like being reminded of principles he grew up on, that were part of the fabric of his political life.

"I was referring to your personal popularity, Mr. Carson. I understand you attract local audiences to your rallies."

Matthias inclined his head slightly, but said nothing. Hargrave was observing him. What was he seeing? A good-looking if somewhat common fellow who might have passed for a well-fitted laborer. But something about the eyes that perhaps made Hargrave uneasy. Did the senator realize that Matthias was not to be underestimated?

"I'm told," Hargrave continued, "you're running quite strong for a newcomer. And while you won't unseat Edward Hills Wason this term, of course, you do seem to have a political future ahead of you."

"I shall certainly try," he replied, leaving it ambiguous whether he was trying to have a political future, or trying to unseat Wason.

Hargrave harrumphed.

Of course Hargrave would be perfectly cognizant that Wason was a weak link, Matthias knew. But the senator most likely was convinced his Party was strong enough to overcome that.

Hargrave rose from his chair and went to the fireplace, taking an andiron and poking at the logs to reposition them. He spoke without turning around.

"We realize that Congressman Wason, with a long and dedicated career, is nearing the end of political service to the Second District. The coming term will very likely be his last."

"I would suggest," Matthias responded, "that the previous term is likely to be his last."

Hargrave remained silent and Matthias wished he could see the senator's face. Finally, the senator said, "You must realize, Mr. Carson, that the Democratic Party in this state has no structure and no strength. The donkey party is never going to carry New Hampshire. Thus, it cannot possibly satisfy your political needs in the long run."

"I'm aware that our state has been traditionally Republican," Matthias responded.

Hargrave seemed to bristle at "our state" and stiffened his back. But his voice was evenly modulated. "If you were to join with the Grand Old Party, you would have a very promising political future in New Hampshire. We could groom you for the highest possible state offices."

As Hargrave turned to face him, Matthias saw him swallow hard as though pushing down the acid rising from his stomach. His expression indicated that he found this task personally repugnant.

"Let me be certain I understand your proposal, Senator." Matthias tapped the armrest of the chair as he spoke. "You'd like me to drop out of the *federal* congressional race for this election and switch parties. For that, I would be ensured of a political opportunity at the *state* level in the next election with the backing of the GOP. Is that correct?"

"You have nothing to lose and everything to gain."

"I'd lose the chance of beating Ed Wason."

"You have no chance there anyway. Congressman Wason will be reelected."

Matthias stopped tapping his fingers. "If you believed that, you wouldn't be making this offer."

Hargrave placed the andiron back in its holder. "It's not that we think you can win, Mr. Carson. We are, however, concerned about the margin of your loss."

Matthias nodded. "You mean you don't want the Democratic Party to gain a foothold here."

"We are prepared to meet your ambitions, Mr. Carson. Isn't that what you want?"

"What I want, Senator Hargrave, is a better life for the working poor in this state."

Matthias had screened the righteousness out of his voice, but he knew his eyes had an intensity about them that held a rebuke, possibly an accusation. He could see Hargrave's facial muscles fleetingly tighten in anger.

"Of course," Hargrave replied, sounding like a professor whose freshman student had just shouted "eureka" to something obvious. "That is our common goal."

"I'm gratified to hear you say that, sir." Matthias rubbed his jawline. "It comforts me that, perhaps, our similarities outweigh our differences." Then he added, "Our Parties' differences, that is."

Hargrave paused uncertainly, then responded, "Then it may not be so unlikely to think the Republican Party can represent some of the same interests you espouse. Perhaps you will consider our offer in this light."

Matthias stood up and said, "Thank you for the invitation, Senator. You've certainly given me a great deal to think about."

"When do you think we might have your decision, Mr. Carson?"

"You can expect to hear from me soon, Senator."

Matthias followed his host to the front door, withholding a smile. He extended his hand and the elder statesman shook it strongly, indicating to Matthias that Hargrave felt he had done his job. He would likely report back to the officers that Matthias might be persuaded to join them. They could rely, he would probably tell them, on the man's cunning self-interest.

So, the Republicans were nervous. Good. He wanted them to be quaking.

Hargrave's manner had brought back embarrassing memories of being treated in law school as if he had dirty fingernails. And here was the state's senator, in his baronial setting, reminding him that Matthias was not of the same social order, but of some lower class. An idiot savant, as it were. Well, he would not accept. He had—no, he *was* something they wanted. And he was going to rub their noses in it in the most genteel way.

He would not make an enemy of Hargrave. No doubt he would have to work with him on the state level in the years ahead. But Matthias's political focus was on Washington not Concord.

Inwardly, Matthias was rejoicing.

• • •

The next morning, he telephoned the senator and was put through immediately.

"Thank you for the kind offer, sir," Matthias said, "but I fear that I'm not Republican material. I think your more refined constituency would find me unsuitable. And in the end, I might do more harm than good to the Republican Party. However, as a Democrat, I look forward to working with you someday soon."

"Thank you, Mr. Carson, for your veracity," the senator said evenly.

Matthias smiled. Only two weeks to the election and he was talking to the senator as a peer. He could imagine Dalton Hargrave clenching his teeth as he hung up.

That night, in the Elk's hall in Raleigh, the audience was filled to capacity as Matthias Carson took his place at the podium. Mira was seated behind him. He scanned the audience for Madeline Abbott. When he did not find her, he felt palpably relieved and then quite pleased with himself.

On November twenty-second, a crowd of hundreds assembled at the base of the steps of the State Capitol to await the announcement of November eighth's federal election results. All the enthusiasts were bundled in warm clothing, cheeks rosy and frosted breaths puffing lightly in the cold air.

Although New Hampshire (and indeed Vermont) obstinately went for Hoover, national voters ushered in not only FDR but also a Democratic majority in the seventy-third Congress as well. For the first time since World War I, the Dems held the U.S. Senate majority, fifty-nine to thirty-six (plus one lone Minnesotan from the Farm Labor Party). In the U.S. House of Representatives, 313 of the 435 elected members were Democrats. Including Matthias Carson.

The crowd cheered. Mira beamed. Matthias stood on the steps with his left arm around Mira's shoulders and his right arm raised in victory.

He was no longer a commoner. A new life had begun.

CHAPTER FIVE

"My crown, mine own ambition, and my queen."

Mira stood in the master bathroom in her white peignoir, brushing her hair in slow strokes, the way she used to do when her hair was long. The rhythm was automatic, soothing. She stared into the mirror unblinking, not seeing herself or watching her hands move across her glossy black bob. All she was aware of was the tumultuous beat of her heart and the dryness of her mouth. Tonight was the victory party for Matt's election. In twelve hours, she would be hostess to a formal dinner for twenty influential people from the right society. And she had never given a party before in her life.

On their engagement, six months previously, Matthias had informed Mira that he had every intention of their becoming the social center of the Democratic Party in New Hampshire, second only to the party chairman himself, Aubrey Dunlop. Regardless of the outcome of the vote, he told her to begin planning a dinner party for the Saturday after the election. If the election turned against him, he said, they would call it a thank-you party for his allies, and better luck next time.

Mira had protested that she had no experience in giving an afternoon tea, let alone a significant dinner party. She had been on the verge of panic, whereupon Matthias reassured her she would receive all the training she needed. He went to Boston the following week and hired Mrs. Greenough who taught etiquette at the city's most prominent finishing school, to help Mira plan the event. He further hired a chef and butler for the occasion and arranged to keep both, permanently. Alva was to be their maid, which made the young girl happy enough because she never thrilled to cooking and had no desire to "buttle." Mira was relieved to have all the help, but still intimidated by the idea of hosting a soirée for people who otherwise would not say hello to her.

Mrs. Greenough had arrived on August first, a day after Mira and Matthias returned from their honeymoon. She would spend all of August with them, returning on weekends to Boston after school began, until the party. Mrs. Greenough was a small round woman with dainty feet and hands that fluttered like butterflies. Her cheerful smile reminded Mira a little of Celia.

Mira's days-in-training were spent in such exercises as 'What constitutes fashion?' How to set a table and use the proper utensils. How to arrange flowers. And constant drills on polite conversation. She was completely awed that there were so many details to even the slightest social activity. It was so absurdly alien to everything she had ever known, it fascinated her. Mrs. Greenough was very patient, having realized immediately that the young woman would have to be educated a great deal in a very short time.

"Mrs. Dunlop, how very delighted we are to have you join us tonight," she practiced. And, "So good of you to come, Mr. Armstrong. Mr. Wentworth. Mrs. Dennisdale."

They walked around the room with grace, sat at the table and unfurled pleated napkins and, most important of all, planned the menu for the party. They made lists, then lists of lists.

But while Mrs. Greenough demonstrated sitting and standing to absolute perfection, Mira often had to hide her amusement at watching this chubby little woman model how to make elegant entrances and exits. The portals were too high for her diminutive height and too narrow for her girth. Her teacher was just not meant for doorways.

How smart of Matt, though, she acknowledged, to hire someone so dear and helpful as Mrs. Greenough. It might have been a Madeline Abbott-type he engaged, and then where would she be? No, he'd deliberately sought out a woman who was just a little like Celia in her warmth and patience. Mira was profoundly grateful for his selection. There were times it seemed Matthias hardly paid any attention to her. But then he would do something as considerate as this.

Slowly, with Mrs. Greenough's help, Mira's apprehension diminished. Until this morning, that is. Now, the day of the party had arrived and Mira felt completely unsettled. She desperately wished her instructor were at her side, telling her what to expect and what she should do next.

Her gaze traveled the length and breadth of their newly decorated bathroom. It was entirely modernized, most of it accomplished per Matt's instructions while they were away on their honeymoon. Every appointment had been replaced. New tile had been laid, an Italian marble floor she found too cold and had covered up with area rugs. Everything was redone in hues of brown and gold. The marble was light beige with swirls of darker brown. The toilet, sink and tub were light brown and the fixtures were brass. The wall tile was brown with flecks of gold. Matt seemed to know exactly what he wanted. She had wanted pink, but he vetoed that. He liked things orderly and spare, so there was no clutter. His toiletries were neatly lined up in the cabinet over the commode. She had one glass shelf on the wall by the tub for her powders and perfumes. He would come in while she was primping and hold up a bottle of perfume to the light to see if it was low. If so, he would discard it and buy her another. She had never been so fussy about such things. Before, she might leave a top off this or that, sling a towel over the bathtub, but she would not dare to do that now. Matt was far too meticulous to tolerate any slovenliness. She was very careful to correct her old habits.

She was not at all sure she could pass muster in everything Matt wanted her to do, and no amount of money could buy her that certainty. She had done well at the rallies, Matt had told her. After a while. All she needed, he assured her, was practice. But there'd been no other parties to practice on. This was her debut.

Mira took a deep breath and looked at her reflection. It used to give her pleasure to see her creamy skin, her large eyes framed by dark lashes, her classic looks. But now she could see the terror in those eyes and it paralyzed her. She stood without moving until she was startled by a knock on the bathroom door.

"I'm going out for a little while," Matt announced from the other side of the door. "You'd better get dressed and get things in motion downstairs."

"I will," she heard herself reply shakily. But she stayed in the bathroom until she heard him leave. She did not want Matt to see how nervous she was. He could always tell.

Mira dressed quickly. Her closet was filled with elegant clothes to choose from, most of which they had bought in Paris and Rome. Matt picked out everything she wore, except for a silk lavender dress that she loved. It had short pleated sleeves and a long waist with a pleated skirt. She had chosen that one herself, and it was the dress she felt most comfortable in, despite the fact that Matt said it made her look like an out-of-date flapper. It was that dress she picked to wear now because, well, she didn't know exactly the reason, but it made her feel better. She grabbed the notebook on top of her bureau, the one Mrs. Greenough helped her organize for the party, and she went downstairs.

First, she had to check on the kitchen. The new chef, Emil, with the right French accent and mustache that curled at each end (where did Matt find him?) had been at work on the desserts. Individual mousses au chocolat mounded in the center of dark chocolate petals with white chocolate veins were lined up on the kitchen table ready for the refrigerator.

"Eeet will haf warm rasp-berry sauce surround." Emil made a fancy circular motion with his finger as he explained his plan. "Et un dollop of whip-ped crème on top."

Looking at the array of desserts, Mira remembered Georgie. This had been his kitchen, now enlarged and so different that he would not know it anymore. The new white stove and restaurant-sized refrigerator, double sink and white ceramic countertops made Mira think of a hotel kitchen. It was a far cry from the little green enamel stove and wooden countertop on which Georgie had cooked all those years. Yet, the memory of his tarts, flaky and hot and filling the kitchen with honest aromas of blueberries, gooseberries, straw-berries, rivaled the dessert of this special chef. They had been Mira's favorites. But Mrs. Greenough had explained that tarts were not for formal dining. Dessert had to be exquisite. Mira had always thought Georgie's pastries were just that. Would she ever know enough of the right things to do and say to fit into her new life?

Chef Emil (she felt awkward calling him that, but Mrs. Greenough said it was proper) was beginning to assemble the hors d'oeuvres as Alva placed the desserts on cooking sheets to put into the refrigerator. Hors d'oeuvres were the trickiest part of the menu, Mrs. Greenough explained. They had to accomplish so much. They must not blunt the appetite, but they must seem like finding a pearl in an oyster—pleasurable, valuable, memorable and portable. Chef Emil was preparing the trays of puff-pastry shrimp, caviar toast tips, finger sandwiches of a duck and fig paté, and smoked salmon with a French Brie and dill on imported crackers. That was sufficient, Mrs. Greenough pronounced, for a small party. Mira had paled, thinking that if this was a small party, what else was in store for her?

She moved through the redecorated living room evaluating the effect. Yellow and white roses and white calla lilies had been im-ported for the occasion, interspersed with candles and sparkling crys-tal lamps to be lighted just before the guests arrived. Mira thought the out-of-season flowers were a terrible extravagance but Mrs. Greenough said that autumn flowers were too common for a formal living room decoration.

The dining room was already set up and the new butler, Lewis, was folding the ivory linen napkins into tulips. Mira couldn't imagine Georgie doing any such thing.

"Good morning, Madam," said the dignified older man who sometimes intimidated her.

"Good morning, Lewis. Everything looks quite ready." She sounded more at ease than she felt and she commended herself on her acting.

"Yes, almost, Madam. Just a few pulls and tucks and we're done."

He had the faintest touch of an English accent. Not so much, Matt had explained to her, to be offensive, but just enough to impress. Mira had to admit that Matt did have a sense of what was needed. They had both come from poverty but the difference between them, Mira realized, was that he had studied the upper class around him while she had avoided them.

What if she did something or said something hideously wrong? Or what if they thought she was ignorant of the social graces? What if she dropped something, or spilled something, or laughed in the wrong place?

Mrs. Greenough had drilled her in all the most likely faux pas. Mira would eat slowly, talk little, laugh softly, and move deliberately. But what if someone asked her a question to which she didn't know the answer? "Be whimsical," Mrs. Greenough had advised, "whimsy always works." They had practiced whimsical responses. "Oh, I let Matt worry about the state and the nation. I merely organize our lives." Of course she had told Matt she might say something of this sort, so he would know how to respond. He had seemed, she sensed, quite approving of her diligence.

But now, with the passing hours, all the rehearsals seemed like fantasy, and she was feeling genuine fear again. She gripped her notebook tighter. She felt she might throw up.

By the time Matthias returned to the house two hours later, she and Alva were arguing in the foyer.

"I'm not wearing that ridiculous get-up!" Alva said, her eyes blazing as Mira held a black-and-white maid's uniform.

"There's nothing ridiculous about it," Mira said. "It's a perfectly respectable uniform."

This had been going on for fifteen minutes and they had reached an impasse by the time Matthias came upon them. He listened a moment to Mira's futile arguments and Alva's staunch refusals. His expression was unreadable as Alva turned to him in hope of securing a favorable opinion.

"Mr. Carson, surely you don't think it's necessary for me to wear this. After all, you wouldn't want to seem too la-de-da, would you?"

Matthias's eyes did not even flicker.

"You have two choices, Alva," he said calmly. "Wear the uniform and serve the food properly, or collect your pay and leave."

Alva opened her mouth as though to protest but then decided against it. She thrust out her jaw, stared at him unyieldingly and said, "I'll take cash." She turned on her heel and left the room.

"What do I do now?" Mira asked imploringly.

Matthias went to the telephone. "I'll call Aubrey and ask him to ask Clara if you can borrow their girl for the evening."

Mira winced at the word "girl." But he seemed actually pleased about asking the party chairman to help them out. It was useful to be in his debt in a minor way, Matthias explained. Now Aubrey would ask him for a political favor that he would willingly oblige. Then Matthias would ask Aubrey for another, and the seesaw would begin. In time, he said, they would "up the ante." The trick was to have Aubrey owe him a very large favor. That would be very useful indeed.

Mira listened but her mind was racing toward evening. Twenty guests for dinner. Would anything else go wrong?

She went through the rest of the afternoon in a swivet. She checked with Chef Emil three times in an hour until she saw he was becoming prickly about it. She rearranged the centerpiece on the dining room table. It was a donkey formed of autumn-colored mums with pinecone ears and orange strawflowers for a mane and tail. Autumn flowers were appropriate in the dining room but not the living room. She personally disliked the centerpiece, but Mrs. Greenough assured her it would be a pleasing attention-getter. They had ordered it from a flower shop in Concord because Matt was sure that the Republican florists of North Conway would not accept the order. Mira was learning politics at every turn.

Mira retreated to the bedroom to dress. She laid out her Paris gown on the bed to look at it again. Was it too revealing? The gown had a high neck and dolman sleeves, but hardly any back to it. And it was beige satin. It would show everything. When she tried it on, it had clung to her breasts and hips like warm caramel. Matt liked the dress from the moment they saw it in a salon on the Rue de Monde and he insisted she wear it to the party. When she showed it to Mrs. Greenough, that consummate lady said very little other than, "Well, you have the figure for it, dear."

Mira laid out the matching stockings and shoes on the bed and went into the bathroom. She used a bar of her best perfumed soap, and afterward powdered and perfumed herself in the same camellia fragrance. Mrs. Greenough told her never to mix scents. Overkill was a common mistake made by ingénue socialites.

"Simplicity is the guiding principle in all things," she'd say.

Just as Mira was daubing the backs of her knees with the glass stem of the perfume vial, she felt her stomach contract. She felt nauseous and weak. Within seconds, she was leaning over the toilet, vomiting.

By seven o'clock, Matthias came in to change to his formal attire, and found Mira sitting in front of her vanity in her silk robe. She was shivering.

"What's wrong? Why aren't you dressed?"

"It's hot. I'm burning up." Mira's voice quivered.

He moved quickly to her side and touched her forehead with the back of his hand. "You don't have any fever. You'd better get dressed. Our guests will be arriving soon."

"I can't. I'm sick." Mira pulled her elbows close to her sides and rubbed her arms.

"You're not sick." He sat down on the bench next to her and looked at her reflection in the vanity mirror. "You're scared. That's all."

She shook her head and her teeth began chattering. "No, I feel hot. I feel terrible. I can't do this."

Matthias frowned, his gray eyes becoming obsidian. "Get dressed, Mira."

"I can't." Mira lowered her head. "I just can't." Her body shook. "Tell them I got sick. I'll stay here in the bedroom, you can host the party."

"Get dressed," Matthias repeated. There was no kindness, no understanding, no forgiveness in his voice. But still, Mira could not move.

"I can't," she said raspily, pleadingly, looking up at him in the mirror.

Matthias spread his fingers and wound them through her bobbed hair to her scalp. He tightened his grip and turned Mira's head toward him.

"You will get dressed. I don't care how sick or how scared you are. You're of no use to me, or yourself, if you give in to this. You were frightened to be on stage at the rallies, but I made you do it and you learned to do it well. After tonight, there will be more and more occasions for you to be frightened. So if you don't get over this right now, you will never, never overcome your fear. Do you understand me?"

In that instant, Mira did not know him. His eyes captured hers and seemed to bore into them. She did not know whether he was threatening her for her good or his own. All she knew, would ever know, was that right now he terrified her more than the dinner party, more than the twenty strangers judging her every move, more than socially disgracing herself in any possible way. Mira clenched her teeth and nodded. As he released his grip, she rose to reach for the gown.

As she dressed and Matthias changed into his black formal suit, she saw him watching her warily. For the first time, she began to wonder what her life was going to become. Appearing at the rallies had been scary in the beginning, but Matt was right, she had gotten used to it. Had even grown to like it. But he really had not expected much of her then, just to look appropriately attractive. This was different. Now she had to perform as the successful politician's wife.

On the other hand, it was euphoric. She had married well, better than she expected. Matt was successful, after all, and now life would be full of new experiences. Plus, of course, they were financially well off. Matt was a catch by any woman's standards. And he was an exciting lover. She liked that part of their relationship very much, even if he was a little rough at times. He may have chosen her for reasons of convenience and because she kept him sexually stimulated, but he could just as easily move on to someone else. She did not deceive herself for a minute. Anything that interfered with his ambitions would be cast aside.

No, she had to do this. Somehow. She shook her head in despair as she slipped on the gown. But as she reached behind her neck to button the one satin button at the top, he was there, his hands on her hands, helping her find the buttonloop, kissing her on the nape of her neck and thrusting his tongue in her ear.

"Just remember," he whispered, "do not throw up, faint or look nervous in front of our guests. Do not offer any political opinions. But don't forget to thank Clara Dunlop for helping us out."

She nodded mutely.

"We won't require Clara's girl to wear a uniform," he added.

"I don't understand. Isn't that why you fired Alva?"

"I fired Alva because she was insolent to you. She was quite correct about the uniform."

Mira stared at the square set of his back as Matthias left the bedroom. He was so perfectly designed for this occasion. His suit emphasized his broad shoulders and trim body. He had a natural military posture, straight and easy within himself. He had no reserve, no hesitancy, no insecurity. How can he be so in control, she wondered. He'd had the same disadvantages as she did, but had somehow overcome them. By sheer will, she told herself. He refashioned himself into what he needed to be. She was determined to do the same.

She felt as though she were back in school and she'd failed her first tests. But there was so much more at stake now than grades. She felt herself go chill again and took deep breaths. Soon she would have guests to greet.

Oh, God, I just want it to be over.

That same evening, Madeline sat on her porch polishing her Grandmother Albermarle's silverware with a chamois cloth while Georgie tended the woodstove and read the Bible. They had passed many such nights in each other's company recently.

They listened to the sounds of owls and the occasional echo of a moose over the water, and nodded to each other signifying recognition. Smoke curled up from the Weekes brothers' houses at either end of the lake but, Madeline noted, none from Celia's house. It was such a cold night that she could not imagine why they were not burning coal. The lights were on in all of the downstairs rooms. It looked like a bawdyhouse. She could see several automobiles pulling up to the house and, as she squinted, she could make out figures moving around inside.

"Humph, a victory celebration," she said more to herself than to Georgie.

"Excuse me, Miz Abbott?"

"Matthias Carson is having a whoopee party."

Georgie nodded with a quizzical expression.

"He's won," Madeline concluded, and went back to polishing.

By seven thirty, the guests had arrived at the Carson house. Mira welcomed them as they came into the living room. She had met most of the husbands at the rallies, but she did not know any of the wives. None of them had ever invited her even to tea. She was afraid they would treat her as Madeline had, and was entirely surprised when they greeted her with polite hugs and airy kisses on the cheek. Her reticence won them over more than if she had been confident and secure. When she confessed that this was her first dinner party, Clara Dunlop put a sagging bare arm around her and smiled.

"We all went through it, dear. You're a political wife now, just like the rest of us."

She looked over at Matthias, who was watching them out of the corner of his eye. He gave her a quick approving nod.

The borrowed maid served the hors d'oeuvres and sweet sparkling white grape juice in wine goblets. Matthias was careful to observe Prohibition in company, although he had a full bar of bootleg liquor for personal use.

Aubrey Dunlop led the toast and there were congratulations all around for Matthias's election and for his helpmate.

It escaped no one's notice that Mira Carson was the prettiest and youngest of the group of women. The men tended discreetly to run their eyes up and down Mira's hips, and wish their own wives could wear such slinkiness. Their wives, however, maneuvered themselves between those lustful glances and the object of their desire, like skilled censors. Mira Carson could not help being voluptuous, but their own men had better not even wiggle a toe in her direction or they just might find it in a sling.

Parsifal Leighton's wife, Gladys, drew Mira aside and asked if she might have the recipe for the fig paté. Mira delightedly agreed.

"Now don't give it to anyone else. I asked first," Gladys giggled, bobbing her unstylish henna curls.

Mira nodded, wondering what she would say if anyone else asked.

"Where is your stove, dear? I didn't see any smoke from your chimney."

"Oh, Matt had a propane tank installed and everything refitted. We use the fireplace every so often, but it's so nice to have constant heat without worrying about wood or coal anymore."

"What a grand idea. I must tell Parsifal."

By eight o'clock, they were seated at the dinner table, remarking appreciatively at the first course. The butler ladled the pumpkin bisque into the gold-rimmed china bowls held aloft by Clara Dunlop's maid, who wore a simple black skirt and white blouse.

The wives complimented Mira on her china and her décor. And that led to Aubrey commenting that women were always impressed with the look of things, whereas men, such as himself, delved much deeper. He said this while spooning pumpkin bisque into his mouth and then nodding.

"Now, that is the real substance of entertaining. Delicious, my dear."

Mira smiled gratefully, as pleased as if she had made the dish herself.

"The way to your heart is still through your stomach, Aubrey," Clara said teasingly to her husband.

"And always will be," he replied, patting his girth.

The ice so pleasantly broken, the guests went on to chatter about the price of food, propane heat, their children's illnesses or grades, and the array of non-political inconsequential dinner-party conversation. Mira marveled at the ease with which Clara and Aubrey had generated such amiability, and how they seemed to work together as a team. She wished that, someday, some new political wife might feel the same about her and Matt.

The soup was followed by salad with fresh fruit (flown in by a pilot Matthias hired) to clear and stimulate the palate.

Mira and Matthias sat at opposite ends of the table and most of the conversation was directed toward him. That was a great relief. All Mira had to do was listen attentively and use the right fork in a polite way. Mindful that her stomach was far too nervous to retain very much, she ate quite scantily but managed to give a good impression of enjoying the dinner.

The entrée was leg of lamb with roasted new potatoes, spinach soufflé and whipped yellow turnip. Mrs. Greenough had insisted that the dinner fare be delicious and colorful but not too exotic. It would not do to show off, or to cause the guests to confront foods foreign to their experience. Moderation in the meal, flamboyance in the dessert. The mousse au chocolat was a rousing success.

In all, Mira did not faint or embarrass herself once. Matt would occasionally catch her eye with a slight conspiratorial smile. She would smile back at him and feel contented. Yet, she could still almost feel the tightness of her scalp where he had pulled her hair.

After dinner, the men retreated to the library and the ladies moved into the parlor and broke into groups of twos and threes, as though this were a well-established habit. Clara Dunlop took Mira by the arm into her small coterie of lumpy matrons.

"Dear, that was an excellent meal. Everything was just perfect."

"Thank you," Mira said and blushed.

Clara peered over her half-glasses as though to make a better appraisal. "You're going to be quite the star in Washington."

"Washington?"

"Well, of course," chimed in Gladys Leighton. "Once Matthias is sworn in."

My God, she thought, *it never occurred to me that we'd live in Washington.* Matt had never said so. She did not know whether to think he assumed she would know, or if he just did not want to overwhelm her all at once.

Clara quickly added, "But you'll adjust, dear. You're young and pretty and Matthias will know exactly what to do."

All Mira could think was whether they could hire Mrs. Greenough permanently. But just as she was feeling her most desperate, a wrinkled little woman began playing the Steinway piano that Mira had added to the room. The petite woman played a soft melodic piece that Mira could not identify but it was calming and sentimental and she could simply listen. She was so grateful to Penelope Dennisdale at that moment, she could have hugged her.

At eleven thirty, the men returned from the library enveloped in pipe and cigar smoke. Some of them seemed a little tipsy, and Mira wondered whether Matt had served brandy. Penelope stopped playing the piano, and the room filled with male voices.

"Time to go, toots."

"What do you ladies find to gab about anyway?"

"I don't know about you, but I'm ready to hit the hay."

Listening to them, Mira suddenly began to think that this was not the high society she assumed it would be. It was only the high society of New Hampshire Democrats. She had yet to face the real thing. She almost laughed at her own naïveté. But then she considered what was ahead of her and her apprehension returned.

By midnight, the house was emptied of guests, the table cleared, the dishes done and the staff gone. As Matthias and Mira stood in the dining room, he plucked a white mum from the centerpiece.

"Congratulations," he said softly to Mira. "You did well."

He entwined the flower in her hair over her ear and kissed her lightly on the lips. Then he kissed her throat and unbuttoned the neck of her dress. It dropped to her waist, exposing her breasts. He slowly stroked her nipples. Mira pulsed to his touch, and her body began to undulate against him. He grew more passionate, more insistent, pushing his tongue inside her mouth. He lifted her and tipped her onto the table. They made love there in the dining room, rocking together, Mira's buttocks slapping against the bare wood.

When it was finished and Matt had collapsed on top of her, she could not help wonder what would have happened had she not done so well tonight.

Later that night, Matthias lay in bed, still awake, while Mira slept soundly next to him. He listened to her soft breath with rising desire. But he pushed the urge out of his mind to concentrate on assessing the evening. It had gone as planned. He believed from the beginning that she had the potential to do what was necessary. Of course, everyone tonight was disposed to be generous to her. After all, he was the new bright light of the party and they would all benefit in the long run. Even Clara Dunlop could see that. As for Mira, she will grow little by little into the role she has to play, he told himself confidently. In two months, he would be where he had always hoped to be, starting his political career. He let himself feel the victory for the first time.

The after-dinner session had gone better than he ever expected. There was no serious internal politicking at this stage of the party's young development. They were clearly the underdog and it was easy to focus on the single goal of increasing their numbers and influence.

In the library that Matthias had designed to resemble Senator Hargrave's sitting room, the men talked about the great change coming with the inevitability of an FDR presidency. There was almost an electricity in the room as they discussed the future. Matthias was the first New Hampshire Democrat in the Legislature with such happy prospects. And he was, in their collective estimation, a team player. There would be good times ahead.

At that point, Matthias mentioned that, except for Prohibition, a little spirits would certainly be nice on this occasion. Not until all heartily agreed did he produce a bottle of Napoleon Brandy he personally brought back from his honeymoon. He could not think of anyone else, he told them, that he would rather share this bottle with. Or the second. Or the third.

He wished briefly that he could share his success with his own family. But he had left them behind when his mother died. His brothers and sisters, well, he was never very close to them anyway. They never understood him. They probably wouldn't care that he was a U.S. Congressman. And they would probably never know. Maybe someday.

His mind drifted to Judge Bennett, the man whose manners and social graces he had keenly studied while in his employ. Matthias had not seen him or his daughters again after that final summer when he drove them home from Saratoga Springs, where they had stayed at the Grand Union Hotel, attended the Saratoga Race Track and took the mineral baths at the spa. Of course, he stayed in the servants' quarters and never went to either the track or the spa. But he watched the parade of gowns, hats and spats and took note. He smiled, remembering Ralph Waldo's last words.

"You're a very keen young man and you will, I'm sure, put that to good use."

It was as close to an admission, Matthias thought, that he would get from his employer that Judge Bennett regarded him as a sentient human being. Then the dignified judge delivered his coup de grâce.

"In all the years we've had chauffeurs and house staff, you are the only one who was able to tell my girls apart."

Matthias was tempted to inform their father just how he accomplished that. But he did not say that he identified Eva because of her larger breasts and a small mole under her jaw—which he could see clearly when she straddled him. Or that Emma had smaller breasts but a larger bottom that he had so often grabbed when mounting from behind, and which he could identify by touch alone.

By now, he imagined, they would be married with children of their own. But it gave him pleasure to think that the Bennetts and née Bennetts were the most likely to have read of his success.

He closed his eyes and soon was dreaming that he was in his plane, flying victory rolls over the capitol.

David was not having such pleasant dreams that night. He was feverish and had been sick since the night before the election. That previous Tuesday morning, he had dragged himself from bed to go to the Raleigh firehouse, where the polls were set up, to cast his vote against Matthias Carson. "Evil to my enemy," he had said under his breath when he marked his ballot. When the newspaper announced that Carson had won by a landslide, the greatest majority in New Hampshire history, David thought he was in a delirium. If Carson had lost, perhaps he might somehow have had another chance with Mira. Not with Carson elected, though. Now he had no chance at all. The evil done was to himself.

Lying wide-eyed in the dark room, alternately sweating and shivering, he told himself there was no point in sticking around anymore. No point at all. He would go back to California as soon as he heard from his publisher. Several weeks before the election, David had posted the finished manuscript to Hugo Rinehart. He should have a check any day now. Then he would pack up and leave. He was tired of cold, gray New England. Tired of being tired.

But, if nothing else, he was pleased with his book. It had turned out well. He'd put everything in it that he knew as a writer. *Nawasta* was a strong story and he had researched the details meticulously. Even more so than his first book. This one would get him a place in literature. That was all that was left to him now. He had lost Mira, but he still had his writing. Maybe he would never have anything else. But that would be enough.

Why didn't life turn out the way you wanted it to?

No one has control over one's life, David admitted. It was hard enough keeping control of a novel. In his book, though, Nawasta did have control over circumstances. He had made his uncle confess. He made something happen. Nawasta was a better Hamlet than Hamlet because he initiated his action. David was satisfied about that. It was not just a mystery he'd written this time, it was a moral paradigm. Despite the headache forming at the base of his skull, he was glad about this one corner of his life: at least he was a good writer.

He could escape into his own creations. Perhaps he would write his next book about Mira and Carson and himself and, this time, she would choose him. David fixated on that idea through his lightheadedness.

Before he went back to California, however, he would have to return the books that Alva had let him borrow. He was not supposed to remove anything from the house, but the library was being remodeled then, and during that time he couldn't get in. So, she'd let David take out several boxes of books.

He'd also taken a box of Celia's papers. He thought perhaps her notes for the bicentennial history might be of use. He had never taken the time to look through them before—he'd been too intent on finishing the manuscript. But now he was bereft of anything to read and was too sick to sleep.

Slipping on his blue and white flannel bathrobe, David leisurely opened the box of papers and sat down to read. The first page he plucked out of the stack of handwritten notes began, "My family has been in New England as far back as the second generation of Puritans. What would they think of our debasement of their heritage?"

"Debasement of their heritage?" he repeated aloud. What did that mean?

He read on. "My father was the last Eastman, so named, but not the last male of our line."

The sentence riveted him. Soon, he was disengaged from the present. His thoughts twined around the thoughts of the woman whose startling words he was reading.

CHAPTER SIX

" . . . foul deed will rise
Though all the earth o'whelm them, to men's eyes."

The day before Thanksgiving, the aroma of apple pie and mulled cider wafted its way from the kitchen where Georgie labored, to the porch where Madeline sat knitting. She was nearly finished with the afghan. With it spread over her lap, she knitted the monogram of "G.S." in dark brown wool on the bottom border. She had decided it was to be Georgie's Christmas present.

Who else could she give it to? She originally intended it for Celia. She had entertained the idea of giving it to David, but she hadn't seen him in over a month and at their last meeting, he had talked about going back to California. She was sure he had left without even saying good-bye. She believed they had become friends, but it was clear now that she had no friends. There was no one in the whole world she could give a gift to, save Georgie. No one who might give any gift to her, save him.

She felt increasingly the regret of her life's course that had brought her to this poverty. Or, if not regret, a sense of final loss. For a brief time, she'd felt she had a purpose, perhaps even a legacy. What would she leave behind her? What act or gift could she give to posterity that would attest to the fact that Madeline Elizabeth Abbott had been here, had added something to history by virtue of her life? In truth, she had neither purpose nor legacy.

Perhaps, she considered, if I were religious I would be content merely to live a Good Life. Everything else, after all, even progeny is ephemeral. How nice it would be to believe in a Heaven that rewarded good and punished evil and provided eternity for the deserving. Then she mused ruefully, I wish I could think that way and mean it. But she couldn't. Of course, she told herself, I'm not one of the Deserving. But I might have been, had I believed it was worthwhile.

She sighed and leaned back in her chair. Her fingers were starting to pain her. She could see the slight enlargement of the knuckles, symmetrically on each hand. The beginnings of arthritis. The symptoms of age.

"My nails are cracking," she muttered as she regarded her fingers. Her hands had been her one vanity. She'd had perfect nails, just the right mound over the fingertips. She would clip and file them just so, snip the cuticles and push them back to the half-moon, and buff them to a shine. She lotioned her hands and, in her youth, slept with white cotton gloves to keep them soft. She'd had the hands of a coquette even if not the face of one.

I should have behaved scandalously when I was young, she mused. If only I had continued to travel as an adult the way I did with Father as a child, instead of being content to read about faraway places into my dotage. But I had no one to go with and I was too fearful to go alone. I would like to have been serenaded by a Venetian gondolier and been painted wearing only a smile by some starving French artist. If I couldn't be good, I should at least have been respectably bad.

Imagine. She chuckled at her own folly and thought how Celia would have enjoyed the laugh with her.

Thus engaged, she was surprised to see a car drive around to her porch door, and even more surprised to recognize it as David's.

David breezed into the house saying, "Hello, lady! Got any time for an old friend? I haven't seen you in a long while so I thought I'd stop by and surprise you."

Madeline smiled readily. "I thought you'd gone back to California."

"Changed my mind."

Without invitation, he removed his coat and hat and sat in Georgie's usual chair.

"How have you been, Madeline?"

"Well, thank you. And you?"

"Fine. Busy," he replied. "You know how it is, you lose track of time."

There was something about the casualness of his answer that sounded a little too glib.

"You've lost weight," she noted.

"Oh, I had a bout of something or other that set me off eating for a spell. That's why I didn't come around."

"I would have sent you an invitation to Thanksgiving dinner tomorrow but I didn't know you were still here. Would you like to come? It will be just Georgie and me."

"Thank you, but I've already made plans."

"Of course," Madeline said, disappointed. "It's very late for an invitation." Then she changed the subject. "Well, tell me, have you finished your Nawasta book yet?"

A pained look crossed his face involuntarily and then he shrugged. "It was rejected. The publisher didn't like it."

"Oh dear," she said compassionately. He had done so much research for the book and, she knew, it meant a great deal to him. "What did they say?"

He shrugged casually, but the hard edge in his voice betrayed him. "They advised me to stick to simpler subjects. They said my 'literary gift' was unequal to my vision."

She paused. "Now what will you do?"

"I will seek to confine my vision." The corner of his mouth twitched. "So what have you been doing with yourself these past weeks?"

"I keep occupied." Madeline indicated the afghan.

"I was just talking with Georgie. He says you don't go out anymore. Except for the occasional shopping trip."

"Georgie told you that?"

"He's mellowed toward me now that Mira's married Carson. I guess I'm the lesser of two evils." They both smiled awkwardly. "You were going to Carson's rallies there for a while."

"For a while."

"But you stopped."

She nodded.

"Why?"

Madeline began folding the afghan neatly into a square. "My own reasons."

"So you gave up."

Madeline stopped folding and looked at him as though he were accusing her of being fainthearted.

"That's not it at all," she said defensively. "I finally decided I may have been hounding an innocent man. And I had to consider the real possibility that I'd manufactured the whole business, and that there was no reason for it except revenge. That is a very ugly recognition. And that's why I stopped."

"And now he's a congressman."

Before she could say that was no fault of hers, he continued.

"I should have guessed from the beginning that he had political ambitions. A man like that wants as much power as he can get."

"There's nothing wrong with holding public office."

"I never expected to hear you of all people say that. Hell, next you'll be telling me you'd have voted for him if you lived over the state line."

Madeline regarded him in silence and David gestured apologetically and got up. He walked to the window and looked out over the lake.

"Have you seen her lately?"

"Not since before the election," Madeline said.

"There was a picture of her in the paper last month. Giving out penny-apples for Halloween." His voice soured. "She seems to have taken to public life rather easily."

"If anything, Mira's adaptable. That's her gift, I suppose."

"She let me use the library anytime I wanted. She wouldn't be there but I could come by in the afternoons. Said she didn't want to 'violate Celia's will.' Carson's words, I expect. At first, every time I went I kept hoping I'd see her. Sometimes that was the only reason I'd go. But after a while, I began to care more about the work."

He trailed off into silence, but just as Madeline was about to say something, he resumed.

"I stumbled on a box of Celia's papers. Things she wrote."

Madeline nodded appreciatively. "She was always writing something. She was doing a pamphlet on the town history. That was the last time I saw her alive."

"She also wrote little sketches about her life. All mixed in together with everything else," he said. "She apparently copied things over three and four times until she got it the way she wanted it. She was fastidious about her writing."

He waited a beat and then glanced briefly toward the doorway as though to make sure Georgie was not lurking there.

"Did she tell you that Georgie is her half-brother?"

"What?" Madeline was as stunned as though someone had sneaked up behind her and clapped her on the back.

"Celia's father was Georgie's father, too. That's why she kept him with her all these years."

"How do you know this?" She was aghast.

"It's in her papers."

Madeline fell silent as she contemplated what this meant. It was almost unimaginable that Celia's father had an adulterous liaison with the Indian woman that produced a child. Not that she had known Celia's father, of course, but the idea of such a thing appalled her. To father a child out of wedlock and let the mother die in squalor, and risk the life of the poor baby? So many thoughts crowded Madeline's mind, she hardly knew where to begin.

"She probably didn't want you to know," David said, echoing her own thoughts. "Not just because her father visited with Muskataqua, but because he let her live and die so abysmally. And because of what happened to Georgie afterward."

Madeline remained silent, thinking about how Celia had kept this from her. From everyone. What shame she must have felt for her father's hypocrisy. And yet, Madeline wondered, was Celia's hypocrisy any less in not publicly recognizing Georgie? Gradually, an idea shaped itself in her mind.

"Could Georgie contest the will now? As her only living relative?" And then pluck the inheritance right out of Matthias Carson's hands?

"Perhaps," he replied. "But obviously she didn't want anyone to know about it. Especially Georgie."

Madeline was still trying to digest this when he took a folded paper from his pocket.

"There's something else. I found this in her things."

"What is it?"

David unfolded the paper as carefully as she had folded the afghan and then read in a resonant, practiced voice:

"Princess Muskataqua's monument stands in the woods at the bog-end of the lake, and she lays there for all time with a view of the things she so cherished: mountains, water, sky. How fleeting is our life, but how happy it must be to spend one's eternity in such a spot. The best resting place in all New England."

Madeline nodded. "Yes, that sounds like Celia." But she was puzzled. Yes, it was nostalgic, for it brought back to her Celia's personality and of course it referred to the statue that Celia had left her. But it was not what she had expected. It didn't say anything more about Georgie and she wasn't sure why David had been so eager to read it to her.

"Don't you see?" he prodded.

"See what?"

"Does that sound like it was written by someone who wanted to be cremated?"

"What do you mean?"

He handed the paper to her. Madeline took it unwillingly, still not comprehending the intent. Celia's precise and artful handwriting covered the page. It was written before her illness, while Celia still had full use of her hands. Such a beautiful script, full of flourishes and swirls. So unlike the otherwise straightforward nature of her friend. It was the artist in Celia showing itself, Madeline decided.

"I know it's not conclusive," David said. "It doesn't actually say she'd like to be buried there. And even if it did, she might have changed her mind. And her ashes were scattered on the lake, but Carson could have put that in. He's clever enough for that. But reading this, I find it hard to believe that Celia didn't want to be buried alongside the lake."

She waved the paper at him. "When did you find this?"

"A little while ago."

"And you're showing it to me now?" Her voice carried the anguish of time spent in agonizing over her actions.

"I didn't know what else to do."

"Are you saying that now you believe he did it?"

David sat down on the edge of the seat looking directly into her eyes.

"I'm saying that now I'm beginning to question, too."

Madeline's hand trembled as she held the paper.

"So now that I've stopped, now that I'm quits with it, now you want me to go after him again."

"That's up to you."

"Is there anything else?"

"No."

She handed back the paper with finality. "Very flimsy."

"' . . . the best resting place in all New England,'" he quoted, putting the paper back into his pocket. "Celia's own words."

"Don't do this to me, David! I've made my finales with this

business."

"It seems all I can think of these days is 'what if?' What if?"

"Please, David."

She dropped her head into her hands and could not look at him. Her heart began to beat as though it might burst. Her temples throbbed and the base of her neck was tight. After a moment, she said, "David, I want you to go now. I need to be alone and you confuse me."

"All right, if that's what you want."

In silence, he took his coat and hat and walked toward the door. "You know where I am if you want me."

Afterward, she sat unmoving, struggling with herself.

It's only supposition again, she told herself. And nothing more. Nothing, nothing more.

"But, oh, the writing," she said aloud. It was like some living part of Celia herself. The tangible proof of her personality. Something that showed that Celia Eastman had lived upon this Earth, had thoughts and expressions uniquely her own, was in fact a real person outside the memories of those who knew her.

Madeline shook her head. But why should she be the one burdened with this responsibility? No one else seemed to care about what happened to Celia. Except David, all of a sudden. But if David is so convinced now that it was murder, why doesn't *he* do something? she argued to herself.

"Why does it have to be me?"

She got up resolutely intending to put it all out of her mind.

But throughout the rest of the day, no matter what she did—iron the embroidered linen tablecloth and napkins for tomorrow's meal, wash the Albermarle china she took from the hutch for the holiday, or sort through boxes in the attic to find the one with the porcelain turkey that had decorated Albermarle and Abbott tables for generations—she continued to come back to the same haunting question. Did Matthias Carson really murder Celia?

How could she ever know? And yet, she had to know. Because no one else would ever question it and, if he had done it, then he would have gotten away with it.

"That can't happen," she said, then realized that she'd been talking to herself a great deal lately. She looked around to see if Georgie were within earshot before continuing. "If there is no justice in this, then there is no justice in the world and we are not civilized human beings."

For the rest of the day, Madeline went about her tasks with a single-minded determination.

"Tomorrow is Thanksgiving, Georgie. I think we should have a proper dinner. I made a list of everything we need."

The morning sun was hovering over the lake and dried pine needles and oak leaves covered the ground, and the smell of the air was like burning wood and mold, as they got into the car and headed for town.

As they drove around the lake road past Celia's house, she slowed down.

"Do you remember last Thanksgiving?" she said. "You sat with Miss Eastman and me at the table and we all drank a glass of mulled cider. I put mulled cider on our shopping list. We have a lot of stops to make."

"Yes, ma'am."

Then they drove to the butcher shop to order their turkey. "Hen," she said to the butcher, "no tom."

They already had squash and potatoes and sweet potatoes from the garden, and bought tins of succotash. Flour and sugar. And cranberries.

Try as she might, Madeline could not pretend enthusiasm for Georgie's Thanksgiving meal.

"Isn't dinner all right, Miz Abbott?" He waited nervously for the answer.

Madeline looked up then finally said, "Oh, yes, Georgie. Everything is delicious. I don't mean to be unappreciative. I'm just preoccupied."

"Yes, ma'am," he replied, looking downcast.

Madeline put down her fork and looked keenly at him across the table. She deliberated before speaking.

"You know, Georgie, I've turned a lot of corners in my mind these past months." She ran her finger over the English silverware that her great-grandmother Albermarle had chosen. "So many, that I'm right back where I started from and I still can't tell north from south."

Georgie brightened. "When you know which side of the lake you're on, you can always tell north." He pointed toward the left side of the room.

Madeline remained pensive. "The mind's compass is not so easily directed." She sighed and then continued. "Miss Eastman used to say you were her link to the past, Georgie. She used to talk to you often, didn't she?"

"Oh yes. We talked a lot, we did."

"What did you talk about, Georgie?"

"Everything. We talked about everything."

"She loved that statue of the princess at the edge of the lake, didn't she?"

"Oh, yes. When Miz Eastman were younger, she spent a lot of time up there."

"Think back, Georgie," Madeline prompted. "Do you remember Miss Eastman ever saying anything about wanting to be buried up there?"

Georgie considered dutifully and then answered. "She never said to me."

Madeline took another tack. "You were with Miss Eastman a long time, weren't you?"

Georgie nodded heartily. "I lived with the mister and old Miz Eastman since I were fourteen."

"What were they like, Mr. and Mrs. Eastman?"

"Episcopal."

Madeline hid a smile. "Of course." Then she continued. "What happened to your own family, Georgie? Your sisters and brothers? Your father?"

"Never had none. My mother died when I was little." It was obviously not a subject he was used to talking about, and he unconsciously shuffled his feet under the table.

"Who did you live with after your mother died?"

"The mister and old Miz Eastman. Mr. Eastman was old, too, and in a wheelchair like young Miz Eastman when she got old."

"No, I mean before that. Who did you live with before you lived with Mr. and Mrs. Eastman?"

His feet strayed away from him under the table. "The home," he answered reluctantly.

"You mean an orphanage?"

He nodded and said nothing more.

"So the Eastmans took you in and became your family. You must have cared for them very much."

He nodded again.

"You know I cared for Miss Eastman, too."

"Oh yes, Miz Abbott."

"And because I cared for Miss Eastman, I have a problem and I don't know what to do about Mr. Carson. I think he hurt Miss Eastman."

Georgie's feet stopped wandering but he began to work his lips back and forth.

"Miz Eastman's dead."

Madeline shook her head. "No, I mean I think he hurt her when she was alive."

"She were very sick then."

"I think, maybe, he made her sicker. Mr. Carson and Dr. Niles, together. In order to get her money."

His face became quiet. "That's a wickedness."

"Yes. And because I thought Mr. Carson made her die, I went to all those meetings he held to get elected, and I asked questions. Do you remember?"

Georgie nodded.

"But then Mrs. Carson came to talk to me, and I began to think that maybe I was wrong about him. And after that, I found out that Dr. Niles didn't hurt old Mr. Prentice, and maybe Mr. Carson didn't hurt Miss Eastman, either. And I felt unhappy about what I was doing."

"You repented of it?"

"Yes. I repented of it. And I didn't go to any more meetings."

"You didn't go nowhere."

"And now Mr. McKay has told me something that makes me think I was right in what I had believed about Mr. Carson. Do you see?"

"You thought you were wrong and now you think you ain't?"

"Yes. But I don't know for certain. So I don't know what to do. If Mr. Carson is guilty, then I'd be doing a good thing. But if he's innocent, I'd be doing a bad thing."

He pondered and then asked, "How bad?"

Madeline fell silent and then broke into laughter.

"Georgie, you're a moral pragmatist! You're absolutely right? How bad? I should have thought of that myself. Georgie, I think you're going to get your rightful inheritance."

"I need only one inheritance, Miz Abbott. To enter the Kingdom of God."

Madeline lifted her glass of cider in a toast. "You shall have that and justice, too. You shall indeed."

When David awoke that Thursday morning, he felt more lonely than he could remember ever having been in his life. The holiday made him acutely aware of how far away he was from family and friends.

Maybe he should have accepted Madeline's invitation. But he knew she would want to talk about Thanksgivings past, and what they had been like for him.

His memories of Thanksgivings at home were among his favorites because all his aunts and uncles and cousins would come to dinner. Christmases were always a private celebration—just Mother, Father, and him—but Thanksgivings were boisterous with the entire clan. They were bittersweet memories now because none of those aunts and uncles and cousins ever invited him to their Thanksgivings, and none, to his knowledge, ever visited Mother in the sanitarium.

Admittedly, he hadn't visited his mother very often either. She didn't recognize him when he did. He was embarrassed to go because she wasn't the mother he knew. The last time he had visited, his mother had lifted her skirt at the attendant and she wasn't wearing anything underneath. The nurse had taken him aside and explained that they had a problem containing her at times. That it was just the disease. She misbehaved that way quite often, sometimes more so. He hadn't gone back and instead left for California, a continent away.

Despite all, he realized that he missed his family today. The boardinghouse was empty by noon. Everyone, even boarders, had somewhere to go on Thanksgiving.

As he sat at the table in the small room, David opened the box in which his manuscript had been returned. Rinehart's letter was on top. He quickly removed the letter, not wanting to read it again. He lifted the five-hundred-and-eight typed pages of his novel out of the box and set it in front of him. He turned over the title page, *Nawasta, The Story of an Indian Brave*. Rinehart didn't like the title either, but David would think about that later. He immediately went to the front page, thinking, I'll try to revise it. Maybe I can make it better.

But the words on the page were too painful to read. They seemed awkward and leaden.

"Back in the days before you or me, or our parents or grandparents and before this nation, these colonies, this New World, there lived a tribe of Indians called—"

He shuddered and stood up. What had seemed so powerful in the heat of creation now seemed turgid and useless.

He checked his watch. Almost one o'clock. Someone, he couldn't remember who—ah, yes, the landlady—had told him that St. Mark's church was serving Thanksgiving dinner to anyone who wanted it today. Maybe that's what he would do. At least he would be in the company of others who were as solitary as himself, looking for some fellowship just for the moment. It was a day when those who were without fellowship or without means would not be outcast. Times were hard; no one would question anyone else's need to be there.

He put on his topcoat and left the room and the manuscript behind him.

It was cold but bright and clear with only a few clouds high in the almost luminescent blue sky. How like a painting the day looked. An end-of-autumn scene, with brown leaves blowing across the last of the green grass, and a white-steepled church in the little village square surrounded by a split-rail fence painted white.

As he walked briskly toward St. Mark's, the curled brown leaves crackled underfoot. A loose line of people were entering the church basement, including families with young children.

At least I'm not too late, David thought agreeably as he fell in behind a tall man in a short brown jacket and green workpants. The man wore a gray felt hat with a broken brim and his black brogans were scuffed at the heel. He began to feel a little uncomfortable about fitting in, but soothed himself with the fact that no one there knew him.

David had not made friends with anyone besides Celia and Madeline since he'd arrived here. He'd met Celia in the library in Raleigh, both looking for the same book. That was right before she'd become ill and took to a wheelchair. They had begun talking about the history of the town and she invited him to the first of many dinners, including Christmas. Who would he spend Christmas with this year?

As he followed the gaunt man with the scuffed black shoes, David descended the stairs into the church basement. There were tables in rows running nearly the length of the room, flanked by chairs of diners on either side. There seemed to be over a hundred people, and he wondered where they'd all come from. There were only a few seats still empty. The room was alive with chatter, children's babbles of play, the clatter of knives and forks on plates and a pervasive hum of adult conversation. It was a pleasurable combination of noises. He looked forward to joining it, to mingling his voice with theirs, indistinguishable and unidentifiable. To abandon his self-imposed isolation, his writer's detachment, and simply join anonymously with the anonymous crowd.

He fell in behind the felt-hatted man at the end of the food queue. As David glanced ahead to the beginning of the line, he froze. His pulse quickened to where he could no longer hear the sounds in the room but only his racing heart. Mira was among the five women serving dinner from the hot trays of turkey and stuffing. Suddenly the pungent aromas of cooked food made him dizzy.

He looked around wildly to see how he could escape without her seeing him. She was, fortunately, completely absorbed in her task of ladling gravy over the filled plates. She looked exquisite. Her hair was bobbed to jaw-length and it swung away from her face and then back like a pendulum as she bent over and straightened up.

The only way out was the way he'd come in. David quickly turned and crossed to the stairs, bounding up two at a time. Finally at the top, he paused to take a deep breath. She hadn't seen him, thank God. He would have died if she had seen him there, desperate and alone, in line for a charity meal.

He opened the door and stepped back out into the bracing air. He took a deep breath of relief and decided he'd better return home straightaway.

As he rounded the corner of the building, David found himself face-to-face with the minister and Matthias Carson.

Carson seemed unfazed. He looked David up and down and then glanced at the basement door of the church. An amused smile played around his lips.

"Enjoy the meal?"

David's face reddened. He couldn't speak. You son of a bitch, he wanted to scream. But he stood mute. Then he rushed past, brushing the minister's shoulder. He walked away as fast as he could, wanting only to disappear from sight. His mind raced. He had never felt such humiliation and rage in his life. He would get even with that bastard if it was the last thing he ever did.

By the time David reached the boardinghouse, he had formulated a plan. Back in his room, he removed his coat and immediately went to his writing table. He unceremoniously dropped the box of typed pages of his Nawasta novel onto the floor. Then he opened a new box of white bond paper, took the top sheet and inserted it in his Underwood.

He typed a new title, *Murder for Money*.

It would not be a psychological study like his book about Maria Danforth. Nor would it be a mythic story like Nawasta. No. This would be a murder-mystery about a lawyer who kills for the inheritances of his clients. There would be a hero. He would be a journalist. No, a proofreader in the Obituaries section of the newspaper, who sees the death notices and puts it all together. He would try to catch the lawyer and his accomplice, a doctor who was not above using his skills for nefarious purposes.

He would set the book in California. And, of course, there would be a woman, the lawyer's girlfriend. But the woman would become suspicious of her boyfriend . . . of Martin . . . that would be his name, oh that was good . . . and she would help the proofreader . . . Johnny . . . no, too juvenile . . . Albert . . . too stuffy . . . Daniel, yes, he liked that. She would help Daniel uncover Martin's misdeeds. She would be just like Mira. He could not even think of another name. He would leave that until later. And, of course, she would fall in love with him, with Daniel, and Martin would be convicted of murder.

David began swiftly typing the opening paragraph. By the time his stomach was growling for supper, he had completed the first chapter. Never before had he written so quickly and easily.

He grinned with the savagery of a boy pulling the wings off flies.

CHAPTER SEVEN
"But my revenge will come."

A week before Christmas, Matthias flew his plane over the little village of Raleigh. He knew he would not have another such opportunity for many months. The winter weather and his new job would see to that. The whir of the engine was the only sound in the sky. If the houses below had not been buttressed with storm windows, the sound might have drawn residents to look out at the rarity of an airplane overhead.

The late afternoon sun cast a rare golden light on everything. The air was still and crisp, perfect for flying. There was little snow yet except on the hilltops. Wearing a cap and goggles, Matthias felt only the cold rush of wind around his nose and mouth. It was almost like skiing. In a way, he thought, that's what I'm doing. He was skiing the air as he dipped and rose, turned and cornered the plane. The Stearman was fully aerobatic and Matthias pushed it to the limit, going for a hammerhead stall. He pulled back on the stick and the plane slowly climbed until it was nearly vertical. Up and up so straight, it defied gravity. Then, at the top of the pitch, he kicked left rudder before the motor faltered and stopped. The plane fell like a hammer. After he pulled the plane out of the dive, he did a victory roll. He could feel every throb and hum of the engine, every move of the aircraft.

He inverted his plane and then flew into a straight eight. He liked flying upside down because everything was reversed. To dive, he had to pull the stick back toward him instead of away from him. To climb, he had to push it forward.

"The high shall be low and the low shall be high," he said aloud, smiling to himself.

He circled around Raleigh before heading back to the airfield, which was merely a landing strip with a windsock, one hangar and tie-downs for six planes. His mind was on Washington now. Tomorrow, he would take the train down to D.C. to meet with U.S. Senator J. Hamilton Lewis of Illinois. The new Democratic Senator from New Hampshire, Fred Brown, had ousted Republican George Moses after a fourteen-year stint. But since Brown was as new to his position as Matthias was to his, Fred could not be much help in the political arena on Capitol Hill. It was Dunlop who had arranged for a meeting with the legendary Lewis to discuss Matthias's "future." Matthias wondered at its prematurity, but Aubrey Dunlop assured him that this was quite a coup. "You are about to be touched with a magic wand," Aubrey told him. Matthias was not exactly sure what boon the magic would convey but he knew it would be heraldic.

He was reminded of how he and his brothers used to play King Arthur and the Knights of the Round Table. He and Luke, his older brother, would squabble to play the king and slay their foes with Excalibur. They had begun the game with a tree branch. But over time, they transformed Excalibur from a strip of wooden molding into a carved sword with a painted handle. That was Luke's idea. Matthias fought very hard wielding that painted sword, and he usually won against his taller, heavier opponent. His mother put a stop to it when he poked Luke in the eye. His brother had to have three stitches just below his eyebrow that cost three dollars at the doctor's. His mother cried all the way there and back. They didn't have the three dollars to spare. That's when Matthias began his paper route at age seven.

Taking a wide swathe to line up for the landing approach, Matthias looked down over the bare, brown, early winter landscape. The lake was frozen around the edges, almost to the center, but they had not yet had a major snow of the season. The landscape was still mottled with leafless oaks, birches and tamaracks, interspersed with green pine and fir. Then, he caught sight of a boom truck. It was crawling up the lake road away from town and it made him curious. There was no logging in that direction. The road simply ringed the lake as far as Preston Weekes's house and then angled off to Wickessett, Vermont.

He pulled out of the pattern and circled around again to watch as the truck pulled off the road and onto a path through the woods. It drove toward the edge of the lake where the princess's monument stood.

The boom truck pulled up to the statue, backed around and stopped. The driver and his companion got out and began taking rigging line from the back of the truck. Matthias recognized Thomas Hingham but kept himself at a distance so that he did not appear to be watching. By the time Matthias had made his third circle, the huge stone statue stood in the bed of the truck, tied securely.

Matthias was now focused on the movement of the truck as it slowly inched its way up the lake road. But Washington, Senator Lewis and his future career were of more immediate concern than the truck that was driving toward Madeline Abbott's house with a stature in its grasp. So, she was claiming her legacy, so what?

By the time he saw the truck pull into Madeline's backyard, Matthias calculated he had enough fuel to get himself back to the field and not enough for another pass over her house. He headed for home. He could not even speculate about what might be on Madeline Abbott's mind. But it mattered little. Tomorrow, he was going to meet Merlin.

• • •

Madeline and Georgie watched the boom truck pull into their yard, the statue of Muskataqua seeming to point the way from the truck bed.

"Excuse me, Miz Abbott, but why have you brung the statue here?"

"To catch the conscience of a king," she answered with a faraway look.

"Is it going to be here always?"

"I don't know yet, Georgie."

The next morning, Mira did not get out of bed until several hours after Matthias had left for Washington. He would be back for Christmas. She reveled in being in bed alone again and sleeping until eleven. She'd hardly had any rest at all since the campaign began. No wonder she was tired. She dressed leisurely in navy-blue silk bell-bottom slacks and a white silk blouse. Then she went downstairs to a breakfast of hot farina and preserved peaches that the judiciously silent Chef Emil prepared. Afterward, she sauntered into the parlor to begin wrapping the Christmas presents she had bought for Matt.

When she parted the curtains of the window overlooking the lake to let light into the room, she gasped. There, in full view, stood the statue of Princess Muskataqua, facing across the lake with her arms outstretched toward her.

Mira's heart beat wildly as she viewed Madeline's handiwork. There was not a moment's hesitation in her understanding of what it meant. It was almost, she recalled, like the statue in front of Sacred Heart Church in Elmira, the statue of the Virgin Mary. But this one seemed not to beckon but to condemn. And she'd had enough experience with Miss Madeline Abbott to know the old harridan had thrown down the gauntlet to Matt.

"Oh why can't you just leave us alone," Mira said with a catch in her voice.

Something would have to be done before Matt came home and it ruined their holiday. But Mira had no intention of confronting Madeline again. This time, she would use an intermediary.

That afternoon, a new maid let David into Mira's house. This one was older with brown hair in a tight bun. Her movements were swift and efficient as she escorted him into the parlor. He wondered what had happened to Alva, but his attention was all on Mira as soon as he glimpsed her. She was standing in her refurbished living room looking out over the frozen lake. She wore a wine velvet suit and sheer black stockings. He observed a Christmas tree in one corner and holiday decorations everywhere. It was a startling transformation from the living room of Celia Eastman.

Without greeting him, Mira turned and pointed out over the lake.

"Have you seen it?"

"Hello, Mira. How've you been?"

"Have you seen it?" she insisted.

"Seen what?" he replied innocently.

"Look!"

He gazed out over the lake at the statue of the princess facing them with outstretched arms and countenance up to the sky. It reminded him of the Statue of Liberty, regal and serene. But with the arms pointing toward them, the gesture seemed one of asking help rather than offering it.

Without waiting for a response, Mira continued. "When I opened the curtains this morning, I saw *that*!" When she turned toward him, her cheeks were flushed nearly the shade of her suit.

"What is the problem?" he said, purposely indifferent.

Mira's voice took on a hard edge as she slowly and deliberately explained the obvious. "The problem is, every time we look outside, we'll be staring at that statue pointing over here at us."

"Merry Christmas," he said smiling at her.

"It's not funny! God, wait till Matt comes home!"

His satisfaction was dampened by the news that Matthias had not yet seen the statue. "Where is he?"

"In Washington. Did you know anything about this?"

Mira went over to the new bar and poured a Scotch and seltzer for both of them. He watched, more than a little shocked, and wondering when she had started drinking.

"No," he answered untruthfully. "Have you talked to Madeline about it?"

"No, I haven't talked to Madeline about it. She doesn't have a damn telephone, and I'm not going over there again. That's why I called you."

"Why me?"

Mira slammed down the seltzer bottle. "You're friends with her. Tell her I want her to move her damn statue."

"Why? It's *her* statue."

She handed him his drink and he toasted, sardonically, "To Prohibition."

She scowled at him then continued, "Are you going to do something about it?"

David shrugged. "What can I possibly do?"

"There must be some kind of ordinance against it. Matt will—"

"That's Vermont, don't forget," he interrupted, "*not* New Hampshire. I expect Madeline is perfectly within her rights. Why are you so upset? It's just a statue."

"That is *not* just a statue. If it were on the town green, it would be just a statue. In front of the Historical Society, it would be just a statue. But over there, pointing across here, it's Madeline Abbott's accusation."

"And what accusation would that be?"

"You know perfectly well what accusation. I thought that crazy old woman had come to her senses. But I guess not." She took a long drink, the ice clinking in her glass.

"I don't know . . ." He glanced at the statue, concealing a quick smile. "I think it has a certain majesty perched up there."

"You would." She scanned his face. "You're always on her side.

Birds of a feather." She glared at him and took another drink.

The clinking ice resonated in the silence between them and her reproach swept over him like a frigid wind. Was that how little she thought of him? David walked over to the window to look out again. All right, if that's what she thought, he would gleefully rub her nose in it. He turned back to her with a scornful expression.

"Madeline is just acting on her convictions. At least she believes in what she's doing. Can you say the same?"

"Just what is that supposed to mean?"

"It means," he said contemptuously, "*you* sold out for cash."

"I did not!"

He sipped his drink and then moved away from the window, circumnavigating the room and constraining his emotions.

"You can't say Carson's wealth hasn't improved your circumstances," he said with a disdainful sweep of his hand.

"Why shouldn't it? I have everything I could possibly want now. I deny myself nothing."

"But self-denial never was your strong suit, Mira. At least not that I ever noticed." Leaning against the fireplace, he fingered a Waterford crystal candleholder.

She simply glowered at him.

"Besides, your *husband*," he pronounced the word snidely, "is the one the statue was meant for. Let *him* worry about it."

"You hate him. Don't you?"

"Not at all. I have no feeling for him whatsoever. But he appears to dislike me." He affected an ingenuous tone. "Why is that? Does he know about us?"

She regarded him haughtily. "What's there to know? All we had were a few laughs in bed. Anything more than that is in your mind. Just like anything to do with Matt and Celia Eastman is in Miss Abbott's mind. As I said, you two are a lot alike. Pathetic."

This time, her words turned him breathless and hot almost to fainting. He clenched his fists to calm himself, harder, harder, until his breathing became regular and he replied evenly, "And I'm beginning to think you and Carson are a lot alike."

"We are," Mira answered without hesitation. "We live in reality. I don't know what you live in. The past. Fiction. You invent the past like she does."

"I didn't invent us making love." He knew that sounded obsequious and loathed himself for it.

"No, but you invented its meaning."

As David searched her eyes, he couldn't see anything in them to show Mira didn't believe what she was saying.

Was that it, then? What had happened to his creation? In writing about Maria Danforth, he had, in his mind, been her charismatic lover, the man to whom she had given all her passion, her body and soul. He was the man to whom she fled, leaving her life and all her responsibilities behind. But here, in the space of this brief afternoon, Mira had turned him from rapturous lover into the sniveling minor character of Maria's scorned husband. The man she couldn't abide. The man she ran away from. The pain was so real, he could hardly bear it. But he would not let her know how much she'd wounded him. If nothing else, he must keep control of himself.

"Well," he finally replied, "I'm a chronic inventor. That's a novelist for you."

"Don't be so self-righteous. For heaven's sake, David, what's happened to you? Suddenly you've got this morality about everything."

"Pity, you don't."

"Well, let me tell you something," Mira hissed, moving closer to him and narrowing her eyes. "Your newfound morality is as boring as your books."

This time, it only took a moment before regaining his composure. When he did, his tone was glacial.

"You missed your calling, *cookie*. You should have been a publisher."

She put down her glass. "I suppose now you won't talk to Madeline for me."

"Ah, the statue again. Lest I forget why I was summoned." He eyed her appraisingly. "But I have no reason to ask her to move it on my account. Do I?"

Mira stiffened. "You mean you want something for your efforts, is that it?"

He moved close enough to touch her hair. "Just market value."

She pushed his hand away. "No."

"And why not?"

"I'm married."

"So?"

"I'm pregnant."

David felt the blood drain from his face. Then he stepped back and snorted derisively. "And I thought he only bought your soul."

Mira slapped his face, hard. His cheek stung and he resisted an impulse to slap her back. Instead, he stepped away and began walking toward the door.

Over his shoulder, he sneered, "Well, let me give you some advice, little mother. Don't put in a nursery just yet. You might be looking for another domicile by baby-time. There's a legal heir to this old homestead."

"What are you talking about?"

"Didn't you know?"

Mira said nothing but watched him with hypnotic attention.

"No?" he taunted. "Well, the fact is, Celia's father had . . . *has* . . . a son. Celia's half-brother."

"I don't believe you."

"As you like."

Mira studied him. "How do you know this?" And when no answer was forthcoming, she asked, "Who is it?"

David remained silent.

"I see," she said, spitting out the words. "That's why you came here so willingly. You couldn't wait to tell me."

"Not you, dearie. Your beloved husband."

He drove away from Mira's house in a vengeful fury. Yes, *Mira's* house, he reminded himself sourly, no longer Celia's. There was hardly anything left of Celia's there now. In just half a year, the things he remembered about the house had been obliterated. The spartan library, the homey living room and the once-amorous Mira he had known were all gone. Not only had she changed the way she looked but even more the way she acted. He had hoped for some small acknowledgment of feeling for him, some subtle sign of distress in her new life with her new husband. Face it, he told himself, you wanted her to throw her arms around your neck, press her face into your chest, and sob an apology for having given you up.

But she had done exactly the opposite.

"Pregnant," he muttered to himself bitterly. It had never occurred to him that she and Carson would have children. He headed home with a sense of futility.

Entering the boarding house, he saw that the landlady, Mrs. Caldwell, had attempted to cheer up the place with Christmas decorations in the hallway and parlor. But it seemed like diamonds around a withered neck. Mrs. Caldwell had been widowed and left with nothing but the house. Although she kept it fastidiously clean, it was still old and drab. What it needed was painting and wallpapering and new carpets instead of the cracked and faded walls and the threadbare coverings. Obviously, she had little means. Her income from borders probably just covered the maintenance. Yet, she soldiered on.

One does what one can against adversity, David decided.

A lesson well learned.

Mira debated how much to tell Matthias when he returned. He would see the statue, of course. But what would he say when he learned that she had called his former rival? She had hoped she would not have to tell him about it, but now she knew she would. Because she had to tell him about the half-brother.

Over the course of the afternoon, Mira drank too many whiskeys. She could not remember how many. She sat in an armchair in front of the window, looking across the lake at Madeline Abbott's house and the statue of the princess.

At intervals, she imagined that instead of an accusation, those outstretched arms were inviting her to something. But what? She was reminded of bowsprits. Muskataqua could have been a carving on the prow of a whaling ship, calling the sea creatures to the ship's harpoons. Or she might be the siren on the watery rock, luring sailors to their deaths. If only her arms were outstretched to the sky instead of toward them.

She tried to fathom what it all meant, the statue and the revelation about Celia's brother. Half-brother.

What is half of a brother? she wondered, fingering the Waterford glass of Scotch.

Before she met Matthias, she had never tasted whiskey. She had not liked it at first, but it was a regular part of their lives now. She had even gotten drunk a few times, more than a few times in private with Matt. He liked her that way. He said she was becoming conservative now that their situation had changed, and he preferred her uninhibited. She had to admit that he was right. She didn't feel as free and uncomplicated as she used to. But neither did he. He was not as willing to be playful or to take the time to wait until she was ready, too. The nights they made love when they were drunk were the best since their honeymoon.

Their honeymoon had been the most exciting time of her life. Going to Paris, Rome, Venice, had been like a miracle. And to be traveling first-class made her feel like Somebody. It had been uncomfortable in the beginning, not knowing exactly what to do or how to behave. So many bellboys, valets, waiters. But she simply let Matt guide her. How did *he* know how to do everything so well? He had come from a family as poor as her own.

They had been poor in different ways, she concluded. He was city poor; she was country poor. When she was seven, her parents and her baby sister burned to death in their shack from a fire in the woodstove. She had been staying overnight at a friend's house, the first stay-over she'd been allowed. She only remembered her mother and father now in brief pictures in her mind. Memories of Mom pushing her in the tire swing in the front yard. Memories of Dad chopping wood in his shirtsleeves.

After the fire, she had been placed with her father's brother, Elmer, and his wife, Jewel. That's when her life became a nightmare of beatings she tried to forget. But now, as she drank, she could not stop remembering.

Elmer and Jewel had eight children of their own, all older than she was, and all hating to share their meager possessions with her. Mira had arrived with nothing but the clothes she wore. In fact, she'd never had a new garment after that until she went to work for Dr. Niles and earned enough for her first new blue wool coat. Her first pair of new shoes, and her first dress were as vivid to her as anything in her memory, except for the daily thrashings she took from her cousins. Uncle Elmer and Aunt Jewel never paid any attention. They only took in Mira because the town gave them an orphan allotment for her. They saw their responsibility merely as making sure she did not die on them. Nothing short of that interested them.

She should be glad, Mira supposed, that none of her cousins had ever attacked her sexually. But it was still a horrible household, everybody screaming at everybody else, slapping, biting, kicking. Hateful.

She was so unhappy during those years that one day she began crying right in class. Miss Darnell sent her downstairs to see the school doctor.

Dr. Roland Niles was the first person who was ever kind to her. He put his arms around her and held her while she cried. He talked softly to her and gave her books to read. Eventually, out of gratitude and sadness, she let him do it to her. He was so gentle and careful, she never felt bad about it. And when she graduated from high school, he hired her as his office assistant. It was about that time that he stopped approaching her, as though there were some ethic about it she did not understand. Later, she realized that she had simply grown up and no longer aroused him.

As she earned a little money and was able to buy clothes and magazines and saw how to dress up, men began to look at her differently. She had her first date with Bobby Thompson, who had his father's touring car and took her to the picture show. She let him kiss her in the car. It made her feel so squirmy and warm that she went on kissing him. It wasn't at all the way Roland Niles kissed her. This was hot and wet and full of urgency. She let him pull down her panties and touch her, and then she wanted more. She recalled the flash of surprise across Bobby's handsome face when she wrapped her legs around him and drew him inside her.

She missed her monthly the following cycle and became frightened. Dr. Niles took care of it immediately and from then on, she took precautions with the device he provided.

There had been an unbroken series of young men as word got around from one steamy-breathed lad to another. And so it went until she came to live with Celia. Then she met Matt.

After that, there had been only him and, intermittently, David. Matt forgave her all of them except David. "What was he like?" he would ask her repeatedly. And she would always answer, "Forgettable."

But that wasn't quite true. She knew she was David's first love, and there had been exhilaration in it. It had made her feel less used.

CHAPTER EIGHT

"For it is, as the air, invulnerable,
And our vain wind blows malicious mockery."

Early Christmas morning as the sun was coming up over the lake, and long before Madeline awakened, Georgie stoked the stove to a roar, baked a final batch of fragrant cookies and quietly left the house. It had snowed lightly, leaving a thick cover of white over everything. He went to collect the holly berries, as he had done every year since he could remember. He would choose the branches with the brightest red berries and the sharpest green leaves to prepare his wreath. This morning, in the bright wash of dawn and the crisp fresh snow, the berries and leaves seemed the purest reds and greens he'd ever found. A smile spread over his face and his eyes crinkled with delight as he sat on the cold ground amongst the fallen and dried leaves and the miniature princess pine that poked up through the snow.

He knew just how to weave his wreath with holly branches

through a circle of interlocking grapevines that he'd prepared early last spring just for this occasion. He never noticed the spiny edges of the holly leaves pricking his fingers as he threaded the branches into the vines. Instead, he thought of the candle service in his church last night and he hummed "Joy to the World" as he worked.

He loved the midnight candle service on Christmas Eve better than any other, even the Easter sunrise service. Everybody was given a small white candle in a white paper collar. After the sermon, the pastor lit the initial candle from the one on the altar. Then he lit the candle of the first person in the first row, who turned to the next person to light that candle, and on and on from one to another until all the candles in the whole congregation were glowing. They turned out the lights in the church and all you could see was the candles flickering and lighting up people's faces as they all sung "*Silent Light, Holy Light*." It was, Georgie thought, the holiest light there was.

"*How precious is thy baby, Jesus,*" he sang, and he was filled with happiness. His fingers tugged and pushed at the holly branches as he thought about how fortunate he was. He had a good place to live, and although he missed Miz Eastman, Miz Abbott was kind to him. It usta be that Miz Abbott didn't have time for no one—but now she was different.

They had exchanged their presents last night, before he went to church. Miz Abbott had given him the brown and orange and blue blanket she made. He knew how long she had been knitting it. Since before last summer. And she gave it to *him*. It was as precious to him as the swaddling clothes the precious baby Jesus was wrapped in when he laid in the manger.

Georgie wished his gift to Miz Abbott had been better. He had carved a loon out of birch because they always listened to the loons on the lake. She said it was a very good likeness and she put it right on the mantelpiece. But it hadn't taken him as long to make it as it took her to make the blanket. Next year, he would make a hope chest out of cedar. He knew where there was a stand of white cedar that he could use, too.

Georgie remembered Christmases with Miz Eastman at her

house and how there would always be lots of people coming to visit practically every day between Thanksgiving and New Year's. And on Christmas Eve, there was always an open house and lots of food and hot cider and wassail and people from church and the historical society and people from town would come. Christmas at Miz Abbott's seemed very quiet compared with the old Christmases. Didn't Miz Abbott like company?

The best Christmas he ever had was the first time he was out of the orphanage and went to live with the old Mr. and Miz Eastman. Their Christmas tree had looked a hundred feet tall to him and it had littler candles than the ones they had at church all over it, and popcorn on a string and candy canes and gingerbread men. And there was a red stocking over the fireplace with his name on it, right next to young Miz Eastman's.

And there was a present under the tree just for him. It was a puppy, a real puppy for him. With black fur and a big chest. He had called the puppy Blacky and Mr. and Miz Eastman said that was going to be his name from now on. Blacky lived to be an old dog and his muzzle turned white before he died with his head in Georgie's lap.

Georgie's eyes filled with tears as he thought about Blacky. Other than his mother—and he didn't remember her—no one had ever died on him before Blacky. But, just as quickly, he remembered again how the little puppy with the red bow around his neck had licked his hand all over, and Georgie smiled again.

After he finished his wreath, Georgie walked back to the house.

"And heaven and earth da-da-da, and heaven and earth, da-da-da, a—nd hea-ven and er-r-r-earth da-da-da-da."

He placed the holly wreath at the base of his mother's statue, just as he had done every Christmas since he was young. Only now, the statue was in Miz Abbott's yard.

Georgie looked up at the face of his mother. Her eyes stared out beyond him, the way Miz Abbott's had when he asked his question about why the statue was here now. His mother's lips were parted as if in prayer. He knew she had died right after he was born and that if he hadn't been born, she wouldn't have died. He hoped she still loved him. He wondered if Blacky was with her in heaven.

"Merry Christmas," he said to the uplifted stone eyes, praying stone lips. He only wished her outstretched arms would fold him to her breast.

The warm smell of fresh-baked cookies drew Madeline out of sleep without her even realizing what had stirred her awake. She thought she might have been dreaming, but she couldn't remember anything specific, and she had never dreamed before. "I don't dream," she used to say to Nathan when her brother would tell her about his nocturnal sleep-adventures. He seemed to have such a good time there. She even envied him the scary nightmares of monsters and being chased or lost or in a place he didn't know, where the ground wasn't solid or the sun was purple. It seemed to her that people who dreamed had another life to go to. Her brother used to say she did too dream, everybody did. But Madeline stoutly denied it. *This* was the only life she had. She wondered if Nathan believed in a hereafter before he died. She wished she did.

As she lay in bed, she gradually realized that the room was comfortably warm and that Georgie must have added a full measure of coal to the stove this morning. Then it dawned on her. *This is Christmas.* But she shrugged in recollection that it would be a day no different for her than any other. Other than she would have a visitor today. She had gotten a gift for David that she hoped he would like.

She and Georgie had already exchanged presents last night. He had given her a wooden loon that he had carved himself. Madeline was quite taken with it. It was beautifully done, with fine markings—the eyes, beak, feathers, were all perfect. She was surprised at his talent.

Although I shouldn't be, she chided herself. Georgie's very good with his hands and he has infinite patience for detail. She saw that in his baking and how light and buttery his pastries always were.

The aroma of cookies came again, working into her consciousness with an insistence. She put on her white chenille robe and blue felt slippers and went directly to the kitchen.

"Georgie?" she called, but there was no answer. "Georgie?" she called a little louder, but still there was silence. He's probably out cutting wood, she concluded and picked up a crescent-shaped cookie from the plate on the table. Oh, it was delicious. It practically melted in her mouth, and the taste was almonds and the aroma was . . . her throat constricted . . . almonds. She stopped chewing halfway through the cookie.

"That's the smell!" Madeline said with her mouth full of cookie crumbs. "Almonds!"

She swallowed quickly and rushed to the sink for a drink of water. She pumped the cold water into a cup and drank it as fast as she could. Her heart quickened and she felt faint. She poured some of the water onto the dishrag and pressed it to her temples.

The smell of almonds was the smell of Celia's medicine, the smell that had haunted her all these months. The smell that was not quite almonds, but so close. She knew that smell.

When she was just a little girl, her mother had had treatments for rheumatism. Fowler's Solution. Wasn't that arsenic? She had a vision of her mother lying in bed with the shades down and the curtains drawn, so pale against the white sheets, her eyes closed, lying so still because every part of her body ached. "Keep her warm and rested, and give her a few drops of this in orange juice twice a day," the doctor had told her father. At only eight years old, Madeline had been frightened that her mother was going to die. She would watch her father use the eyedropper to put the medicine into the juice, and she remembered the faint smell of almonds.

Her mother's sickness had lasted a terribly long time and it seemed like forever before she died. There were days when her mother seemed not to recognize her or anyone. Days when her father sat in the darkened living room all evening and never spoke. Days when she and Nathan tiptoed around the house. But finally one spring morning, her mother got out of bed and began cleaning house. Washing curtains, walls, linens, rugs. She took out rodent poison and set mousetraps as though the house was infested. She never explained why. But the recovery was temporary.

Madeline's chest heaved with deep, rapid breaths. "They killed her. I know they did. Now I know how."

But what should she do? She knew the truth, she told herself, but she could never prove it. She stood riveted in the middle of the kitchen, tugging haplessly at the neck of her flannel nightgown. She felt as powerless as she had as a child, hearing her mother throw up in the bathroom from the medication. But she couldn't give in to that feeling. She had to do something. But what?

Then her eyes widened as she remembered David was coming to see her this afternoon. She would ask him what she should do next. Moving the statue from the woods to her yard had been an empty gesture. It would probably be nothing more than an irritant to Matthias Carson. Now was the time for a better strategy.

Matthias sat on the sofa watching Mira on the floor in the center of the living room, which was draped with looping garlands of pine and holly. She was surrounded by gift-wrappers flung off in haste, red velvet ribbons and bows strewn around the room, and piles of presents.

He watched her tear open the embossed paper and gleefully lift off the top of the largest box under the Christmas tree. As she pulled aside the tissue paper, she shrieked with delight at the glittering gown inside.

"For the Inaugural Ball," he said, both anticipating and instructing her. He looked almost paternal in his pleasure at watching her.

"I love it, Matt! It's beautiful!" She held the beaded and sequined dress up to her chin.

It was the most beautiful, most expensive gown he could find. It was iridescent black, a black that shimmered blue and opal, and matched the black iridescence of her hair. The neckline was straight across and the dress was held up with slight, sequined straps. On the empire bodice were small seed-pearl roses with gold embroidered stems, and the hem was a handkerchief style with swirls of sequins and bugle beads in rose patterns.

"It will be the most glamorous night, won't it?" But then her expression became serious.

"I won't look too fat, will I?" Her hand went automatically to her stomach.

"No one could ever tell," he replied, eyeing her still-flat stomach. It was barely her third month. Even by the March inaugural, the style of the gown would hide her pregnancy. He'd planned it that way. "And yes, from what I hear, it will be very glamorous. Music by Rudy Vallee and Guy Lombardo. Tom Mix will lead the parade. And there will be a gold and silver train from California to Washington with all the stars and starlets they can fit."

Her eyes danced at his words as he lightly stroked the calfskin briefcase on the set of luggage she had given him. The smell of new leather, he decided was like the smell of new money. He glanced at his new gold pocket watch—another of Mira's gifts.

"Time to put everything away. The Dunlops will be here any minute." He stood up and called, "Lewis!"

Within seconds, the butler appeared at the door.

"Put the luggage in the hall closet, Lewis, and have Maureen put Mrs. Carson's presents in the bedroom."

"Yes, sir," the distinguished gentleman's gentleman replied as he assembled the pieces of luggage and began carrying them out of the room.

A cloud passed over Matthias's face as he watched his butler. Was there a slight arrogance in the man? Did he, so smooth and flawless, think he was better than his employer? Matthias fixed on the square shoulders and straight back of the man carrying the luggage.

But he dismissed the idea because he was still happy from his meetings in Washington. They had gone so well, his return home had been delayed and he'd only arrived an hour ago. Matthias couldn't recall ever being happier in his life than he was at this moment.

Mira still held the dress to her chest, asking would they go to the White House? Would she meet the President and Mrs. Roosevelt?

Matt simply nodded and offered her his hand.

"Up you go. It wouldn't do for our guests to find you on the floor."

Mira took his hand and he lifted her to him. He took a step back, admiring the dress she still clutched to her.

"You will be the belle of the ball," he said pleasingly.

Laughing, Mira swirled around and around, with the dress floating out in front of her. She cocked her head at him and purred. "Shall I wear it tonight?"

"No, save it for the ball. I have something else for you to wear tonight."

"What?" Mira asked, looking around for another present.

"Under your pillow."

Just then, Maureen, the bun-haired maid, appeared at the doorway.

"Begging your pardon, Mr. Carson, Mrs. Carson. Lewis said I was to bring Mrs. Carson's things to the boudoir."

"That's right," Matt answered. "I want everything put away before the Dunlops arrive."

As Maureen took the dress and box, he was gratified that he did not have to struggle with her the way she did with Alva. He still rankled when he recalled the other maid's defiance. "Would you like to pour me a drink?" Mira purred.

"Later," he answered in a low voice. "After they're gone."

David drove from town on the lake road, heading for Madeline's house. But, as he neared Mira's house, he could see the lights on in every room. He wondered what she was doing right this minute. As much as he tried to block it out, he could not think of Mira in there on Christmas Day without thinking of Carson. Doubtless they were together. He shook his head, as though the image of Mira and Carson together were a stereopticon picture that he could rattle out of the viewer. But the image persisted.

He impulsively rolled to a stop just before coming into full view of the house where he had spent so many hours visiting Celia and reading in her library. He told himself that he needed to see Mira again.

Dare I peek through a window to look in? No, they might see me.

But it was tempting. He could leave the car here and walk up to the house. He might be able to get away with it.

Then he frowned. Why was he torturing himself? Looking in their window would be like watching a picture show of other people's lives, where he could only be the audience, never a player. No, he didn't want to see them together. Maybe she would be in his lap, or he'd be kissing her. Did he really want to see that? No, he told himself. "No," he said loud and clear. But he *did* want to see. He wanted to look. To know how they lived. How they were together.

As David sat gazing toward the house, he felt a charge of electricity as he made his decision. He *would* do it.

But just as he was about to open the door, he was startled by another car coming up behind him. It pulled even with his own and the older woman passenger rolled down her window as her jowled husband leaned across her.

"Do you need help?"

David rolled down his own window. "No, thank you. I was afraid I might have hit something. A raccoon. But I don't see anything."

"Oh, that's good," the gray-haired woman said. "Well, Merry Christmas."

"And to you."

She rolled up her window and the car drove on a hundred feet and turned into the driveway.

Visitors! David took a deep breath and blew it out slowly in profound relief. His face felt numb. They surely would have caught him. He could never have explained it. He shook his head again and started up the car. As he backed around, he did not even allow himself to look back.

He drove without consciously noticing where he was or what he was looking at until he reached Madeline's house. He pulled up next to the statue in the back. As he walked to the door of the house, he noticed a holly wreath at the base of the statue and assumed Georgie had put it there. A flash of pity swept through him for the man who never knew his mother or father. And hadn't known, nor ever would, that Celia was his half-sister.

David had brought a present for Georgie. It was just a small gift, but since he was bringing a present to Madeline, he didn't want Georgie to feel left out. He had very little money these days. The publisher had let him keep the advance he'd been given on the Nawasta book, as an advance on this next book. It was generous of Rinehart, he realized, and he would not disappoint him again. But he had to be very frugal. So he'd wrapped up a brown woolen scarf and cap that his parents had given him many Christmases ago but he hadn't worn in California. There wasn't anything else he had to give.

Finding a present for Madeline had been more difficult. There was hardly anything she needed, and he couldn't afford anything really nice. So he wrapped two books for her. One was the copy of his failed manuscript, *Nawasta*. The other was a copy of his first book, *The Descent of Maria Danforth*. He inscribed in the manuscript, "*Dear Madeline, I hope some day this will have value. Your friend, David.*" In the second book, he wrote, "*Dear Madeline, In search of truth. Your friend, David.*"

He suddenly had second thoughts about giving her *The Descent of Maria Danforth*. Would Madeline see the similarities between Maria and Mira? Perhaps so. He felt as if anyone who might read his book, and knew Mira, would ferret him out. It would be as if they were voyeurs in his fantasy. It might be better, he decided, if he didn't give Madeline that book after all.

Georgie came to the door within seconds of David's knock. He ushered David in and showed no particular expression as David slid the telltale book into his empty coat sleeve.

David handed Georgie the box with the cap and scarf.

"Merry Christmas, Georgie. This is for you."

"Thank you, Mr. McKay. I wasn't expecting nothing. I don't have nothing to give you for Christmas," Georgie said in a somber voice.

"I'll bet you do, Georgie."

Georgie shook his head, his eyebrows coming together in bewilderment.

"Did you bake something for me to eat while I'm here?" David asked.

Georgie nodded. "Christmas cookies."

"Then that's my present," David said enthusiastically.

Georgie looked quizzical and then his face brightened. "I can put some cookies up in pretty paper. You can have some to take home."

"Why, that would be wonderful, Georgie, thank you. I will enjoy them very, very much."

Georgie nodded happily, took his gift, and walked toward the kitchen as David proceeded into the living room.

Madeline was sitting in a large armchair that obviously had once been a very expensive piece of furniture. The rich dark wood around the top and the tips of the arms and the legs was still shiny. David had never thought much about Madeline being well-to-do, but he realized that she must be.

"Merry Christmas, lady." He proffered the manuscript.

"Oh, David, thank you, and Merry Christmas to you, too," she said gaily. She reached over to the table beside her and pointed to a large box wrapped with shiny white paper and a green velvet bow. "You'll have to lift it yourself, I'm afraid."

It was a very heavy box, the size of a carton. David looked at her inquiringly, but she merely gestured for him to open it. As he pulled away the paper, there was indeed a cardboard carton underneath. There were no markings on the outside, so he continued to pull open the glued flaps of the box.

As he removed the cardboard protector on top, *The Tempest* stared up at him. And next to it, *Love's Labors Lost*. There were two equal stacks of half-size books with blue cloth covers and gold lettering. The complete works of Shakespeare.

He stared at the books with a mixture of emotions. Embarrassed, because his present to her was, by comparison, a paltry offering. Then, after his discomfort in receiving such an expensive gift, he had a second reaction: *humiliation*. The books made manifest, with devastating reality, the truth that he could never expect to come within a shadow of Shakespeare. They unyieldingly erased all fantasy, all hope and ambition of being a great writer. They declared him unworthy of even aspiring to greatness. Nothing he could write would survive for three centuries; perhaps not his own lifetime.

He touched the top book with his fingertips. If not for this tangible reminder, he might have kept his delusions. One somehow can in the absence of irrefutable proof. But no longer. Forever altered, he now would have to carry this knowledge like a scar.

"Do you like it?" Madeline asked eagerly.

"Oh, yes, very much. What a wonderful gift."

He knew she had meant it only as encouragement. He would never tell her it was the most terrible present he'd ever had.

"When I knew you were going to be here through Christmas, I ordered the set from a bookstore in Montpelier. It just arrived two days ago. I was worried it wouldn't be here in time." Madeline began opening the little bow on her present.

"It's a very thoughtful gift, thank you, Madeline."

"You are most welcome," she replied as she removed the paper from his manuscript.

"I'm afraid my gift doesn't compare with yours."

"On the contrary," Madeline said, running her fingers over the manuscript's title page. Then she turned to his handwritten inscription to her. "This is lovely, David." She then turned another page and read the typed dedication, *"For Celia, for so much."* She looked up at him. "If only she had lived to see it. Thank you so very much, David, I will cherish this."

"But it isn't fit for publishing."

"That doesn't matter to me. It's very special."

David felt a deep gratitude for her saying that. And yet, he tried to tell himself that the book he was working on now was the one he cared about most.

• • •

As Georgie brought in the tea service and a platter of cookies to

Miz Abbott and Mr. McKay, they were deep in conversation. On the platter were not only the almond cookies he had baked today, but the cookies he had baked all week—apricot bars, pecan sandies in powdered sugar, gingersnap Santa Clauses with lemon icing beards, chocolate drops and rum butter cookies in the shape of bells and wreaths and stars coated with sugar crystals.

"It was the smell of almonds," Miz Abbott was saying to Mr. McKay. "That's the smell of arsenic."

"Are you certain?" Mr. McKay asked.

"I'm positive," Miz Abbott replied.

And then neither of them said anything more.

Although Georgie did not think he had done anything wrong, he reckoned that they both looked unhappy. He remembered Miz Eastman saying that Miz Abbott said that almonds are for holidays. So he had waited until Christmas. He was so sure he had done the right thing. But then why were they both looking so unhappy? They hadn't tasted his almond cookies yet, so they couldn't know if something was wrong. He had eaten one himself and it seemed all right. He thought they all were good. He thought she would like them. It was a holiday.

"The thing to do," Mr. McKay said, "is to invite him to come here."

"Come here?" Miz Abbott answered.

"For tea," Mr. McKay said.

Georgie was relieved, if a little confused. They weren't talking about his Christmas cookies no more. He poured the tea and wondered who else was going to be invited.

"Do you think he'd come?" Miz Abbott asked.

"Without a doubt," Mr. McKay answered. "He'll want to gloat over his election. That's the one thing he won't be able to resist."

"But what motive will he attribute to me for inviting him?" Miz Abbott asked.

Georgie watched Mr. McKay choose a gingerbread Santa Claus from the plate as he said, "To apologize, of course. And offer him an olive branch."

Miz Abbott nodded. "I think you're right."

Mr. McKay bit the head of the gingerbread man and smiled.

Georgie left the room contented. Miz Abbott and Mr. McKay obviously believed Mr. Carson could not resist his Christmas cookies.

CHAPTER NINE

"For murder, though it have no tongue, will speak
With most miraculous organ. I'll have these players
Play something like the murder of my father
Before mine uncle: I'll observe his looks;
I'll tent him to the quick: if he but blench,
I know my course."

Two days after Christmas, it began to snow lightly as Matthias Carson drove the lake road past Chester Weekes' house. The Weekes' cottage was an eyesore. Better to have an unspoiled landscape, he mused. So, too, with Preston Weekes' cottage at the north end of the lake. Neither would be missed.

Anticipating his tea with Madeline Abbott, he smiled with the satisfaction of having the upper hand. All her conniving—at his rallies and now with the statue—had come to naught. He had bested her, bested them all. He had clawed and scratched his way up to the top of the pile of toothless aristocrats and it felt good. He would not be contemptuous toward her—it would not befit his new station. No, he needn't do that. He could afford to be charitable.

He evaluated his trip to Washington with satisfaction. When he had arrived at the capitol, the city was already bustling with talk of the upcoming inauguration on March fourth of Franklin Delano Roosevelt, President of the United States. These were heady days. It was, as Matthias had calculated, the right time to be a Democrat. The incumbent Congressional Democrats were welcoming the newcomers to a society of the successful. All would share in the spoils of victory.

The House speaker-to-be, Henry T. Rainey, met with all the Democratic representatives-elect and outlined the initial programs that the new president would present to Congress and what was expected of the new brethren. He was quite pointed about their obligations. The most important issues were the economy and social programs. Putting everyone back to work. It was, indeed, going to be a New Deal—not the least of all for the Democratic Party.

Rainey had served in the House for nearly thirty years and at seventy-two, with a shock of white hair and an Illinois twang, he addressed the new Democratic legislators firmly, describing their role in the governmental pyramid. It was a primer on how they were connected to the national Party.

Matthias listened to the recitation of the various committees and studied the roster of incumbents both in-term and reelected. He would be very wise, he told himself, to choose his friends well. As he estimated his peers, he gauged which of them he would cultivate. From his list, he noticed there were a number of Democratic representatives from New York. They were the ones he'd get to know first, he decided. New York was, after all, the home state of the new president. He ticked off the name of Emanuel Celler, a ten-year veteran of the House who opposed national origin quotas established by the Immigration Act of 1924 as selectively denying admittance of Catholics and Jews into the United States. From what he knew of

FDR, he believed the new president would engineer the rescinding of the Act. Matthias would make a friend of Celler.

"This is what I was made for," he exulted, "the high-stakes game."

After his orientation with Rainey, Matthias had gone directly to his appointment with James Hamilton Lewis, late of Illinois but originally from Virginia and Georgia. The senator's office looked as though it belonged to a business executive rather than a public servant. Matthias wondered casually who had paid for the plush forest-green carpet that matched the walls, the cherry-wood desk, matching chairs and paneling. There were built-in bookshelves and brass fixtures on every drawer of the wooden cabinets, and there was a brass scale held by blindfolded Justice on the top bookshelf. The only objects on the desk were a green blotter, a jade pen and ink-well set, brass lamp and telephone. The very orderliness of the room appealed to Matthias as he sat waiting for the senator to finish his telephone conversation. The senator, who had retained something of his Southern drawl, was referring to a senate bill only by number. Something, Matthias deduced, to do with farm subsidies.

The senator finally put down the phone and looked at Matthias over his half-glasses. Lewis had a full head of red-auburn hair although his mustache and neatly trimmed square beard showed some of the graying expected of a sixty-nine-year-old man. Lewis was known collegially as Pink Whiskers, a name he would not deign to acknowledge. He surveyed Matthias intently and Matthias recognized the look. It was the same look he had received from every judge he had appeared before to plead a case. Sizing him up. Taking his measure.

"So you're the junior Democrat from New Hampshire in the House this term."

Matthias knew what was expected of him. He did not react to the slightly patronizing tone of "junior" Democrat. He responded the same way he did before the bench when he could not tell which way the judge was leaning.

"Yes, sir, I am. Matthias Carson, Senator."

"You've had your ballerina lessons from Rainey, I expect."

Matthias allowed himself to show amusement without openly smiling. "Yes, sir, he was quite thorough."

Lewis snorted. "Well, you can forget most of that flap-doodle. Rainey thinks the Legislature actually has some power." Then he laughed. Almost, Matthias thought, as though he were enjoying a dirty joke. "Nothing gets done in the House that can't be undone by the Senate."

Leaning across the desk, Lewis stared at Matthias dead on. "What House politics is, is boot camp." He held up two fingers in an emphatic gesture. "Two terms. That's all. You stay two terms, get your stripes, and move on. You understand that?"

Matthias nodded. He did not mention that had already been his plan.

Then Lewis leaned back in his chair, stuck his thumbs in his red vest and seemed to examine the ceiling. "That means you have to distinguish yourself in a relatively short period of time."

"Yes, sir."

The senator dropped his gaze from the ceiling to look at him again. "I don't know where you'll wind up, representative-elect Carson, but the party plans to keep a stream of candidates in the pipeline now that we're in command. You may as well be one of them." His remarks were said in a tone that indicated the interview was concluded.

"That is my intention," Matthias said evenly.

"*What* is your intention, Mr. Carson?"

"To go as far as I can, sir."

Lewis paused a moment before speaking. "Do things the party way, and the party will support you."

"I'm counting on it." Matthias made this sound unassuming.

The majority whip pursed his lips. "You realize that New Hampshire is a very small state, Mr. Carson."

"Yes, sir, it is. But New England is a very populous region. With a long tradition of notable statesmen."

Lewis folded his arms and leaned back in his chair. "You went to a mediocre law school, and interned at a mediocre law firm. You're a junior legislator from an insignificant state. You're not even *nouveau riche*, Mr. Carson, you're *nouveau* middle-class. What makes you think you have a promising political future?"

"I'm the common man, Senator. The common man who represents the common man. Except for one thing. I have uncommon ambition to have a seat at the table."

Lewis smiled benignly. "Well, you have a long way to go, Mr. Carson. But you have made a beginning."

Matthias rose and extended his hand. "Thank you, sir, for your time."

Lewis smiled and his eyes formed a crinkle at each corner. He rose to his feet and shook Matthias's hand. "I suppose I'll see more of you, Carson."

"I hope so, Senator."

"I hear you have a very beautiful wife."

Matthias inclined his head, not knowing how to take this.

"Use her to your advantage."

"Yes, sir. She is anxious to help."

Lewis nodded absently, sat down and began dialing the telephone.

Matthias left in high spirits. The meeting was promising, if not heraldic.

During his short sojourn in D.C., he had seen a house he aspired to in the right neighborhood. It was an old Williamsburg-style colonial, suitable for entertaining, but not too ostentatious. He and Mira would live there during Congressional sessions and return to Raleigh for intercession and summer vacation. He would send her back periodically as his aide to perform some deed or another, to keep in touch with his constituency and keep his name prominent in their minds and the newspapers. He would represent them as no one ever had before. His future was coming together.

He knew, too, that he needed one act of moderate flamboyance to draw attention to himself. As he drove the lake road toward Madeline Abbott's house, he considered what that would be.

"I think," he mused with a nod, "I'll have a bronze cast made. A coiled rattlesnake with the inscription, *Don't Tread on Me.*" He would keep it on his desk next to the plaque he already had, which read *Live Free or Die.* He rather liked the idea.

He was very pleased with himself by the time he reached Madeline's house. The snow was coming down quite heavily by then and he vowed to stay just a short time.

He entered Madeline's house by the back porch, where a tea table was set with fine china and ornate silverware. She greeted him cordially enough. But then, she would, of course. She gestured for Matthias to warm himself at a chair by the woodstove as she sat across from him. There was a third chair with a colorful afghan on the back of it, and a Japanese-style folding screen off to the side, to keep the heat centered where they sat.

Georgie came in with the tea tray just as Matthias was replying to Madeline, "Yes, I *was* somewhat surprised to receive your invitation. But I'm glad to have the opportunity to talk with you." He nodded to Georgie. "And you, Georgie, how have you been?"

Georgie did not respond.

"Georgie," Madeline coaxed, "Mr. Carson asked you a question."

"I'll be getting more wood now, Miz Abbott." And without anything further, he left the room.

"You must excuse Georgie, Mr. Carson," Madeline said as she poured the tea. "He has his ways."

"You may call me Matt."

"But it *is* Matthias, is it not?"

"Formally."

"Is that a Biblical name?" Madeline asked disingenuously.

"I really don't know. Is it?"

"I don't know either. I'm not much of a Bible reader."

"That amazes me," he said, with a hint of derision.

"I shouldn't have thought you'd amaze so easily. Do you take milk?"

Madeline passed him the milk pitcher and then offered him the tray of cookies and pastries.

"Do help yourself. Georgie's bakeries are perfectly wonderful."

"Yes, I know. Thank you." He took a flaky gooseberry tart and put it onto the plate but did not immediately eat it.

"I haven't seen Mira in quite a while," Madeline said, sipping her tea, "but I understand she is *enceinte*."

At his uncertainty, she clarified, "With child?"

He bristled at her tone, but replied cordially. "Yes, she's due this summer. We're hoping for July Fourth. Our anniversary."

"How very nice," Madeline said insincerely, glancing away toward the Japanese screen. Then she continued. "How do you find your tea?"

"It's very pleasant."

"It's English. I've developed a fondness for it. Celia always served it. I seem to be acquiring many of Celia's attributes. I suppose it's because I can't abide having her disappear past all recollection. Sometimes I think I'm becoming her. Extraordinary, isn't it?"

Madeline caught herself glancing at the screen and immediately looked away. Behind it, David sat on a wooden kitchen stool, listening to the conversation and waiting for Matthias Carson to incriminate himself. Madeline was convinced she could accomplish that. His story of Nawasta had given her the idea and he, after the humiliations at Carson's hands, was a willing accomplice. He'd parked his car on the far side of the house where Matthias wouldn't see it and she had told Georgie not to say anything about David being there.

He took me rather literally, she mused, and said almost nothing at all. Rather that . . .

Mindful that David would be rather uncomfortable sitting on the stool trying not to move or make a sound, she proceeded.

"Tell me," Madeline said, "do you think that being a Congressman will meet your expectations, Mr. Carson?"

"For the time being."

"For the time being? Then you plan to move out of politics eventually?"

"Up. Rather than out."

"I see. Up." Madeline scowled. Was there no end to his ambition?

Matthias looked out the porch window, past the statue and across the lake through the falling snow. "With all my campaigning, we never got the use of the lake this past summer. Next summer, though, I expect to spend a lot of time at home after the recess. Do some fishing off the dock. Of course we'll have the baby then. I guess this place will see a little life to it for a change."

Madeline waited for him to remark on the statue.

"I've bought out the Weekes brothers, you know. They'll be gone by the first of the year. We passed papers before Thanksgiving."

"You did?" Madeline was nonplussed.

"Umm hmm. I thought surely you would have heard about it."

"No."

Madeline glanced automatically out the window although she could not see either Weekes house from hers. "I can't imagine them selling out. Each one owns half the other's property. How did you get them to agree? They never agree on anything."

"This once they did. Of course, it took some negotiation on my part. The irony is neither of them ever wanted to stay. They just hung on out of orneryness. They're going to move to Nashua. Different addresses, naturally." He calmly sipped his tea.

"Preston and Chester." Madeline shook her head in disbelief.

Matthias eased back into his chair and crossed his legs.

"You know, if you ever want to sell, I'd be interested in your property as well."

"You already own a sizable piece of New Hampshire," Madeline snapped. "You're not planning to run for office in Vermont, are you?"

Matthias laughed. "Neither Vermont nor Massachusetts."

"But Boston was home, wasn't it?" She wondered why he didn't try his hand *there.*

Matthias shook his head. "Not originally. I was born in Lowell. My mother was a mill worker there." Then, as though rubbing her nose in it, he concluded, "*This* is home, as far as I'm concerned."

Madeline was not to be outdone. So his roots were in a poor immigrant mill town, and he was ashamed of it no matter how he acted.

"Do you still have family in Lowell?"

"Four brothers and five sisters. My mother's dead."

"And your father? Is he still alive?"

"I didn't know my father." Then Matthias leaned forward. "Much like Georgie."

So there, Madeline thought, he's thrown down the gauntlet, and it's time to take up the challenge.

"You haven't mentioned anything about the statue," she said slyly.

He leaned back in his seat again. "What is there to mention? I've seen it."

"You're not going to petition me to move it, or take it down?"

"Why should I?"

She scanned his face for a sign of what he was thinking, but found she could not read him.

"Then it doesn't bother you?"

He shook his head.

"But it bothers Mira, I understand."

"When she first saw it, I suppose. But she's grown accustomed to it since then."

"Oh." Madeline sipped her tea in defeated silence.

"I understand that it's a statue of Georgie's mother," Matthias said.

"That's right."

"But there's no birth certificate for him, you know." He said this gently, almost consolingly.

He had obviously prepared for this and she had lost the element of surprise. She had hoped Celia's family Bible might have provided some genealogy that included Georgie, but it hadn't. He'd outflanked her.

"If there isn't," she finally responded, "I suppose it's because she died in childbirth in her cabin and he never got recorded."

"Technically speaking," Carson pronounced confidently, "without documentation, he has no known mother. Or father. I'm afraid Georgie doesn't exist as a legal entity."

"I expect that can be rectified."

"Not without difficulty. But you can always take up the hopeless cause. You seem to have a penchant for that."

"You think I'm an odd duck, don't you?" she said, taking a new tack.

"Some of your activities have struck me as erratic."

"Did I cause you some concern?"

"No, actually not," Carson answered and he sounded quite genuine. "I think Mira was a little upset. But candidly, she was the only one who took you seriously. The audiences didn't."

Madeline looked at Matthias with the realization that her visitor might be right, and that she had deceived herself about her effectiveness. Perhaps her soul-searching decision not to attend any more rallies was really inconsequential. Perhaps nothing she did, or could have done, would have changed the outcome of the election. Her spirits plummeted. Perhaps there would *never* be anything she could effect.

"I've occasionally wondered," Matthias continued, "what made you decide to stop coming to my meetings. Not that it made any difference. I'm simply curious."

Madeline nodded somberly. "Which is why you accepted my invitation today."

"In part."

"Then let me satisfy your curiosity." She would not tell him of Mira's visit, only of its result. "The fact is, during the course of my mission, I came to a point of agnosticism, shall we say. One sometimes does. I couldn't proceed with doubt in my mind. Are you a pursuer of truth, Mr. Carson?"

He looked at her askance. "I like to think so, since I've been trained to the law. I don't journey into metaphysics, however, if that is what you mean."

Madeline put down her teacup. "I myself have never pursued anything with great vigor before. Whether out of cynicism or laziness, I can't say. I am rather old to have this responsibility thrust upon me, and I was ill-prepared, perhaps ill-natured for it. However, there it was." She paused in reflection.

"You're speaking of this Eastman business."

"I am speaking of my friend's murder."

"Not that again—"

"Allow me to finish, please," she interrupted. "My friend's murder. Knowing it was murder, and knowing who committed it, what to do?"

She offered him more tea but he declined, so she poured for herself and continued.

"Georgie and I have talked at length about it. Crime and punishment. Divine Will. He believes in vengeance being the Lord's, so he is untroubled. As for me, I am much troubled. But I find, to my mortal despair, there is nothing I can do."

She paused a moment to see what reaction her words had elicited. She saw that he was listening carefully.

"So, I am willing to concede defeat. You can go your way, Mr. Carson, without interference from me. I'm done with it."

He made no response.

"Given that," she went on, "there is only one thing I would like from you in return."

"Which is?" he said noncommittally.

"I need to know that I was right. That I was, in fact, pursuing Truth."

After taking her meaning, Matthias said, "You mean you want me to confess?"

"That is the price of freedom."

He gave a short mirthless laugh. "I would almost pay it." Then he added, "But I didn't commit any crime. Least of all, harm Celia."

"I don't believe you."

"I know you don't," he said without rancor. "But it's a minority opinion."

"David McKay doesn't believe you either."

"Your friend McKay believes whatever suits him. That's why he's just a hack."

Madeline's eyes inadvertently shifted to the screen and she immediately pulled them away as Matthias continued.

"His is not a very reliable partnership. He's just fueling your imagination for his own purposes."

"What would he have to gain by that?" Madeline could feel her voice grow sharp.

"A motive doesn't have to be grandiose. It all depends on what is wanted."

"I don't have anything that David wants."

"But *I* do. I have Mira. He'd do anything to get back at me for that." His tone became sardonic. "Have you read his *Maria Danforth* book? I'll gladly loan it to you. You might be amused. You see, he describes a seductive, raven-haired beauty with 'eyes like blue gentians' and 'a full-bosomed body of Venus.'" Matthias smiled and gestured across the lake. "Now who does that sound like?"

His smile broadened. "McKay was clearly in love with his invention. The man is pathetic. I'm afraid Mira and I have had many a good laugh at his expense."

Even Madeline was startled at the sound of the stool toppling over as David, unable to contain his anger, flung away the screen like a pleated curtain.

"Who the hell do you think you are?" David shouted, confronting Carson.

"What the hell are *you* doing here?" Carson snarled, looking back and forth between him and Madeline.

"I came to witness a confession!"

"You're mad! Both of you! Truly mad!"

Carson began to rise from his chair, but David held him down at the shoulder.

"Sit down, we have something to discuss."

Carson knocked his hand away and got up.

"We have nothing to discuss."

"Oh, but we do." David blocked Carson's exit. "You just lied to Madeline about me."

"That was no lie, Shakespeare. You are a pathetic hack." Carson pushed him out of the way.

David tried to block him, but Carson shoved him back.

"Until now," Carson said menacingly, "I haven't tried to do anything about you. For Mira's sake. She felt sorry for you. But this is the end." He included Madeline in his furious gaze. "I'll bring charges against both of you!"

"If you do," David replied, "I will swear I heard you tell Madeline you're guilty. I'll say how you bragged about it. How you fooled everyone. How you financed yourself to the Congress by killing an old lady."

"You lying bastard!"

Matthias lunged at David, hitting him in the stomach with his fist. David doubled over.

"Stop it! STOP!" Madeline shouted, rising to her feet.

As David struggled against Matthias, it was clear to Madeline that he was no match for his opponent. Carson was a street fighter and took advantage of every opening.

David rammed his shoulder against Carson, forcing him against the wall. Carson pressed his hands around David's neck, cutting off his breath.

"Georgie!" Madeline yelled in terror. "GEORGIE!"

Heedlessly, Madeline inserted herself between the two men in an attempt to separate them and protect David from a thrashing. She placed a hand on each of their chests and tried to push them apart. As David lunged forward to grab his opponent's neck, Matthias instinctively flung Madeline out of the fray. She toppled backward against the tea table.

• • •

Outside, Georgie heard Miz Abbott's frightened yell. He ran the few steps to the house, still holding the armload of wood he was bringing to the stove.

As Georgie entered the porch, he saw Mr. Carson hit Miz Abbott. He saw that Mr. McKay could not protect her. Mr. Carson might kill her. Without hesitation, he dropped all the wood except for one piece and rushed forward. With a downward blow, Georgie whacked Mr. Carson on the head. Mr. Carson immediately went limp and fell to the floor.

Madeline yelped and covered her mouth as she watched Matthias crumple and lie still at her feet. Georgie held the wood in his hand, frozen in place.

After a long shocked silence, David finally moved forward and bent over the fallen man. He investigated the outstretched body.

"Is he all right?" Madeline whispered.

He took Matthias's pulse at his wrist. After what seemed like eternity, he finally looked up at her and shook his head.

"He's dead."

"Oh, no," Madeline cried.

Georgie dropped the bloodstained wood. "I didn't mean to harm him. As God is my witness." He sank into his chair, stricken.

David stood up, silently looking down at the body.

"We'll have to contact the police," Madeline finally said.

He slowly shook his head. "We can't."

She looked at David questioningly. He walked over to her and drew her aside as Georgie sat transfixed by the body.

"We have to think about Georgie," David said softly. "He's killed a man. If he doesn't wind up in a loony bin, they'll hang him instead. They'll say he did it for the inheritance. They'll say we were his accomplices."

"But he doesn't even know about the inheritance."

"It doesn't matter. They'll say he did. That's what happens. Mira will tell them she told me. And that I told you. And that you told

Georgie."

Madeline was horrified. It was on her behalf that Georgie had done it.

"Don't you see?" David explained. "Carson's a politician now, and that means publicity. They'll dredge up all the past accusations you've made against him. Your appearances at his rallies. Everything. They may even say it was premeditated. That we lured him here to kill him. We can't go to the police."

"But what'll we do?" Her whole body trembled.

"We've got to get him out of here."

David noticed the afghan on the back of Georgie's chair. He tugged it away.

"We'll take him out in this and put him in his car. Then I'll drive it down the road from here. I'll make it look like an accident or something. Then I'll come back and get my car and leave."

He covered the body with the afghan. "It'll be hours before Mira gets worried enough to call the police. When they get here, tell them that Carson never showed up."

Madeline nodded, trance like. David walked up close to her and spoke in a whisper.

"You have to convince Georgie not to say anything. Can you do that?"

Madeline looked at Georgie huddled in the chair. "I don't know." Her voice was flat.

"It's for his own good. You have to."

She looked at him, not wanting to make that decision.

"There's no other way," he urged.

Madeline took a deep breath and then approached Georgie. She leaned over him.

"Georgie, the police will come tonight or tomorrow. You must tell them that Mr. Carson never came to tea. You and I were alone here all day. Mr. McKay was never here either. Will you say that, Georgie? It's very important."

"That would be a lie." Georgie was now in tears.

"You didn't mean to kill him, Georgie. It was just an accident,"

Madeline said. "But the police won't let it alone. They'll take you before a judge and the judge will commit you to an institution for the rest of your life."

Georgie looked terrified as she continued. "I can't let that happen on my account. Mr. Carson is dead and nothing is going to bring him back, and you should not suffer for what was not your fault. So we're going to tell a small lie. You must say he was never here, Georgie. Do you understand?"

Still tearful, Georgie looked up at her trustingly, and Madeline nodded to David.

David unfurled the afghan. "Georgie, help me lift Mr. Carson out to his car."

When Georgie didn't move, Madeline gently touched his shoulder. "Georgie, help Mr. McKay."

Slowly, Georgie rose and walked over to the body. David rolled the body onto the afghan and he took one end of it. Georgie took the other and they both lifted.

Madeline sat in Georgie's chair and held her arms. She was terribly cold.

Outside, more than three inches of snow coated the ground, and it was coming down even harder. David and Georgie struggled to load the body into the passenger side of Carson's car. Trying not to look at Carson, David set the body upright on the seat and removed the afghan. As he closed the door, the body tilted against it. David turned away and glanced across the lake at the light in Celia's house. He wondered, almost perversely, what Mira was doing now. Probably sitting in front of the fireplace in a huge stuffed chair, waiting for her husband to come home. At least the drapes were closed. She wasn't looking over here.

He handed the afghan back to Georgie and walked around to the driver's side of Carson's auto. In the rearview mirror, he saw Georgie standing there, holding the afghan in his hands as though he were holding a baby.

David found himself unusually cool and collected as he drove down the deserted road. He had formulated his plan even before leaving Madeline's house. Formulated it, in fact, as soon as he'd checked Carson's heartbeat. Though still pulsing, it was weak and irregular. It wouldn't take much for it to stop. All he had to do was to crash Carson's car into a tree. Then he would surely be dead. It would look like an accident on the slippery road. Neither he nor Georgie would be suspected.

And, with Carson gone, his way back to Mira would be clear and his revenge would be complete. It was what he had always wanted. Everything was now within his grasp.

He felt, he realized, godlike.

It was nearly dark at four o'clock but the thickening snow seemed to highlight the woods. He would drive halfway down the road, turn around as though Carson was heading for Madeline's house, and push the car off the embankment. It would look like an accident in the slippery snow. Then he would walk back to Madeline's, get his own car and go home. No car tracks or footprints would be visible after the storm.

He passed the perfect spot, a bend in the road that a car could easily miss and go careening off into the woods. He turned around and started back.

Unexpectedly, around the curve, car headlights came into view from the opposite direction. The lights blinked in courtesy. David was startled but as the other car passed, he quickly turned his head so that his face could not be seen.

His first reaction was panic. Then he began to think it would all work out perfectly. Now, there'd be a witness to say that Carson was driving toward Madeline's house when he went off the road.

He pulled over and looked down the embankment into the woods. There was a steep drop. A car would fall at least forty feet before it hit a tree—with enough momentum to cause a head to crash into a windshield.

David left the motor running as he got out of the car. He leaned across the seat, pulling Carson's body over to the driver's side. He carefully aligned the body with the steering wheel. Then he turned the wheel to aim the car toward the trees at the bottom of the slope. He released the brake, slammed the door and gave the car a push.

The car slowly pitched forward and then picked up speed as it rolled down the slope. It crumpled against a large tree with a reverberating thud, shaking the snow from the pine needles onto the roof and hood of the car.

Just before the moment of impact, David thought he heard something. Something unexpected. Was that a groan? No, it couldn't be. He felt suddenly nauseous. The sense of power he'd had a moment ago now vanished like a vapor. Perhaps it was just his mind playing tricks on him. But he could not help thinking, *What if he's still not dead?* Like a sleepwalker, he began plodding slowly down the slope.

As he neared the car, he began to tremble. Leaning against a tree for support, the word *pathetic* kept repeating in his mind. *They both called me that, both of them. Is that what I am?*

Memories of his embarrassing encounter with Matthias on Thanksgiving Day flashed into his mind, followed by Mira's brutal rebuff, the humiliation of his book rejection, the shame of his father's suicide and his mother's breakdown, the grinding poverty of his day-to-day life in a boardinghouse of old bachelor men whose shirts were stained with tobacco juice and breakfast.

Is that all I am? he asked himself again.

"No," he said aloud into the rough bark of the tree. "No," he repeated in a whisper, "not anymore." He was, he reminded himself, the master of this situation. He was the one in control. Forcibly, he pushed himself away from the tree and continued the final steps down the slope.

At the car, he stood looking impassively in the window. Blood was matted on the back of Carson's head where Georgie had hit him, and blood streaked out of his nose where it had collided with the steering wheel. There was no sound in the woods. No birdsong, no wind in the branches, no chattering squirrels, just the silence of snow falling.

Then . . . another faint groan.

David felt nothing. All sense of foreboding was gone, replaced by—by what? Detachment? He wondered, because he had no misgivings. He knew what to do. A simple act, really. After all, hadn't he already made the decision to kill Carson when he pushed the car off the road?

Madeline was sitting stiffly in her chair when Georgie finally came back into the house. The woodstove crackled in the silence. He stood there still holding the afghan with Carson's blood on it.

Silently, she got up and took the stove door-opener from the table. She slipped the metal lever into the slot and opened the door of the woodstove. The fire sparked, leaping higher with the draft of air.

"Burn it, Georgie." She had already burned the log that he had used on Carson and cleaned the floor of Carson's blood. No log, no afghan, no visitor. Nothing had ever happened here. She glanced at him briefly and then looked away. "I'm going to bed. I'll see you in the morning."

She left the room as Georgie stayed behind, staring into the soothing hypnotic flames.

CHAPTER TEN

"And even like the precurse of fear'd events,
As harbingers preceding still the fates
And prologue to the omen coming on,
Have heaven and earth together demonstrated
Unto our climatures and countymen."

Mira's first thought was that the road was too dangerous and he had decided to stay at Madeline Abbott's house until the storm was over. And, of course, Madeline did not have a damn telephone. Mira was certain that was what had happened. She would just have to be patient.

The snow continued to a depth of fourteen inches over the course of the following day. At times it would turn to sleet and form a crust, and then change back to snow and settle on the crust until another sleet came, like geological layers in antediluvian rock.

It was only later, the following day, that Mira entertained the notion that perhaps Matt might have had an accident in the storm. But she dismissed that idea. The answer had to be simply that he had stayed put.

Despite her conviction, she paced from window to window, trying to glimpse any sign of his car on its way home. Finally, her concern won out and she called the police. But Chief Tanner told her not to be alarmed; that her husband was probably safe and would stay there until the road was open. The Chief promised he would drive up to the Abbott house as soon as he could.

It was not until the second day after the storm ended, four days after Matthias Carson left home for his tea with Madeline Abbott, that the tractors with plow blades came to clear the road.

Technically, the town of Raleigh was responsible for plowing the portion of the lake road only within its boundaries. However, the Wickessett town barn and snowplows were housed at the north end of the lake. The two communities had an agreement that Raleigh would plow up to Madeline Abbott's house and Wickessett would plow down to meet them. But Wickessett was always late.

Thus was Matthias Carson's car discovered by Master Thomas Hingham of Raleigh, who had shifted from seasonal chauffeuring and trucking to winter snowplowing. It was late afternoon when the observant young man spotted the top of the black car at the bottom of the slope at the tree line.

He set the gears, jumped from the tractor, and slid down the slope to investigate. Peering in the window of the damaged car, he saw Congressman Carson slumped over the steering wheel. Dried blood was streaked over the side of his face. Young Hingham, being a farm lad, did not flinch at the sight of blood or death. He did, however, mutter a quick *Our Father* before climbing up to his tractor. He turned back toward Raleigh while the second and third plows of his two brothers continued on toward the Abbott house.

As Chief Tanner drove up the cleared portion of the lake road in search of Representative-elect Carson, he was confronted by a snow-plow coming toward him in high tractor-speed. He swerved the car just in case Tom Hingham couldn't pump those brakes hard enough to stop. But Tom was a marvel with machines and he brought his big snowplow to a halt, allowing for slippage, just where he wanted it.

Chief Tanner followed him back to the scene of the crash. More slowly than his agile companion, the chief shuffled down the embankment to the collision. One look told Tanner that Matthias Carson was long dead. The other look told him that he was in Vermont.

For expedience, because the Wickessett plows had not yet opened their section of road in the impassable snow, the body of the Legislator-elect was removed from the car and transported to Raleigh by the volunteer fire department.

Chief Tanner then performed the odious task of informing Mira Carson that her husband had died from injuries sustained in an automobile accident in the slippery snow. He called the Wickessett police station as soon as he got back to his office. They were content to let Tanner handle the paperwork and the inevitable calls once the press learned of the death of the new young U.S. Congressman.

After the county medical examiner arrived, the body was immediately transported to the main hospital in Concord. The car was winched onto a trailer and carted to the Raleigh town barn. The Hingham brothers continued to plow through the night.

That evening in bed, Madeline heard the snowplows coming nearer and nearer, their engines loud and irregular, not like her car motor but more labored. Then there were the sounds of the plows scraping over the ground when they moved the snow. It felt like a monstrous army was coming for her. She, who had been so dedicated to Justice for Celia, now felt herself the object of a seeking hand of retribution.

It was not my fault, she pleaded silently into the dark.

But on they came, on and on. She heard the tractors move slowly and inexorably up the hill. They stopped directly in front of her house, rumbling like hungry animals outside her door. She lay still, waiting for what awful thing would happen next. But the tractors withdrew, turning and proceeding back down the road. As they ranged into the distance, she fell fitfully asleep.

As dawn edged over her windowsill, she told herself it was silly to have been so fearful. But she breathed deeply in relief, regardless.

During the night, Chief Tanner received a call from Dr. Eugene Fox in the morgue of the state hospital and early the following morning, the chief drove to Concord.

The state pathologist pointed out that Matthias Carson's head wounds were inconsistent with a car accident. It was what the county medical examiner initially suspected so Tanner had arranged for the post mortem not because he really believed the medical examiner (who was not a doctor), but because the chief was a careful man. This dead legislator was a most visible public figure and he was not going to have anyone say that Raleigh was remiss in any detail.

"You see this blow to the back of the head?" The pinched-faced man in his fifties, with thin tousled graying hair and steel-rimmed glasses, pointed to an indentation. "And these," he moved his hand toward the brow, "are blows with a blunt instrument. Here and here and here."

"You're sure of that?"

Dr. Fox straightened up his five-foot-four-inch matchstick frame and peered up over his glasses at the officer standing next to him. "Quite," he replied sternly, leaving no room for equivocation.

Tanner had not expected to hear anything but the obvious, that Carson died in the crash. He sighed deeply. Now this was going to be a blankety-blank mess. First and foremost, there was a jurisdictional problem. The body had been found on Vermont land. He would have to turn everything over to the Wickessett police. He grimaced. They were even more inexperienced than he was. Dr. Fox would have to declare it homicide but would the Wickessett police accept that without requiring their own autopsy?

If it was murder, who could possibly have done it? There hadn't been a murder in Raleigh since before he was born, when some outraged wife had killed her philandering husband. That didn't apply here. In fact, when he first went to see Mrs. Carson to tell her the terrible news, her reaction had been so pitiable it touched his heart. Mrs. Carson had sunk to her knees, holding her stomach, and wept. He had lifted her to her feet and helped her to a chair as she tried desperately to regain her composure. "No," she kept repeating, "no."

As soon as he was through here in Concord, he would go back to Raleigh and drive over to speak with Miss Abbott. Then he shook his head.

I probably won't be able to talk with her if Wickessett takes over, he thought. *She's in Vermont. Not that it makes much difference for certainly she didn't do it.*

Mrs. Carson had said her husband drove off alone. But, obviously, someone else had come along. What motive could anyone have had to do this? Anger, revenge, greed? What else was there to kill for? And how would someone like that be riding with Carson?

Tanner had not found anything notable in Carson's effects. He reminded himself to ask Mrs. Carson if her husband had carried a wallet without telling her, yet, that her husband had been murdered. There hadn't been a wallet on the body, but that hadn't seemed important when they believed it was simply an accident and the man hadn't been all that far from home.

As for motive, he would have to learn a lot more about the deceased first.

But what can I do, he wondered glumly, if I don't have jurisdiction? Well, Miss Abbott may not be in New Hampshire but the Weekes brothers were. He could at least talk with them.

Tanner's manner was all cooperation as Detective Brandt came to his station. No Wickessett police officer had ever been to Raleigh in an official capacity or met Police Chief Tanner.

"As you know," the younger man said deferentially, "we had to move the body to Montpelier for our own post mortem. No offense, it's our protocol."

"No offense taken. I assume the findings are no different from ours."

"No different."

The two men were silent. Then Brandt said, "I was informed that you already interviewed the Weekes brothers, so it may not be necessary for me to duplicate your interview if I may use your notes."

Tanner flipped open his notebook and read aloud, "'At about four fifteen that afternoon, Preston Weekes was pulling up his lines from the hole near the middle of the lake. He was ice fishing for the last time. In another week, he would move to Nashua. But today the fishing was good. He sat on a wooden bench with a warmer underneath. The snow was accumulating and as he looked skyward, he saw it was not going to stop for a long time.

"'As he looked up, he saw a man's figure walking north on the lake road coming from the direction of Raleigh. It was too gray and snowy to make it out. Preston thought it very peculiar for anyone to be walking up the road in such weather. And he confirmed that no one came to his house.'"

Tanner looked up from his notes. "Then I talked to Chester. Chester was driving from Wickessett back to his house about four o'clock when he passed a car coming in the opposite direction. Obviously Carson's. He says he saw two people in the car, although he couldn't see their faces."

"Are we thinking that the passenger and the man on foot are the same?"

"It would seem so. But it doesn't add up," Tanner said. "The lake road ends at Preston's house so the only place a hitchhiker could have been going to is Wickessett. No offense, but why would anyone want to go to Wickessett? And the only thing beyond Wickessett is mountains."

Brandt shrugged. "There are a lot of hoboes crisscrossing the country nowadays. Maybe this one didn't realize where the road went."

Tanner shook his head. "We didn't get any report of a stranger in Raleigh that week, and I know you didn't get any in Wickessett afterward. Where'd he disappear to? Into the woods? Is there any other town east of you that he could've cut through the woods to?"

Brandt shrugged. "There's Hillsdale. But it's a good twenty-five miles through forest. And it was snowing bad that night. Even if you knew where you were going, you'd get lost or frostbit."

"Exactly. Let's suppose for a moment that it wasn't a hitchhiker," Tanner suggested. "That it was someone who knew Matthias Carson. And perhaps knew his itinerary that day."

Brandt frowned. "The only ones we've got on the lake are the wife, the Weekes brothers and Miss Madeline Abbott."

"And Georgie Skates who works for Miss Abbott. I think we can rule them out."

"I'll talk with Miss Abbott and Mr. Skates. Perhaps they know something or saw something. I'm assuming Carson's death was robbery, pure and simple. It has to be a hitchhiker."

"Then where the hell did he go?"

Brandt shook his head.

Chief Tanner pulled his mouth into a bulldog expression. "If we categorize it as a crime of opportunity by a hitchhiker, we're at a dead end."

Brandt leaned back in his seat in shared frustration. "And there was nothing in the car that could help us."

Tanner shook his head. They had gone over the car meticulously. Obviously when it had been transported to Wickessett, they had no better luck.

"I can't figure it out," Tanner said. "Let's say there was a passenger. So the passenger does what? Hits Carson over the head and goes off the road into a tree with him?"

"Maybe he hits him when the car stops to pick him up and then pushes the car off the road afterward."

Tanner shook his head. "Then what? Takes his wallet. Bops him over the head a few more times? Why? What was the weapon? Our pathologist says it was a blunt instrument."

"Ours thinks perhaps a rock," Brandt offered. "There's plenty of rocks to pick up if he needed one."

Tanner tapped his fingers on the desk. "Doesn't make sense to me."

"We know he had a passenger," the young detective argued. "And he didn't start the trip with a passenger. So it was someone he picked up after leaving his house. That leads right to a crime of opportunity. If not greed, what was the motive?"

"Anger, revenge."

"No," Brandt said, "the only one who'd have killed Carson for his wallet would have been a hitchhiker. As for anger or revenge, for *what*? He hadn't taken office yet."

Tanner fleetingly wondered if Mrs. Carson would have a reason to plot her husband's death. But he thought not. And what about Madeline Abbott? Less than a year ago, she had sat in this very office and all but accused Matthias Carson of murdering Celia Eastman. After that, he'd heard stories about her going to Carson's rallies to make trouble. And now she was inviting him for tea? Of course, she wouldn't have killed him herself. Could she have put Georgie up to it? That could happen. She could have had Georgie walk up the road. Surely Carson would have stopped to give him a ride. Then Georgie could have hit Carson with the rock, pushed the car off the road and walked home.

But Georgie wouldn't do that, Tanner reminded himself, he hasn't got a violent bone in his body.

The theory would work, but not with Georgie. Tanner sighed. "I don't know what to think."

"Me, neither," Brandt admitted. "But we'll keep looking for a hitchhiker."

"There's just one thing," Tanner added, and Brandt looked at him inquisitively. "When Chester Weekes saw Carson, he was positive it was four o'clock."

"Right," said Brandt.

"And Preston Weekes was certain it was four fifteen when he saw the walker."

"Right."

"But Mrs. Carson said he left at two o'clock. It would only have taken him about half an hour to get to the crash site. So what happened in that extra hour-and-a-half?"

"I don't know," Brandt admitted.

"The only possible explanation is that Carson went somewhere else before he started out for Miss Abbott's house. And wherever that somewhere was, he got himself a passenger."

"So where did he go?"

"That's the question," answered Tanner. "It could only be somewhere in Raleigh. So I'll work this end of it and you can work the other. I would make one suggestion, however. I think we should keep the fact that it was a murder under wraps. At least for the time being. If Wickessett is anything like Raleigh, the rumors will corrupt the investigation. Not to mention the calls from the big city newspapers."

Detective Brandt nodded.

Mira had no idea what funeral arrangements to make. She was further distressed by the fact that the police chief hadn't released Matt's body. Why was it taking so long? She was so distraught, she called Roland Niles and asked him to help her.

"Of course, Mira dear," he'd said, "I'll do whatever I can. Shall I come over?"

The sound of his voice unnerved her, the suggestively solicitous voice he'd used when she first came crying to him in school. "No, thank you, Ro, that's not necessary."

"Well, just keep it in mind. If there's anything else you need—"

"I'll be all right. Thanks for your help. I'll talk to you later."

She knew he had sensed her vulnerability. She felt as though she were stepping back in time. Then something cold and clammy washed over her. Her legs felt wobbly. She sat down as she became dizzy. Instinctively, she put her head down and breathed deeply. It felt as though she was holding onto a branch as she swirled down the river, bobbing up and down. She held her head with her hands, almost ready to pass out. Gradually, in slow-motion time, the feeling began to pass.

She sat in front of the fireplace, leaning back with her hand on her stomach. Even though it was early in her pregnancy, she believed she felt the baby growing inside of her. She gently rubbed her stomach as if consoling the child and telling him that Mother was still there, even if Father was not.

She badly wanted a drink. She had been crying for two days and she was exhausted. Her skin felt dry, her eyes were sore and swollen, her nose was runny. Her whole body ached. But Ro had cautioned her about what to do for a healthy baby, and drinking liquor was not prescribed.

He, the baby—for she was certain it was going to be a boy—was all she had now.

Along with the terrible wracking grief, there was a small part of Mira that was released from a future she had not known whether she could survive. As exciting and attractive as a life in the social whirl of Washington promised, she did not know if she was up to it. Matt had believed she was. But that worried her, too. His expectations had been so high.

She began to cry again, for herself this time. And for her fatherless baby. And for Matt. And for a life she did not know if she really had wanted.

"Now what will we do?" she said imploringly into the air.

Surely, one drink couldn't hurt.

A week had passed since Carson's death and David was nearly finished with his new book. He had been writing furiously since Thanksgiving, day and night. Almost clinically, he knew he had to finish while the fervor was still in him. He was afraid it would dissipate with Carson's death. And there would be no revisions this time. He sensed this would dilute the energy of the writing. So it would be sent as written, and be damned.

Typing the words "THE END" at the bottom of the page, David

sat back and rubbed his neck. This afternoon, he would mail the manuscript to Rinehart.

He got up and stretched and walked around the room several laps to loosen his muscles. Then he flopped on the bed and let the feeling of completion wash over him.

"Now," he told himself, "I can let myself think about her." He wondered if he should send a condolence note first, or simply appear. This was the second chance he'd been waiting for and he didn't want to do it wrong this time.

Inadvertently, he began visualizing Carson's automobile crashing headfirst into the tree at the bottom of the slope. He pictured himself walking, sliding, skidding down the incline to where the car had landed.

He deliberately cut off the images that followed and concentrated on the walk back up the hill to Madeline's house and to his car. It had taken him nearly an hour to get back, walking into the storm, the snow crusting his eyebrows and whipping against his unprotected face. When he finally got back to her house, he had not gone in. He'd gone directly to his car, hidden on the opposite side of the house, and begun the difficult journey back down the lake road, fearful lest anyone see him.

He recalled passing the bend where he had pushed Carson's car off the road. The tire tracks were already covered by the snow, as his own tire tracks would soon be. His windshield wipers had sounded like his heartbeat. But he had made his way down the road and back to his room without encountering anyone.

"Thank you God for the storm," he whispered. Or, he thought fleetingly, thank Lucifer, fallen from grace.

Madeline appeared at the door behind Georgie as the young man was saying, "I'm Detective Brandt, from the Wickessett Police Department. You must be Mr. George Skates." The officer stood with his feet apart.

"Are you looking for me, Detective?" Madeline interjected, stepping forward.

"Miss Abbott?"

"That is correct."

Georgie did not move. He continued staring at the policeman with widened eyes.

Madeline moved in front of Georgie as he faded back against the wall. "Wickessett Police?" she repeated.

"Wickessett, Vermont. Your house is in our jurisdiction. You do know that."

Madeline fixed him with a javelin stare. "Of course I know I'm in Vermont, young man, I've lived in Vermont for more years than you have been alive." That wasn't quite true, but she'd made her point.

"Sorry, ma'am." Brandt's feet came together and his shoulders lost their starch.

"Now, if it's donations you want, I'll be glad to help out."

"No, ma'am, thank you. That's not why I'm here."

He pulled out a notepad. "I expect, Miss Abbott, you've heard about Congressman Carson's automobile accident."

"Yes," she replied weakly, "on the radio."

"I understand from his wife that you entertained Mr. Carson that day."

Here it was, Madeline thought. Ever since she heard the brief report on the radio that Matthias was found dead in his car, this was the moment she had been dreading. She tried to stay calm. Georgie was well behind her. She wanted to turn and look at him, reassure him, but she couldn't. She took a deep breath before answering.

"Actually, no. He was supposed to come, but he never showed up." She must be careful not to give anything away.

"Didn't you find that odd?"

"Not at the time, not with the weather that day. It was a very bad storm."

"Didn't you think it was rude of him not to let you know he wasn't coming?"

"I don't have a telephone."

"Was there anyone else here that day?"

"Just Georgie and myself."

"All day?"

"Yes, all day." She could feel her temples throbbing.

Brandt turned to Georgie. "What about you, Mr. Skates? Did you see Mr. Carson or anyone else that day?"

Without looking up, Georgie shook his head.

Brandt turned back to Madeline. "What time was Mr. Carson supposed to be here?"

"For afternoon tea, Officer, at two forty-five."

"Detective," Brandt corrected, putting away his notebook. "According to Mrs. Carson, Mr. Carson left home at two o'clock. Apparently, he only got as far up the road as the town line. The snowplows found his car in a gully about three-quarters of a mile from here."

"How dreadful." Madeline's voice quivered nervously. "He must have been on his way here when he had the accident. I feel terrible."

"Mr. Chester Weekes passed Mr. Carson on his way home from Wickessett. Carson was motoring up the road toward your house about four o'clock. Chester saw two people in the car. A half hour or so later, Preston Weekes saw a man on foot walking up the road. Preston was ice fishing on the lake, too far to get a good view of who it was. But it had to be after the car crashed, so obviously it wasn't Carson. Did *anyone* come to your house that afternoon?"

"No, no one," Madeline said, realizing that both the second man in the car and the one on foot was David.

"The man on foot," Brandt was saying, "must have been his passenger. But you say you weren't expecting anyone else?"

"No."

"Mr. Carson was alone when he left the house, according to his wife. We don't quite understand what accounts for the delay if he was to be here at two forty-five, but we think he must have picked up a hitchhiker along the way."

"And you think the hitchhiker was coming to my house for some reason?"

"We don't know, ma'am." Brandt directed his attention to Georgie. "And you were here the whole day, Mr. Skates? You didn't leave for any reason?"

Georgie shook his head.

"I've already told you that, Detective," Madeline said. "He was not away from this house the entire day." Except for the early morning, this was entirely true. She was suddenly afraid they might think Georgie was hitchhiking back to her house. Maybe they suspected the blow to Carson's head was not from the crash. Then it would all come to the same end, even with David's efforts to disguise what had happened.

Madeline's mind was reeling. Now the police were looking for a hitchhiker who did not exist. This was an awful turn of events.

"Do you have any idea who it might have been?" she asked.

"Not yet, but we're working on it. Got a little jurisdiction problem with the Raleigh police. Mr. Carson lived on their side of the line, but the car crash was on ours. We aren't always in step, if you know what I mean. But we'll work it out. Anyway, thank you for your time, Miss Abbott."

She drew a deep nervous breath after he left. She disliked lying as much as Georgie did, but she had to protect him, just as David told her. If only David hadn't come from behind the screen so recklessly, she might have had a confession *and* a witness. But Matthias had not confessed. Nor, she had to admit, had he even appeared guilt-stricken. The man either had no conscience or—

She immediately dismissed the thought.

Georgie melted back into the house as Miz Abbott was saying good-bye to the policeman. He went directly to his room, put on his jacket, the cap and scarf that Mr. McKay had given him, and the gloves that Miz Eastman had given him many years ago. He left the house by the back door without knowing where he was going.

He could not bear his deceit.

Outside, he headed down the road as the police car drove off in the opposite direction. He walked harder and harder until he was running on the packed snow. He exhaled bursts of white air. All he could hear was the sound of footfalls and his own breathing. He ran downhill, the incline so steep that his steps became farther apart. He felt as though he were almost flying. He wanted to go so fast he would leave his body behind.

He ran and ran until he reached the bottom, and then he turned into the woods. He ran on the path to the edge of the water, to where the statue had stood and now was gone. He bent over, resting his elbows on his knees, and breathed in gasps until finally his breaths began to slow.

Then he went to the nearby pine tree. It was old and thick around the middle, with branches close to the ground larger than his thigh. As he had so many times before, he began to climb.

Hand over hand, he climbed the tree, his foot finding each branch with practiced precision. Only the ends of the branches had crusted snow on them and, as Georgie climbed, they quivered and the snow fell off in clumps. Up he went to a height of twenty feet to the crook of the highest branch that would safely hold him. And there he stayed, looking over the lake, looking at his mother across the water, and crying. He told her of the soul-sinning act he had committed, and that he knew he was damned forever.

One month later, there were still no headlines in the Wickessett newspaper to indicate anything new about Matthias Carson's death. Madeline was immensely relieved. She had begun a subscription to the weekly *Gazette* right after Detective Brandt showed up just so she could follow the investigation.

With each issue, she had chided herself, "Have I no remorse for the murder of this man?" She had a fear of discovery, she acknowledged, but that was not necessarily the same thing. And still there was that singular nagging doubt—there had been no hint whatsoever of guilt in Matthias' expression or behavior. What if Matthias Carson were actually innocent of Celia's death? What if he were simply an egotistical, detestable, ambitious man driven to succeed but not to kill?

She badly wanted to talk with David for reassurance, but she had neither seen nor heard from him since that afternoon. Where was he? Had he left and gone back to California? Perhaps it was prudent, she supposed, that he didn't contact her, so as not to raise suspicions. But she was worried to think that someone whom she knew so little, a stranger really, had her and Georgie's fate in his hands.

In Raleigh, David bought another issue of the *Raleigh Sentinel*. He folded the paper carefully and left the corner store with a mixture of relief and frustration. The obituary for Carson simply stated that he was found dead in his car. Wordsmith that he was, David would have liked it to read that Carson was found dead in a car crash. "Found dead" did not have the finality of exculpation he would have preferred. He knew instinctively that Carson's death was suspect. He could tell that by the omission of the word "accidental."

Of course he hadn't counted on one of the Weekes brothers seeing him in Carson's car. But there was no way he could have been recognized. If only he hadn't been seen, there would be no doubt about its being an accident. But then there was the wallet.

It had been stupid of him to take Carson's money. Why did he do it? Because he needed it. It was nearly one hundred dollars. A small fortune in his penurious circumstance. But it wasn't only that. He did it because it was Carson's. Afterward, he had thrown the empty wallet far into the woods away from the crash. If he had not taken the money and hadn't been seen, they would have believed it was an accident, and it would be all over. Now, they thought it was robbery.

"How could I have been so stupid? And so greedy?" he castigated himself as he walked back to the boardinghouse. Then he realized that perhaps it was a good thing he did take the money since the Weekes brothers *had* seen someone.

If I hadn't taken the money, he rationalized, there would have been no motive to ascribe to some random hitchhiker. At least now, if the police were suspicious, they'd think a stranger killed Carson for money. And that was logical.

Yes, he had done the right thing after all.

He had not gone to Carson's funeral. He knew Mira would not have wanted him to. He badly wanted to see her, to go to her house and offer his sympathy. But it was too soon. He had written her a note saying he was sorry for her loss and telling her to let him know if there was anything he could do to help her. She had not written back, and he had not expected her to. He would wait a little longer; then, he would go to see her.

But first, he would send her flowers. Bought, unavoidably, with her husband's money.

When he reached home, he found a letter from Rinehart on the tray of mail in the foyer, and his heart leapt. It wasn't the returned manuscript. It was a thick letter!

He grabbed it off the tray and bolted upstairs to his room. As soon as he closed the door, without waiting to take off his coat or boots, he ripped open the envelope.

Inside was a contract for his new book reflecting the change in title that his editor suggested from *A Murder for Money* to *A Legal Murder*. There was also a check, and a personal note from Rinehart:

"*Great villain. Good formula, David. Keep them coming! -R.*"

At first, he was euphoric as he looked at the check. Then he sighed. Although he was gratified to have the money, it really was barely enough for him to live on until he wrote another book. And as he reread the note, the remainder of his elation dissolved.

"*Great villain. Good formula.*"

The words made him seethe. Formula, indeed. He hadn't intended it as a formula. He'd put so much of himself into this book. Himself, Mira, Celia and Madeline. And he didn't want Matthias to be a *great* villain. He thought he had written him as merely pernicious and repugnant. He was torn between the accolade for having written a great villain, and the resentment of having Matthias best him even in his own book. Too, he realized that he was stuck on a treadmill now. He had hoped to write something more meaningful to follow-up on *The Descent of Maria Danforth*. Something more literary. But from Rinehart's letter, he was now expected to write another murder mystery. With the same "formula."

His thoughts drifted inexorably back to Mira. What would she do now? Would she stay here in Raleigh, in Celia's house? It occurred to him that she would have inherited Carson's estate. Celia's money. Enough money, perhaps, for him to write the book he wanted to. And live the way he wanted to—not like some pawnshop pinchpenny.

That just sweetens the prize, he thought. He would not to wait any longer before beginning his courtship.

CHAPTER ELEVEN

"That we would do,
We should do when we would . . . "

When winter was spent and the bare ground spread like molasses on bread, and the trees began leafing as tentatively as baby hair, Madeline again took to sitting at her window overlooking the lake. It had been nearly five months since she'd come back there to spend the day. The porch was the coldest room in the house and, facing east, the short days of winter made it dark and inhospitable by mid-afternoon. Yet, in the morning, the view captured the rising sun and she could sit there bathed in light.

The first Sunday afternoon she ventured back was disquieting as she looked across to Mira's house. She was unable to think about anything other than the fact that this room was where Georgie killed Matthias. As much as she tried to put it out of her mind, there were moments of anxiety that swept over her. She felt like a passenger in the very car that rolled faster and faster down the slope into a tree. She had more than once dreamed of herself sitting next to the body as it plummeted down the hill and, at the instant of impact, Matthias turning to look at her.

It wasn't that his death was unjust—it was unplanned. She believed with every breath that Matthias Carson deserved his fate. She had to believe that. It was tragic, however, that it had to be Georgie's doing. And still, she told herself, Georgie had acted honestly and, in her mind, was blameless.

Getting rid of Matthias's body had been David's idea, but of course it was necessary to protect Georgie. What else could they have done?

She had not seen David in all these months. Not a sight. Not a sound. As if he had dropped off the face of the earth. Or she had. But, as she looked across the lake wondering what happened to him and whether she should try to contact him, she observed a pregnant woman and a man with a gray fedora hat walk around the back of Celia's house. She instantly recognized Mira. But the second figure startled her into a panic until she reminded herself that it was impossible. Matthias was dead. No matter how much the figure looked like him, no, it couldn't be.

As she squinted, it dawned on her that it was David. He was holding Mira around the waist and supporting her at the elbow.

There was something bone-chilling about seeing the two of them together. Her hands gripping the arms of her chair, she did not know quite what to think. Of course she knew how he'd always felt about Mira. But it never occurred to her that he would pursue the woman again. Not after what had happened.

How could he be with her and keep that terrible secret? Would he break down and tell her everything? No, Madeline decided, for then he would have to reveal his own part in the affair, and surely he would not want to do that. But how could David look at her and not remember it all? How could he be with her while she was carrying Matthias's child?

She watched as David helped Mira into the back of a rowboat—the one that Matthias had used to row out to the middle of the lake to scatter Celia's ashes. As Madeline thought back to that day, the air in her lungs expelled like a dying breath.

"That was the beginning of it all," she said aloud.

She watched David push the boat away from the shore and step in. He sat down facing Mira and dipped his oars in the water. They began gliding across the water.

"And this is how it ends," she concluded.

It was an ending that troubled her, and she was uncertain exactly why. Obviously, Mira and David were content. Matthias had been punished for his crime and Georgie was spared incarceration. And she had no more obsession with it. Of course, there was still Dr. Niles, but Madeline was fairly confident he was just a dupe. He had gained nothing from Celia's death—that she knew of. But he *had* been an accomplice, so she should have the same determination to see justice meted out to him as she had to Matthias. But she had simply lost the ambition for it. What was bothering her was not that Niles went unpunished. What it really was, was Georgie.

Georgie had changed. He had grown thinner and somehow older. His hair had begun to gray and his pallor was dull. He seldom made eye contact with her. He had a haunted look about him now and he rarely talked anymore despite her attempts to engage him in conversation. He did everything around the house that he was supposed to do, but clearly there was no satisfaction in it for him. He seemed to take no pleasure in anything he accomplished. And he had stopped going to church. Madeline had offered to drive him there but he declined, saying he would walk. But he always returned home too soon. There was no possible way he could walk to Raleigh, attend services, and walk back in less than four hours. Yet he had consistently been back after an hour or two.

A few weeks ago, she'd spoken to him over dinner. It was the one meal a day they ate together, and the silences had been disturbing her.

"Georgie, you worry me," Madeline had said softly. She had mentioned nothing for a long time about her concern, half from her own pain and half from guilt. "You don't talk two sentences together in a day anymore. And you look so tired."

Georgie dropped his head. "I don't sleep so good no more. I get bad dreams. About Mr. Carson."

"That's all over with, Georgie. The police have given up."

He put down his fork. "You don't understand, Miz Abbott. I lost my redemption and I lied. The policeman asked me, 'Was Mr. Carson here?' and I lied."

Madeline leaned across the table. "There was nothing else you could do."

Georgie shook his head sadly. "I shouldn't have hit him like that. I should've just held his arms. I don't know why I hit him."

"Why do we do anything, Georgie?" Madeline replied, her shoulders hunched in resignation. "Sometimes we can't help ourselves."

Georgie remained silent for a moment and then spoke remorsefully. "Because we're imperfect. The Bible says that's what we are."

"Is that it? Perhaps so."

As Madeline recalled that conversation, her attention drifted once again across the lake. Then her gaze fell upon the statue. *Help me*, the outstretched arms seemed to be saying, *Help me*.

Help you do what? Madeline pondered. Return to your gravesite? Protect your son? Proclaim his birthright?

She had never seen the plaque at the base of the princess's statue in the woods, but would not have been surprised to read that Muskataqua was *The Last of Her Kind*. Madeline would have felt a particular affinity for that. She herself was, she had come to believe, the last of *her* kind, as well.

Georgie stood at his mother's gravesite in the woods, not knowing what to do there. Only the cement base with the inscription remained; he had made no effort to tend the grave. Although his mother's body rested there, it was, to him, as if her spirit were in the statue. When he prayed to his mother, he had always looked at her. He needed to talk with her more than ever before.

He had added another lie to his lie about that day. He let Miz Abbott believe he was going to church. It wasn't an outright lie. She never said, "Georgie, how was church today?" to which he would have had to say "Fine." No, she never asked. But she offered to drive him in the cold weather and he'd said, "No, I'll walk." That was a lie. He didn't walk to church. He walked here, and here he stayed.

He could not enter the presence of the Lord with such a mighty sin on him. Could not take communion. Could not sing "Holy, holy, holy," and could not look at the Reverend without telling him everything. But if he told everything, he knew Miz Abbott and Mr. McKay would be in terrible trouble, and it was Miz Abbott he worried about. He could not cleanse his soul at her expense. How could he save himself and damn his friend? The whole world would go wrong if he told his secret. No, this was his burden. He did what he should not have done and he would bear this alone. Every week that passed, though, the burden seemed to grow heavier instead of lighter. He felt as though there was a never-ending war inside his head.

As he looked out over the lake to where his mother stood, he saw the boat with Miz Carson and Mr. McKay in it. Mr. McKay was rowing. Miz Carson, he observed, was going to have a baby. Mr. McKay looked very happy. Miz Carson looked at the sky.

Mira had closed her eyes to let the sun warm her face as David rowed. It was the first day the temperature was above seventy and he had insisted she get some air. She had been cooped up far too long, he'd said. But women in her condition, she argued, seldom went out. Not accepting her demurs, he'd bundled her up in a coat and scarf and led her to the water.

She had to admit David was right. The air was fresh and there was only the slightest breeze. The sky was so clear and blue, it made the surface of the water glisten in perfect reflection. With her eyes shut, Mira could feel her skin tingle with the sun and soft wind, and all she could hear was the rhythmic splash of the paddles. She held on to the sides of the boat for balance. She was afraid the weight of her pregnancy could tip them one way or the other.

Nearly five months had passed since Matt had died and her life had changed almost immediately. At first, the Dunlops had visited once a week. After a month, Clara came alone a couple of times. Then she stopped. By the end of the second month, she had no visitors at all. She'd dismissed her staff. There was no need for a butler, cook or maid anymore.

After Matt's death, it occurred to her that no one really cared how she was. She was using Roland as her obstetrician, but that hardly counted. And as for David, she hadn't seen him since their fight before Christmas. The truth was, she had no friends. No family. And no idea of what to do. Should she move to North Conway? Or perhaps to Concord? She had enough money so she didn't need to work. But she was lonely, terribly lonely.

Then David had shown up. He appeared at her door two months after Matt died to offer his help. But she had not been receptive. Had not wanted to do anything unseemly and she definitely didn't want to encourage any advances. But he came every day. She tried at first to tell him she was not up to company. But, after two weeks of turning him away at the door every day, she finally let him in. Just for a moment. And after another week of letting him stay just for a moment, he stayed a little longer. The afternoon visits stretched into evenings.

He entertained her, made her laugh, held her when she cried, and talked to her. He had begun another book, this one a story about the Gold Rush in California. Two men who are partners come from Vermont to search for gold and get into a fight. One kills the other and runs away. He would read her sections of it and they would talk about it, and he'd tell her about California. She would like it there, he said. Maybe we should move back there. Her baby would grow up in sunshine.

It happened so gradually that he began talking about "we" that she hardly noticed it. *We*—Mira, the baby and David. And the more time he spent with her, the more chores he did around the house, and the more they did together, the more they became *we. Us.*

It had been about three months after David began seeing her again when he suggested it was time to clean out Carson's things. She hesitantly agreed. She led him into the bedroom and opened the closet door on his side of the room. She sat on the bed as David took out the first suit and removed the hanger.

It was Matt's election suit. The navy pinstriped suit he wore the day he claimed victory on the steps of the state capitol. His wardrobe had been impeccable, the best of everything.

As David laid the suit over the back of a chair and reached for another, he tentatively said, "You know, Matt and I are about the same size." Then he fingered the silky luxurious material.

She felt herself recoil, but tried not to show it.

"They're perfectly good suits," he added. "It's a sin to see them wasted. That is, unless you don't want me to have them."

He held the jacket up and assessed it. Slowly, he slid his arm into one sleeve and then the other. Yes, it fit perfectly. He held the trousers to his waist. The right size, the right length.

He's right, I suppose, she thought. It would be sinful to throw them away, or even worse to donate them to a charity and see someone else wearing them.

From then on, David wore Matthias's suits, gold cufflinks and then even his underwear.

In the end, instead of it being repellent to see David in Matt's clothes, Mira found it oddly comforting. And it was a respite not to have what amounted to another funeral in disposing of her husband's belongings. The first funeral had been more than enough.

The funeral had been held in Concord. It was then, when the undertaker asked about his family, that Mira realized Matt had never mentioned them. She did not even know their names. Didn't know his real name, even. So she couldn't identify them, whoever they were. But the Dunlops came, and Ro Niles, and some of the people who'd come to Matt's victory party. And two society matrons whom Mira did not recognize and who looked like twins.

But it was a smaller turnout than she had expected. Although elected, Matt had never served. He couldn't do anything for the party anymore—concerned now with the politics of appointing a replacement. It was, she decided, a portent of her new circumstance. Chief Tanner had been there, and the Weekes brothers, come from their new residences in Nashua. She wondered if they sought social occasions like this just to renew their distance, for neither ventured within thirty feet of the other. But it was, all in all, a meager showing, and she was glad Matt couldn't see it.

Afterward, David seemed to flow into the void that Matt had left in her life. He was so solicitous, far less demanding, and she knew he loved her by the way he always seemed to anticipate her needs. Only last week, he had reminded her they needed to have a nursery for the baby, and they had begun fixing up the maid's room. He drove into Concord to buy a crib and brought her home a mail-order catalogue so she could pick out whatever else she wanted for the baby.

David had moved out of his room in the boardinghouse in Raleigh and in with her. She was certain she'd be labeled wanton by the Dunlops and friends of Matt, but she didn't care. Let them gossip all they wanted. David had asked her to marry him and she said she would think about it after the baby was born.

As she sat quietly in the boat, she opened her eyes and looked around. David smiled at her and she smiled back perfunctorily.

"Feel all right?"

"Wonderful," she replied.

She did not mention that she was having heartburn and hadn't slept well last night. Her hip hurt from sleeping on her side and her back hurt when she walked. Only a month-and-a-half to go, she reminded herself, and I'll be back to normal. Then she amended it to, *Well, not exactly normal, I'll be a mother.* The enormity of that overwhelmed her sometimes. Maybe that's why she should say yes to David's proposal right now.

But I have to see how he acts with the baby, with Matt's baby, she thought. *That* was why she had to wait to give him an answer. She would not marry David if he weren't good to the baby. That's what's important, she decided, then took a deep breath. *I guess I've become a mother already.*

• • •

David had never been happier in his life than this very afternoon. Here was his dream come true, the two of them in love, floating serenely on the lake on a day in May. And a world of prospects ahead. He felt as though he were first in the Olympic track race with the finish only a body length away. Or maybe a boat length, because there she was, sitting just a few feet from him, her face upturned to the sun like some—he broke off as the upturned stone face of the princess Muskataqua caught his eye. And beyond that, Madeline's house.

He had not seen Madeline since that day. He would have to face her some time, but he wasn't ready yet. Not until things were settled with Mira. He already had Mira convinced that he would be a caring father to her baby and he was confident that marriage was just a few short months away.

No slip-ups, he cautioned himself. Everything was going so well.

He set the paddles in the water smoothly, dipping in and out with barely a ripple.

As Madeline watched the rowboat disappear around the bend in the lake to the north, she heard a car motor in the near distance, echoing through the stillness of the day. The spring peepers had come and gone. The songbirds were beginning to trill, but the most pervasive sounds were the constant chirruping and clacking and hum of insects calling to each other, and the rusty squawk of the redwing blackbirds. The car motor could almost have been another such noise, some swarm of wasps or honeybees flying up the road in formation. But no, it was unmistakably a motor. Occasionally, in the past, Chester might have driven by on an errand in Wickessett or Preston on his way to Raleigh, but they were gone now.

The motor slowed as it neared her house and stopped. How odd, she thought. Then there came a knock at the door and, Georgie being somewhere other than at church, she answered it herself.

She had no trouble recognizing the heavyset man she hadn't seen since Celia died over a year ago.

"Chief Tanner, what brings you so far from town?" She hoped her face did not betray her panic.

"May I come in?"

"Yes, of course," Madeline replied with a little catch in her voice. "I was just sitting on the porch. Please join me."

She led the way through the house as he followed. She made no attempt at small talk, feeling that she really should say something but no words came to mind. All she could think was *Why is he here?* over and over. He was not in uniform. Was that a good sign?

She invited him to sit down, saying how comfortable it was out here in this weather, and watching crestfallen as he removed his jacket. That meant he intended to stay awhile.

"It's quite a surprise to see you," she tried again. "What brings you out this way?"

Tanner lifted his pant cuff and laid a chunky calf over the opposite knee. "Well, Miss Abbott, I'm interested in talking with everyone around here about that day when Mr. Carson died."

"Oh?" Madeline said slowly, trying to detect any suspicion on his part. "I thought that had been investigated by the Wickessett police."

"Yes. They've closed the book on it, so to speak. They never found any information about any hitchhiker, so they determined he was long gone."

"And you think otherwise?"

"Well, I just thought I'd go over it one more time and see if we get any new ideas. I hate to give up on a puzzle. Makes me awfully cranky, Nora says. That's my wife."

"I see." Madeline was not sure she saw anything other than her own cold fear, but she kept herself under control. "And how might I be of assistance?"

"I thought, if we could go over the details of that day, it might help me."

"Help in what way, Chief Tanner?"

Tanner rubbed the back of his neck, as though the matter were of importance only to him. "Just some loose ends, that's all."

"Such as?"

"The hitchhiker. You see, no one saw him before or after that day except for one glimpse in the car by Chester Weekes and a sighting of him on foot by Preston Weekes. So, would you mind, Miss Abbott, telling me everything that you can remember about the day of Mr. Carson's death? I know you talked with Detective Brandt, but please indulge me in this. Who knows? Maybe we'll turn up something."

Madeline steeled herself and then reiterated what she had told Detective Brandt. But Chief Tanner kept asking her about Georgie. Where had he been? Did she think he could have been away from her sight for an hour or so? Was she sure?

She parried all the questions but she was frightened. Why was he concentrating on Georgie? Although he seemed satisfied with her answers, she felt shaken.

All these months, Matthias's death had been almost a private affair. Something that involved only her and Georgie and David. Detective Brandt had come and gone like an inquisitive raccoon finding no food in the cupboard. Even Mira was a distant concern. What had happened to Matthias, in her mind, was just a small drama, like watching an anthill. But now she was unexpectedly confronted with the fact that none of that was true if Chief Tanner was still investigating the matter. This was the death of a public figure; of course there would be intense scrutiny.

How could I have been so dim-witted? she thought nervously. She looked into Tanner's full-cheeked face and debated telling him everything. He was a man who would understand. Then she looked away toward the lake.

Tanner followed her gaze and as he did, a rowboat came around the bend from the northern end of the lake, heading home. She watched him squint to see more clearly.

"That's Mrs. Carson, isn't it?"

"Yes."

"And who is that with her?"

"I believe it's Mr. David McKay."

"The writer fellow at Mrs. Caldwell's boardinghouse?"

"Yes."

He turned toward Madeline. "Are you acquainted with Mr. McKay?"

Madeline debated what to say. To deny knowing him would be folly. "Yes."

"How did you meet him?"

"Through Celia Eastman. He used Celia's library."

"And didn't Mrs. Carson work for Miss Eastman?"

"Yes."

He looked back out the window. "Is he courting her?"

"I wouldn't know."

"A little premature, don't you think?"

"I couldn't say."

"When was the last time you saw Mr. McKay, Miss Abbott?"

Her face darkened. "He was here on Christmas Day."

"Then he's a friend of yours?"

"I," she began, and for the first time the words faltered. "I . . . have had occasion to . . . have him visit. But I really haven't seen him in months."

"Why is that, Miss Abbott?"

She regained her composure. "I presume he has been otherwise occupied."

"I presume so," he said as the rowboat docked.

They were both silent and then Tanner said, "There's just one thing more, Miss Abbott."

She looked at him inquiringly. While his face seemed kindly with plump cheeks and a wide brow, his blue eyes held hers with a direct unblinking gaze.

"How was it you happened to invite Mr. Carson to tea?"

"I beg your pardon," she said, stalling for time to think.

"Well, I recall when you came to my office last year. You were pretty angry about what had happened to Miss Eastman. You seemed to blame Mr. Carson for the disposition of her remains. And I heard you went to some of his political rallies and asked him questions about inheriting her money. So, I'm curious. How was it you invited Mr. Carson to tea when you obviously hadn't been friends?"

Madeline felt a headache moving up from the back of her neck to her forehead as he spoke. She knew she might be asked this question someday.

"You're exactly right. We weren't friends. But I didn't wish to have continued hostility between neighbors. I wanted to assure him that I was ready to make an effort to overcome past differences. I thought the holiday season was the time to smooth the waters." Her head was pulsing with pain as she tried to sound convincing.

"I see. Then what did you think when he never came that day?"

"As I said to Detective Brandt, I wasn't really surprised, given the weather. And I don't have a telephone so he couldn't call me." Could he see her head throbbing?

"What about after the storm, after the road was open? Didn't you expect to hear from him then?"

Madeline passed her hand over her pulsing temple. "No, Chief Tanner. By then, I assumed Mr. Carson chose not to accept my invitation."

"But wouldn't that have been insulting and rude?"

"Yes," she answered simply, implying that Carson was capable of such discourtesy.

Tanner nodded. "Then you must have felt badly when you found out he died on his way to see you."

"Yes, it weighs heavily on my mind." She pressed her fingertips against the vein in her temple.

"Well, you mustn't hold yourself responsible."

"It is tragic, nonetheless."

"Oh, yes," he said as though reminding himself. "What time had you expected him?"

"By tea time. Two forty-five."

He nodded again. "Well thank you for your time, Miss Abbott."

"I'm sorry I couldn't be more helpful."

"Yes. For in the end, all we really know," Tanner said, "is that somebody bludgeoned Matthias Carson five times, took his wallet and money, and then disappeared."

Madeline sat bolt upright, startled beyond breathing. "*What?*"

"It's been officially declared his death was a homicide by an un-known personage. Most likely the hitchhiker. For his money. At least that is what the Wickessett police have determined."

"You said he was bludgeoned five times?" Her chest felt strangled.

"Yes. Five blows to the head."

Her breath came now in shallow gasps. "It just doesn't seem necessary."

"Necessary?"

"Necessary to hit him more than once." Madeline shivered.

"Oh." Tanner simply nodded and looked again out the window. "Yes. That is what I thought." He rose to leave. "Well, thank you for your time. Where is Georgie, by the way?"

"He likes to be outdoors."

The Police Chief nodded.

After she had escorted him out, Madeline returned to the porch and sat with her head in her hands.

"But why?" She repeated, "*Why?*"

CHAPTER TWELVE

*"O God, I could be bounded in a nutshell
and count myself a king of infinite space,
were it not that I have bad dreams."*

Tanner drove back down the lake road from Madeline Abbott's house mulling over what pretext he could use to stop in to see Mira Carson. Maybe nothing more than friendly official interest would be necessary, he decided. He had told her earlier, as he had just told Miss Abbott now, that they believed her husband had been killed by a hitchhiker. She had not taken the news well.

He was still not completely reassured by his conversation with Miss Abbott. It wasn't anything concrete. It wasn't even anything in particular. Only a sense that she knew more than she was saying. She looked as though she'd gotten a migraine as soon as he had asked her why Carson was coming to see her. He didn't feel she was being completely honest about that, but he couldn't refute anything she said.

He pulled into the newly graveled driveway and went to the door intent on examining Mrs. Carson's suitor.

She graciously invited him into her living room, introducing the two men with no hint of reticence. Tanner had seen David McKay around town, but only from a distance. Now, his impression of the writer had to do with his olive-green suit. Tanner recalled seeing the newcomer in ordinary clothes on the streets of Raleigh, clothes that marked him as a man of modest means. The suit he had on now, however, was custom-made fine wool. Almost like silk. Very European looking, or what Tanner guessed would be European. He had never had such a suit himself. Even if he could afford one, and even if it was tailored to his large girth, he could not imagine wearing it.

"Please sit down, Chief Tanner."

Mrs. Carson sat in her own chair with a stretch of her body that indicated physical discomfort. She automatically rubbed her hand soothingly over her stomach.

Tanner immediately thought about Nora, when she was carrying their daughter, and how he had watched her belly enlarge with absolute wonder. He had felt privileged to put his hand there to feel the baby move.

"Have you some news?" she asked with what seemed to be genuine anticipation.

"No, I'm afraid not, Mrs. Carson." Tanner watched her face fall. "The Wickessett police have given up the search for the hitchhiker. I was going over the details to see if we might have missed anything."

He sat in the chair next to hers and McKay took a seat opposite on the sofa. Tanner watched him as McKay ran his fingers down the crease of his trousers, and he could not help observing that he had very expensive taste for someone who had lived in one room of a rundown boardinghouse. He wondered if Mrs. Carson were buying Mr. McKay's clothes now. It occurred to him that the suit could be Carson's. But that was highly unlikely. What sort of man would do that?

"I've just come from Miss Abbott's house," Tanner explained, "and last week, I spoke with Preston and Chester Weekes in Nashua. But neither she nor they were able to shed any new light on things, I'm sorry to say."

"Does that mean," McKay asked, "that the investigation is over?"

"In Wickessett. Not in Raleigh."

Did McKay's eyes flicker just a little?

Mira sighed and looked at Chief Tanner with resignation. "It's been five months now. The hitchhiker is five months' gone. What more can you do?"

There was something innately wrong with a world that would let such a crime go unsolved and unpunished. For a moment, she felt dizzyingly close to Madeline Abbott. Had she not used much the same language about Celia Eastman's death? Mira wanted to believe with all her heart that Celia died naturally, that there was no malice in it. But Madeline had always believed otherwise. And now Mira knew how she must have felt.

There were times when her own conviction about the cause of Celia's death wavered. Times when she wondered if, in fact, Matt had anything to do with it. These times had been fleeting, had come upon her after some flash of anger she had seen him conceal, a side-wise glance that could paralyze her in an instant. There was much about Matt, no matter how intimate they were, that seemed concealed from her.

David, however, was entirely different. There were no shadows with him. She never felt the same tension around him that she'd always felt around Matt. David wasn't hiding anything from her. She knew exactly what he was thinking. Granted, there wasn't the thrill as there had been with Matt, never knowing what would happen next. Even David's lovemaking was tender and stroking, not full of passion and fury. Maybe she *had* been a little afraid of Matt, quaking sometimes at the glower in his eyes. Yet, there had been an excitement that she would never have with David. But, she cautioned herself, excitement was not what she needed any more. She needed a man who was kind, who'd be a good father to her child, with no uncertainties. At that recognition, Mira knew she *would* say yes to David's proposal.

The conflicted look on Mrs. Carson's face convinced Tanner that whoever conspired to take her husband's life, she was not privy to it. He counted himself a good judge of character. He had a sense about people. Tanner would not allow that he had intuition; that was a woman's province. But he had a gift, he acknowledged, for knowing human behavior. It was this perception forged of experience and natural ability that enabled him to do his job—whether it was catching Ethan Farrell for jacking moose out of season or arresting Bobby Thibidoux for barn burning. It was the same sense that had nagged at him when he was with Madeline Abbott, as he noticed her voice sharpen and hands tremble when he told her about the killing. The same sense that, at this minute, made him wary of David McKay.

It was the suit, of course. Somehow it epitomized his misgiving. Wherever he had gotten it, it told Tanner that this man was opportunistic. Like a tick.

Should he reveal, Tanner deliberated, his skepticism about the hitchhiker theory? It might be too soon. Yet, he would like to see how McKay would react.

He found himself replying, "To tell you the truth, Mrs. Carson, I'm not entirely certain it was a hitchhiker who killed your husband." He focused his attention on his quarry.

"What do you mean," she demanded in an agitated voice.

But Tanner was watching McKay's mouth open and then shut. Nothing more. And yet, it was everything. The man knows something, he told himself.

Tanner turned to the widow. "There are some ways in which a hitchhiker wouldn't behave, Mrs. Carson."

"Are you suggesting," McKay said evenly, "it was a premeditated murder?"

Tanner turned back to him, hearing a note of urgency in the question. Rather than answer directly, he said, "I beg your pardon, Mr. McKay, but do you have a special interest in this matter?"

"My interest," David responded, "is in Mrs. Carson and her well-being."

"Of course."

"Tell me, Chief Tanner," Mrs. Carson asked, "what would make you think it wasn't a hitchhiker committing a robbery?"

Tanner cleared his throat. "It wasn't something I felt you had to know at the time, Mrs. Carson, but when I had a hospital pathologist examine the body, he found that your husband had been struck five times in the head." He found himself repeating Madeline Abbott's words. "It just doesn't seem necessary. One blow. Two. But not five. Not just to take his money."

He saw Mrs. Carson's fingers dig into the arms of the chair and her pallor change to flour-white. The room was quiet except for the ticking of the grandfather clock in the corner, an ornate standing timepiece with scrolls of parquet wood in the mahogany cabinet.

"But who would have done such a terrible thing?" she cried.

"It could have been someone deranged, couldn't it?" McKay's voice knifed through the hanging silence, much to Tanner's irritation.

"I mean," McKay continued, "a hitchhiker out in that weather, in the middle of nowhere? After all, what *is* a hitchhiker? Just somebody walking who wants to ride. Maybe this was some escapee from an asylum or something. Has anybody checked the asylums?"

Tanner nodded slowly. "We checked the asylums. And the prisons. Within a hundred-mile radius."

"But what if he escaped from some loony bin farther away?"

"We can't check all of them," Tanner admitted grudgingly.

McKay leaned back in his chair, gesturing *There you are* with his hand.

"Then it *is* possible," Mrs. Carson asked in a near whisper, "that it might have been some crazy person?"

"Of course it's possible," McKay interjected. "It's the likely thing. Wouldn't you say so, Chief Tanner?"

"It's possible."

"I'd say your madman is long gone, Chief Tanner. Or perhaps he froze to death somewhere in the woods."

"Possibly," Tanner said noncommittally, but he was not happy about this turn of conversation. It was true, none of his ideas about motive made any difference if they were dealing with a madman. There was no normal rationale to a killing by a crazy person. He had to acknowledge there was a chance, a reasonably good chance, that the hitchhiker was an insanity case. And yet, sitting across from David McKay, he could not help feeling he was in the presence of an unscrupulous man who had something to hide. He wanted to ask him where *he'd* been that day, but he didn't want to telegraph his suspicions to either McKay or Mrs. Carson. Instead, he appeared to agree with what was said.

"It is likely that no reasonable person would be walking on that road unless he had a destination on it."

"Given the weather, in particular," McKay added.

Tanner let himself look thoughtful and then befuddled. "Of course, it wouldn't have been snowing very much yet at the time Mr. Carson left the house. Or even at the time a hitchhiker would have begun walking up the road." He looked at McKay as though for assistance.

"Which is probably why he was hitchhiking," he complied.

Tanner shrugged one shoulder. "Can't help wondering how he got to the lake road in the first place." McKay said nothing in response. "Or how he got off it." More silence.

"Some storm that afternoon," Tanner persisted. "Glad *I* wasn't out in it. Never been much fond of snow. My daughter, she loves it. Goes out tobogganing with her friends. Not me, I stay indoors with a hot cocoa and read while my wife makes raisin cookies. That's *my* idea of what to do in a snowstorm. What about you, Mr. McKay? You like that kind of weather?"

"Hardly," Mrs. Carson interjected. "He's from California."

"That so?" Tanner said. "Guess you don't get snow there. This your first storm then?"

"No," McKay replied casually. "I was here last winter."

"I don't think we had any storm quite like this one last year. You didn't get caught out in it, I hope."

"No, I went home. That is, after it started coming down hard."

"I expect that's the best thing to do if you're not used to snow. Lucky you weren't far from home and could get back in time."

"Yes, it was."

"You live at Mrs. Caldwell's?"

"I did."

Mrs. Carson discreetly lowered her eyes.

Tanner was afraid he had already alerted McKay too much, so he dropped it. He had learned as much as he could have hoped for. The suitor had been away from his room until mid- or late afternoon. Motive and opportunity. By now, he felt absolutely certain that David McKay had murdered Matthias Carson. But how could he ever prove it?

David was palpably relieved when Police Chief Tanner finally left. It was apparent that the chief viewed him with a certain amount of suspicion. He should have realized that his liaison with Mira would make him an object of inquiry. However, he was pleased with his own performance under duress. He had always relied, he thought with some pride, on his nimble mind. And thank heaven he had corrected himself about his whereabouts on the day of the murder. Someone might have seen him leave the boardinghouse. Out in the morning, back in the afternoon. That was all Tanner had asked. Now he had time to decide where he'd been. As long as he didn't say he was someplace that could be checked, he'd be fine. Nothing could ever be proven. He wondered if Mira had understood Tanner's suspicions.

"The chief seems a competent sort," David offered, waiting to judge her reaction.

"Yes," she said solemnly. "I know he's trying his best, but by now, I think it's quite hopeless. Don't you?"

Despite knowing that she wanted him to contradict her, he said lugubriously, "I'm afraid so."

Mira nodded slowly in final acceptance as she stared at the patterns in her Oriental carpet. Tears welled up in her eyes.

"I think I'd like to take a nap now."

"I'll take you upstairs," David said immediately, rising.

She smiled wanly at him and took his outstretched hands to help her out of the chair.

Georgie had stayed longer than he intended at his mother's grave. Miz Abbott must be wondering where he was by now. And yet he did not want to leave. To leave the woods was to go back to his torment.

What if I just walked out into the lake and kept walking until the water was over my head? he asked himself. Would his soul be damned forever? Wasn't it damned already? Never in his life, not even when he was in the orphanage, did he have such thoughts. Maybe he could be damned just for thinking this way. How far from grace he had already fallen.

"Lead us not into temptation, but deliver us from evil," he murmured. Why had he been tempted so, to have Mr. Carson placed in his path? And why hadn't he been delivered from this evil? Was he so unworthy? If he were so unworthy *before* he killed Mr. Carson, what possible worthiness could he have now? None. None at all.

Georgie looked at the water softly lapping at the shore. It reminded him of Blacky drinking at his water bowl. They called this side of the lake, the "bog end." But there was no more bog. Maybe there had been, once upon a time, but it had long since drained and become just woods. Only the place where the water met the land was still boggy. He could walk out into the middle of the lake and let the water close over his head, but he would have to step on the spongy soil to get there. And what if the bottom of the water was still boggy? He could get in up to his knees or his hips and not be able to walk any farther through the muck. What then? He would have to stand there, stuck, until someone found him. And then everybody would know what he did.

He knew he shouldn't be thinking like this. It seemed as if he'd taken one step onto the wrong path and now he couldn't find his way back. He stood by his climbing tree but instead of going up, he leaned his back against it and slid down into a sitting position, knees bent.

"I wish I was a bear," he said aloud. "I would eat blackberries and scratch my back on this tree." He wiggled his back against the trunk, moving his head from side to side as though he really were a bear. "I don't want to be Georgie anymore."

And suddenly, Georgie leaned over onto his knees and put his hands on the ground. He arched his back and began to move on all fours. Lumbering over to the base of the grave, he smelled the stone and then licked the cold granite. It tasted of leaves. His hands were prickled by the pine needles and his pant legs were moistened by the wet ground. He felt clumsy and slow and didn't know what to do next.

Then he sat back on his heels and began to sob. "I ain't a bear."

Madeline sat on the porch, shaking her head as if to deny what she had heard Chief Tanner say. "Five blows." It was a vengeful and loathsome thing to do. What could David have been thinking of? The man was dead, why did he have to—? She stopped abruptly. What if Matthias hadn't been dead? Could it be that Georgie's blow didn't actually kill him?

"Oh no," she said aloud. It couldn't be. There had to be another explanation. But she couldn't erase the images that came to mind of him bashing Matthias's head. Could David really be that evil?

Madeline caught herself up sharply. I mustn't do this. I mustn't do this again, she thought. Would it never end? Why was *she* the one who always had to ferret out the evil deeds? Well, not this time. This time, she would stay out of it. If David did this to Matthias, it was for a reason. To make it look like a hitchhiker. What was wrong with that? Matthias was already dead. It was unpleasant to think about, but he was already dead. He was already dead.

Suddenly, Madeline was overwhelmed with a feeling of constriction in her chest, as though her body were helpless under a mighty stone. She could only think of the Puritan stories about people being pressed to death for their crimes.

"Help me," she cried out involuntarily. Her pulse throbbed and her head felt swollen. It seemed, for a moment, that she might explode. Never had she been in such fear. It was not the fear of dying, but rather of having committed a great and irreversible wrong.

She staggered up from her chair and gasped for air, shuddering. Her fingertips tingled. At that moment, she did not care if she lived or died. It would be a welcome release from this agony.

Slowly, over the course of the next minutes, her heart stopped racing and her breaths became regular. She still had a pounding headache, but the feeling of being pressed to death abated.

She sat down again and the time passed in infinitely slow motion. She remembered that she had cried out, "Help me." But to whom? To God? But had God answered her? Or had the attack simply run its course? The latter, she concluded. For God had never answered any of her prayers, ever. She had long since determined that He, if there were such a One, had no interest in her. And now, after all the harm she had caused, she had proven Him right.

Her life had accomplished nothing. She had not only failed to help better the world in any way, she had actually made things worse. And there was no going back.

For over an hour, Madeline was occupied with such thoughts. Finally, it was the sheer weariness of feeling so abject that made her stop.

She scanned the room for her knitting bag. Ah, there it was next to the stove. She picked it up and set it on her lap. She opened it and rummaged through. There were three full skeins left, one of each of the colors of the afghan.

What shall I make? she mulled, fingering the yarn. She considered another afghan and dismissed it. A sweater. Perhaps she could begin with just two colors and send for more wool. She would put her life back in order, she decided while beginning to ball up the first skein of blue yarn.

She had begun the second row of the front panel of the sweater when Georgie returned. She greeted him but he simply stood in front of her saying nothing. Seeing his tear-streaked face, Madeline put down her knitting in alarm.

"Georgie, what's the matter? Are you all right?"

"I didn't go to church." He mumbled the words and the tears began again to course down his face.

"Why not, Georgie?"

"Couldn't." Then he looked at her pleadingly. "I'm sorry I lied."

"It wasn't really a lie," Madeline reassured him. "I never asked you where you went. And I knew you didn't go to church."

"You knew?"

"Yes. And I understand." All too well, she added silently.

Georgie's tears poured out and he fell to his knees in front of Madeline. "I don't want to be Georgie no more," he wept and lowered his head.

Madeline felt her throat catch and her own eyes fill with tears. She reached across and touched his shoulder in consolation. Georgie leaned forward and rested his head on her knees, crying in muffled sobs. Madeline laid her hand on his head and let him stay.

If only there had been someone to comfort *her* that way. To lay a hand on her head and tell her everything would be all right. That she was forgiven. And overcome her sins and sorrows.

But there was no one to do that for her. Yet her own suffering was nothing compared with his. She knew then that she would have to do something to help Georgie.

CHAPTER THIRTEEN

*"So shall you hear
of carnal, bloody, and unnatural acts,
of accidental judgments, casual slaughters,
of deaths put on by cunning and forc'd cause,
And, in this upshot, purposes mistook
Fall'n on th' inventors' heads."*

On Monday morning, Madeline left a letter for the postman to pick up in her mailbox and deliver to "Mr. David McKay, c/o Mrs. Caldwell's Boardinghouse, Raleigh, N.H.," not knowing, of course, that he was no longer there. In the letter, she had written an invitation for him to visit her, alone, as soon as possible.

In the meantime, she had an important errand to do.

• • •

Madeline drove to North Conway rehearsing what she would say to Dr. Roland Niles. But when she arrived at his clinic, the waiting room was filled with patients.

"Tell him I need medical attention right away," Madeline told the pretty young receptionist. The girl looked no older than fifteen. Madeline presumed she could certainly intimidate this youngster into letting her jump the line. But the girl was resistant.

"I'm sorry, ma'am. Unless it's an emergency, you'll have to wait your turn."

"I've driven here from a very long distance. I have to see the doctor immediately."

"I'm sorry, ma'am. So do they," the receptionist answered politely.

As Madeline looked around the room, she saw the hostile stares of four other people, two women and two men. She could not tell what their medical needs were, but it was obvious they were not inclined to be generous and let her in first.

She sat down in the chair farthest away from the receptionist and pulled her face into a knot. She did not move for the next two hours.

Finally, at the end of the afternoon, it was her turn. She was glad there was no one after her. She didn't know how long she might take.

It was evident to her that Dr. Roland Niles was more than a little surprised to see his last patient of the day sitting across from him.

"I'm not here as a patient, Dr. Niles. But I do need to talk with you."

"What can I do for you, Miss Abbott?" he asked cautiously.

"I need to know why you gave arsenic to Celia Eastman."

His mouth opened in astonishment as she continued. "Arsenic or Fowler's Solution, or whatever."

He blinked and shook his head. "I never gave Miss Eastman arsenic or any derivative of arsenic. What makes you think that?"

"I smelled it in her medicine bottle," Madeline replied sternly.

"No," he protested. "There was no arsenic. Miss Eastman did not have any condition that required arsenic."

"I smelled it," she repeated.

Her eyes were sharp and cold as blue topaz, but he again shook his head. "I'm sorry, but you're wrong. The medicine I prescribed for Miss Eastman was laudanum. For pain. There was absolutely nothing else I *could* give her. I just tried to make her comfortable."

Madeline went pale. The room spun.

"Miss Abbott? What's wrong? Do you need smelling salts?"

She took a deep breath and gathered her thoughts. "Does laudanum smell like almonds, Dr. Niles?"

"Why, no."

"Does arsenic?"

"No."

"Are you sure?"

Niles reached behind him and took a brown glass bottle from his cabinet. He removed the stopper and offered the bottle to her. "Here is my Fowler's Solution, Miss Abbott."

Madeline took a deep breath and shook her head. "I was so sure . . . I was so sure I smelled almonds."

He put the stopper back in and placed the bottle back in his cabinet. Then he removed another blue glass bottle and did the same.

"Laudanum," he explained.

She sniffed the bottle and widened her eyes in instantaneous realization.

Laudanum! Not almonds. Almonds were for holidays. She had confused the smells. The Christmas she turned ten she'd had to bake the holiday cookies because her mother was taking laudanum and had become addicted to it. How could she have forgotten? She hadn't wanted to remember how her mother had gone into a stupor, vomiting and crying and ranting. How it had robbed her and her brother of a normal childhood. The reason *she* had to take care of her brother was because her mother was always sick. Her mother would sleep most of the day with the shades drawn. And there were the bottles of medicine on the bed table. She had confused the smells. There were no almonds. No arsenic either.

It was laudanum in Celia's medicine.

She remained silent for a moment then rose shakily to her feet. There was one final thing she had to know.

"Tell me, Dr. Niles. Do you think Celia really wanted Matthias Carson to have her money?"

He looked befuddled, then answered, "It hardly matters now, does it? He had such a brilliant future." He rubbed his eyes. "Miss Eastman spoke of it many times to me. She was a remarkable woman. I think she knew she hadn't long to live. And I think the idea of helping Matthias in his career made her happy. She was, as you well know, a very giving woman."

"Yes," Miss Abbott concurred in a quaking voice. "She was."

Madeline had no memory of how she got home. *We have killed an innocent man*, was all she thought over and over.

Days passed and David did not show up at Madeline's house. By Thursday morning, she was infuriated as she sat on the porch, her knitting needles striking each other like slaps in the face. She was seriously considering driving to Mrs. Caldwell's and confronting him there. She might just do it this afternoon, come what may.

As she deliberated what to do, she heard a car drive slowly up the road. It pulled into her driveway. She rose to answer the door.

Entering the house, David was barely apologetic for not having come sooner and nonchalantly explained he only received her note this very morning.

"I posted the letter Monday morning. You should have had it by afternoon."

He seated himself comfortably near the windows and smiled. How different he looked. She noted that he was dressed in a handsome tweed jacket and fine wool pants. His shoes were new and shined. But it was more than that.

"Yes," he answered easily, "but it was addressed to the boarding-house. I'm not living there anymore. So it had to be forwarded."

The import of his words registered with Madeline as she returned to her seat. Of course. He had moved in with Mira. That was the next logical progression. How is it, she fretted, that we blind ourselves to the things we wish not to see?

"What did you want to see me about so urgently, Madeline?"

She watched his eyes instinctively flicker around the room as if to reassure himself that he was not in the same situation as Matthias Carson had been.

"Chief Tanner was here last Sunday," Madeline began, but David interrupted her.

"Yes, I know. He came to our house after he came here."

Madeline blinked at *our house*, but did not falter. "I wanted to see you because he told me something that concerns me."

"Which is?"

"Chief Tanner said that Matthias had been hit on the head five times."

She looked for a reaction but he gave none. "He had been hit only *once* when you took him out of here, David."

"So?"

"Why did you hit him four more times?"

He paused and looked at her levelly. "It had to be done."

"Had to be done? What do you mean, 'had to be done'?" When he did not answer, she pressed him. "Was it because he wasn't dead after Georgie hit him? Was he still alive, is that it?"

He regarded her as though she were becoming overwrought at nothing.

She persisted. "Matthias was still alive when you took him out of here, wasn't he?" When he did not deny it, she said, "Why did you hit him again? You could have taken him to a doctor." Madeline's voice rose in anguish. "You might have saved him."

David's voice was impenitent, almost clinical, as he said, "Georgie's blow wasn't fatal, but it was bad enough. A decision had to be made.

Think about what he would have told the police if he'd lived. About his visit here. The whole episode. I had to finish him off. It would have been much worse if I hadn't."

"Finish him off!" Madeline pulled at her knitting so hard it almost pulled apart. "What a convenient euphemism!" She glared at him and leaned forward. "All these months, you've allowed poor Georgie to think that he killed a man when all the time it was you! How could you?"

"I did it for Georgie. And for you."

"No," she said contemptuously. "You did it for yourself."

"Not at all."

How dare he? Madeline was incredulous over the calm, deliberate manner of the man she'd thought was a friend. Her own emotions were roiling and uncontrollable. Slowly, she gathered her thoughts. Her fingers played at the yarn, tugging, tugging.

"Then tell me, David, what's become of Celia's papers? The ones that prove Georgie is her half-brother?"

He crossed his knee. "We, that is Mira and I, donated all Celia's books to the Historical Society. I think she would have liked that. As for her personal papers, well, there wasn't anything worth saving."

"I see," Madeline said acidly. "So you finally got what you wanted. Mira *and* the money. Was that your intent all along?"

David's expression hardened and his eyes narrowed into glass daggers. It made her shiver. She tried to match his composure but her hand betrayed her as she clenched her knitting.

"Let's not lose sight of the fact, Madeline, that it was *your* notion that Carson murdered Celia. *You're* the one who went to his rallies. *You* set up our little rendezvous that day. That was *your* doing. *You* told Georgie to stop him. And *you* began this avalanche. I only jumped out of harm's way."

She was stunned by the accusations because she had been making them against herself.

"So, what are you going to do now, Madeline? Hunt *me* to the ground?"

When she did not answer, he continued. "Maybe things didn't

turn out exactly the way you wanted them to. They seldom do. But it's all over and the end has worked out just fine. Carson has suffered justice. Mira and I have a comfortable life together, thanks to Celia. It's what she always wanted for us. And you have Georgie. As for Georgie, he doesn't need anything more than what he's got."

"What he needs is his salvation," Madeline said savagely, "and we took it from him."

"Then give it back."

"I intend to do just that."

"What does that mean?"

"Georgie didn't kill Matthias Carson. You did. And that's exactly what I'm going to tell Chief Tanner."

His lips curled into a smile but his gaze remained fixed on her.

"And just how do you think you can prove anything? By your own declaration, Carson wasn't even here that day. And neither was I. You'd have to change your story, and then it's just your word against mine."

"My word and Georgie's."

"Georgie will swear to anything you tell him. He's already demonstrated that, so who could believe *him*?"

He rose from the chair. "I'm sorry, Maddie, I have to get back now."

She gripped her knitting needles tightly.

"I would suggest," he said on the way out, "that you let sleeping dogs lie this time. After all, it was *your* meddling that caused it all."

Madeline sat very still as the screen door closed behind him. The windows were raised and she could smell the spring smell of the lake and everything coming into leaf and flower. The season mocked her with its life and resurrection.

Georgie, she knew, was in his room. He had hardly come out since Sunday. She called to him and heard shuffling in response as though he were getting up from bed. There was one thing she could do, at least. She could spare him further anguish.

Georgie came onto the porch. Lumbering like a bear, Madeline thought.

"Georgie, there's something I have to tell you."

He looked at her without expectation as she explained haltingly about what really had happened the night of Matthias Carson's death.

"Then after you hit Mr. Carson, Mr. McKay hit him more," Madeline concluded. "Yours was a severe blow Georgie, but it was Mr. McKay who killed him."

She watched Georgie try to assimilate this, and continued. "And *I* arranged the circumstances. So we are both responsible for Mr. Carson's death, both Mr. McKay and I. But not you, Georgie. Least of all, you."

"But did Mr. Carson murder Miz Eastman?"

Madeline paused. She was convinced otherwise now, but she was not going to let Georgie suffer for her misguided thoughts. She was going to tell the second lie of her life.

"I believe so, Georgie. Because I believe that God would never let you do anything wrong. Others of us, yes. But not you."

She looked down at her knitting and saw the wool was so tightly wrapped around the needles she would have to undo all of it.

Georgie sat down in his chair. "But what about Mr. McKay? Did God let him do that?"

"No," Madeline answered quickly. "What Mr. McKay did was very wrong. His actions were intentional."

"He did evil?"

"Yes, he did an evil thing."

After a moment, the furrows in his brow flattened out, giving him an expression of childlike expectancy.

"Then we should tell," he said.

Madeline sighed. "For myself, I would, and take the consequences. But I don't know what will happen afterward to you, Georgie."

"We should tell," he repeated with conviction.

How could she tell him it was useless?

"The problem is, Georgie, I doubt if anyone would believe us."

She began carefully unraveling the knitting row by row. "If we said it was Mr. McKay who did it, he would deny it. And we haven't anything to prove what really happened that day. Not even that Mr. Carson was here."

"Not even the blanket that had Mr. Carson's blood?" Georgie asked urgently.

"You burned it, remember?"

"No, I didn't. I got it under my bed," he answered apologetically.

"You kept it, Georgie?"

He nodded.

"Why?"

Georgie wrapped his arms around his torso.

"You sewed it for so long. It was my present. I never had such a wonderful present. So I didn't burn it. I was going to wash it, but you said to burn it, so I didn't know what to do. I didn't burn it and I didn't wash it. Is that okay?"

Madeline's face brightened. "Yes, Georgie. Yes, indeed. Tomorrow, we'll go to Raleigh to talk with Chief Tanner. And we'll take the afghan. And we'll tell him the truth. Everything. We'll tell him everything. Is that what you want to do?"

Georgie nodded happily.

I just hope he believes us, she worried.

CHAPTER FOURTEEN

Why, as a woodcock to mine own springe, Osric;
I am justly kill'd with mine own treachery.

"Damn that old woman," David said aloud as he drove back from Madeline's house along the lake road. He slowed around the curve where he'd pushed Carson's car off the road and into the tree, but he did not look down.

What if Madeline went to the police, he thought, what would he do? He would have to make Tanner doubt her word. But how?

He could say it was Georgie who finished off Carson outside the house when they were putting him in the car. But then he would be admitting that he was there and knew all about it, and how could he explain that to Mira?

If he denied being at Madeline's house, he'd have to come up with a reason why they were saying he was there. A reason that would make Tanner believe she and Georgie were lying. Maybe that

Georgie killed Carson so they had to blame someone else, and David was the most likely one.

None of this sounded very convincing.

Wait a minute! What if he said he'd been taking a ride to visit Madeline and he saw Georgie pushing the car down the hill, and Georgie had seen him? Then he shook his head. No, he'd still have to face Mira's asking why he hadn't turned in the man who killed her husband.

No, he had to come up with an explanation that didn't jeopardize his relationship with her.

He was beginning to sweat now. He wiped his forehead with the back of his hand and then distractedly wiped it on his trousers. It made a stain above the knee.

It looked like the only thing to do was to deny it completely and let Tanner figure Georgie did it. But it was still their word against his. What he needed was an alibi. Somebody who would say he was there that day, not at Madeline's. There was only one perfect alibi—Mira. Could he convince her to lie for him? She always thought the worst of Madeline. Would she believe that Madeline was lying to protect Georgie and frame *him*? It was, David realized, his only chance.

Police Chief Tanner stood in Mira Carson's living room and accused David McKay of murder on the say-so of an eccentric old busybody and her handyman.

This morning, Tanner had sat across the desk from the most unlikely pair of conspirators he ever saw—the tall, thin gray-haired woman who would strike terror into a hornet's heart, and the thick-set simpleton who probably wouldn't swat a hornet if it bit him twice. And the story they had told him was as bizarre as the Brothers Grimm. They had laid a stained knitted afghan on his desk that they tried to convince him had been soaked with the blood of Matthias Carson.

It was totally implausible, and yet he believed them. Believed every syllable. Because it all fit together, and that's what he had been looking for. He had felt it was David McKay, right down to his socks. Finally he had something to go on.

But now, as Tanner assessed McKay face-to-face in Mira Carson's living room, he was surprised the man wasn't fazed in the slightest by the police chief's accusation about McKay's actual whereabouts the day of Carson's murder.

In Tanner's experience, even an innocent man quivered at such a confrontation by the authorities. But McKay stood his ground and asked what evidence Tanner had to make such a statement. And when Tanner related what Madeline and Georgie had said, he shook his head in pity.

"Poor Madeline," McKay said. "She wants so to protect Georgie. He's the logical one, of course. Madeline was fixated on thinking that Matthias Carson killed her friend, Celia."

Tanner nodded in acknowledgment. "But Miss Abbott and Georgie both say you were at her house when Mr. Carson actually came there that day."

"I don't doubt it. Madeline . . . imagines . . . things, you know. Sees demons all over the place. And as for Georgie, well . . ." He lifted a hand in dismissal.

If Tanner had expected quaking protestations, or an earnest confession, he knew he wasn't going to get it.

"Where were you that day, Mr. McKay? You did tell me you were away from the boardinghouse."

"I was here, Chief Tanner. Right here. I came by mid-afternoon to return the books I had borrowed from Celia's library. Mrs. Carson invited me for a cup of coffee and we talked for a while, a couple of hours, actually, and by then it was snowing so hard, I left to drive back to town."

"And Mrs. Carson will verify that?"

"Mira?" he called, raising his voice slightly. The two men stood in silence until she came to the doorway.

"Yes? Oh, hello, Chief Tanner." She wore an apron over her protruding stomach and she was holding a towel to wipe her hands. "I'm sorry, I didn't hear you come in. I was in the kitchen." She smiled almost bashfully. "We let the staff go. We didn't really need them."

Tanner hardly had time to wonder at that when David spoke up.

"Mira, Chief Tanner has asked me where I was the afternoon Matt died. Would you tell him, please?"

Mira looked back and forth at them.

"David was here, at the house," she said timidly.

"You're certain of that?"

"She said so," McKay interjected. "Now, Chief, we would appreciate it if you finished your business and left."

Tanner was baffled. Why in God's name would she have lied for the man who killed her husband? Mira Carson had sounded like his own daughter the time she had told him and Nora that she didn't eat the cookies before dinner. "Rusty did it," Elinor had said timidly, blaming their Irish Setter. He liked to tease Elinor by calling her dog Rust Bucket. He *should* suspect that Mrs. Carson was in collusion with her lover in the murder of her husband. But not the way Madeline Abbott had told it. According to Her Nibs, Mira Carson was completely unaware of what happened. There was no reason for him to think otherwise, and nothing to do but leave.

"I can't believe it!" Madeline blurted as she faced Chief Tanner on her porch. He had come there directly from the interview. "I don't understand. What in the world would possess her to lie for him? Do you think he threatened her?"

"I don't think so. I would've picked that up." Tanner shook his head. "I think he convinced her it was Georgie who did it. And that you're protecting him. So she's going to protect McKay. And there's no way to charge him with anything when he has no apparent motive and an irrefutable alibi."

"*No motive?*" Madeline surprised both of them by slamming her fist on the table alongside the chair. "*Every* motive!"

"I agree," Tanner said to calm her. "But it isn't that easy. We're talking law here."

Madeline gritted her teeth and then took a deep breath and tried to speak slowly. "Yes, I know. But we have to do something."

Tanner ran his fingers through his thick graying brown hair and looked across the lake.

Madeline followed suit. The sun was directly overhead, she surmised, by the full orb that floated atop the still water.

"The only possibility to convict him is if Mrs. Carson changes her story."

"Tells the truth, you mean," Madeline amended. "Perhaps I could speak with her alone."

"That presents a problem. She now believes you were instrumental in covering up for Georgie in her husband's death. And McKay doesn't let her out of his sight."

Madeline rubbed her chin absently. "What if you could arrange to bring David to your office for questioning? Then I could see Mira. I'll tell her everything I told you. Could you do that?"

"I suppose," Tanner agreed. "I could keep him away from the house for at least an hour."

"Good." A small shiver of anticipation ran through her. "When?"

"Too late today," he said. "Tomorrow."

The following afternoon, Madeline stood on Mira's doorstep, knowing that, of everyone on earth, *she* was the last person Mira would expect to see. Or would want to.

"What are you doing here?" Mira did not even make a pretense of courtesy.

Madeline cleared her throat. "You once came to me to plead for your husband and I listened. Now I've come to you to plead for Georgie. You know Georgie. Surely you couldn't want him to be hurt. All I ask is that you listen."

Mira rubbed the sore spot on her lower back.

"How would Georgie be hurt by me?"

"Chief Tanner is about to take him into custody for murdering Matthias," Madeline lied. "Georgie did not kill your husband. I swear to you, he didn't."

"*I* didn't accuse him."

"Please let me in to explain."

"All right, come in. The baby's kicking and I need to sit down."

Mira walked flat-footed into the living room without looking behind her, as Madeline closed the door and followed.

Everything in the house had changed since Madeline had been there last. It seemed like such a long time ago. The rooms were completely redone and, she had to admit, elegant. The living room was repainted and papered in cream and pale green, with an Oriental carpet to match. The grandfather clock in the corner struck twice with a musical gong.

Mira gestured to a chair and Madeline sat down gingerly. The sofa was covered in pale green velvet, and the chairs in matching green and cream brocade. Ivory lace curtains fluttered slightly in the warm spring breeze, but the deep green taffeta valence and weighted end-panels did not move.

Madeline looked keenly at the young woman. She was really quite beautiful. Hadn't she ever noticed that before? And she was quite large with pregnancy except for her thin arms and face.

Madeline had struggled all night with the question of why Mira would protect her husband's murderer. She had tried to imagine the widow as a conspirator, a collaborator. But she couldn't, no matter how she cast it. She had tossed and turned on the matter, but Madeline finally saw the logic. The only possible answer was that Mira really had no idea David killed Matthias. And moreover, that Mira had been duped into believing that she, Madeline, was protecting the real killer, Georgie, by accusing David. Of all of them, Mira, despite her flagrant promiscuity, was the most innocent.

"What is it you wanted to tell me?" Mira asked, fidgeting for a more comfortable position.

Madeline realized that what she was about to do to the mother-to-be was going to upset her young life yet again. She stared at Mira, reluctant to begin. So she began at the beginning with the scent of almonds in Celia's medication, and ended with her last conversation with Chief Tanner. She left nothing out—her own guilt, Georgie's actions, David's complicity and murder.

Looking across at Mira, who sat with her eyes closed in pain, Madeline wanted to put an arm around the girl and comfort her. But she didn't. She contented herself with saying, "I swear that everything I have told you is true. I was obdurately wrong in trying to blame your husband for Celia's death. I set in motion a series of actions that have had terrible consequences and I will have to live with that for the rest of my life. But neither you nor Georgie should have to pay the penalty for my stiff-necked faults."

Mira sat perfectly still for the thirty minutes that Madeline Abbott took to explode her world. The only things she was aware of were the older woman's scratchy voice and her baby moving around inside of her. Then, as Madeline finished, and the clock struck the half-hour, Mira felt waves of panic. The baby stopped moving and it seemed like time stood still.

"You're not lying to me?" Mira finally whispered.

Madeline shook her head. "I swear on Celia's life."

Mira slumped and closed her eyes. David had told her Georgie killed Matt. Because Madeline had told Georgie he should have inherited Celia's estate. Mira hadn't known until yesterday that Georgie was Celia's half-brother—which David said was the motive. He made it seem so plausible that the Georgie she'd always thought of as timid and withdrawn *could* do such a thing.

And given that, and given Madeline's protection of Georgie, David had said, who better to throw suspicion on than himself? People would think he was the other man all along. It would not be too hard for anyone to believe that she and David had been having an affair before Matt died.

"You see," David had argued, "Madeline could turn everything around to make it look bad for both of us. She will say we conspired together."

What he needed was for Mira to say he was with her, so he couldn't possibly have been the killer. Because he'd just been driving to the bookstore in North Conway that day when it began to snow and he turned back, so no one else saw him. He needed her for his alibi, and she believed him.

Twice, Madeline Abbott had accused the men in Mira's life of murder. She was wrong the first time, about Matt. Was she wrong this time? Mira felt completely out of her depth. She didn't know anything. She was not capable of making these decisions. Yet she had to make a decision now. Madeline's story sounded true. But so did David's.

Madeline was saying, " . . . neither you nor Georgie should have to pay the penalty for my stiff-necked faults."

"Penalty? Me? What penalty would I pay?"

"David hated Matthias. What kind of father will he make to Matthias's child?"

As though she had not had enough fateful news to contemplate, this new insinuation struck her like a bullet. This was the one thing she feared most. It was the one thing that had made her wait before agreeing to David's proposal. The thing that was the voice in her head saying, *Beware*. It was the thing in her that knew, deep down, that David was not to be trusted, not with her baby.

She opened her eyes, saying in a dazed voice, "What do you want me to do?"

"Just tell the truth. Nothing more," Madeline said earnestly. "David is with Chief Tanner right now. Call the chief and tell him that David really wasn't here with you that day."

"But—"

"We both know he wasn't," Madeline interrupted. "But you are the only one who can prove it. Just tell the truth."

Mira looked away. How could David have done this? How gullible she was. All those times she thought how uncomplicated and forthright he was, all deceptions?

"Mira—ask yourself why David waited till now to tell you the real facts around Georgie's birth."

If David could hide the truth from her about Georgie being the half-brother until now, Mira realized, he might be capable of anything.

"All you have to do," Madeline repeated, "is pick up the phone and call Chief Tanner. Just tell the truth, Mira."

The truth was that David had been jealous of Matt from the beginning. She knew that. He'd wanted her and he'd probably wanted the money, too. As for Georgie, the money would have meant nothing to him. Georgie kill for money? No, of course not.

But how could she destroy David? She loved him.

Was that the truth? Or was it simply that she didn't want to be alone, with nobody to care for her, to love her. That what she wanted most was a father to her child.

Just then, the baby began kicking again, as if to say: "Yours and *Matthias's* child."

How could she let the man who killed her baby's father raise his child? Not even if he were the best husband in the world, not even if he treated the baby as his own. Nor could she ever face her child and confess she had done the unthinkable by marrying his father's murderer.

As her hand went to her stomach, Madeline reached over and took the other one. Mira would have imagined the old woman's hand would be rough and unyielding, but it was soft and warm. She must go to bed with Vaseline and gloves on, Mira imagined, to have such soft hands.

"I will do whatever I can to help you through this, Mira."

Her eyes welled up with tears. Madeline's voice was compassionate, the way Celia's had been, and her hand was soft and warm, and Mira believed her. She tightened her hold on Madeline's hand and nodded.

As David sat impatiently in Chief Tanner's office, repeating his whereabouts on the day Carson died, the phone rang. Tanner answered and then simply listened. David waited for the call to be finished. The chief did not converse with the person on the other end, but merely voiced "Um hmm" at intervals. Then, finally, he said, "Thank you very much," and hung up.

"Where were we?" Tanner addressed him.

"I was just telling you for the third time," David said in exasperation, "my entire whereabouts that entire day."

"Oh, yes." The chief leaned back in his swivel chair and it squeaked with the movement. "You know what I can't figure out?"

"No, what?" David grunted.

"What I can't figure out is: If Carson never went to Madeline Abbott's house, and Georgie is the murderer, we have a time problem. You see, Carson left his own home at two o'clock. But Chester Weekes passed him heading up the road at four o'clock. What happened to the intervening time?"

"How would I know?"

"On the other hand, if we believe Miss Abbott, we have no problem with the missing time, we have you as the culprit, and everything falls into place."

"Except," David said through clenched teeth, "that I wasn't at Madeline's house. I was with Mira."

"So you say."

"So *she* says."

Tanner's swivel chair squeaked again. "I'm afraid not."

David felt a jolt in the pit of his stomach. "You're afraid not, what?"

"I'm afraid Mrs. Carson has just recanted. That was her on the phone."

David said nothing, unable to trust his voice.

Tanner went on, "She says you asked her to alibi you, so she did. But the fact is, she never saw you that day, or any other day until months later."

"She said that?"

Tanner nodded.

He wanted to cry out in unfathomable pain from the pit of his stomach, but no sound emerged.

Why had she turned on him? What could have happened?

Everything had been going so well. How could this be? He had come so close to fulfillment. It had all been so perfect after his year of agony. What had he done that was so terrible? He'd merely dispatched an already dying man. A man who had corrupted the woman he loved, a man who poisoned his dearest friend, a man who would have led the state, perhaps the nation, to ruin.

How could she betray me, my Maria?

No sound was equal to the absolute despair of his life. He sat mute.

Georgie helped Madeline out of the car when she returned home at day's end. She immediately told him what had transpired.

"Chief Tanner says Mr. McKay will be convicted and will go to prison for his crime, but you are blameless for what happened to Mr. Carson, Georgie. You were simply defending me. As for me, he thought there would probably be no charges." She paused, not feeling it necessary to say that she would do lifelong penance inside her own prison for her transgressions.

"We will have to help Mira now," she concluded. "I will visit every day and knit her baby clothes and we can bring her dinners and later, if she permits, we will help her with the baby."

She'd made a terrible mess of Celia's plans and she had much to atone for. *I will try to make this up to her. Celia would have wanted that,* she thought.

As they began walking up to the house, Madeline's glance fell on the statue of Princess Muskataqua. Lit golden by the setting sun, her face looked, Madeline thought, almost beatific.

"I think she should go back where she belongs now. What do you think, Georgie?"

Georgie nodded in eager agreement. She was relieved that he seemed more like his old self again.

They walked a little farther toward the house when Georgie volunteered cheerfully, "I could do some baking if you want."

Madeline stopped, looked at him, and could almost visualize the burden lifted from his spirit. Although she did not feel herself unburdened, she nodded to encourage him. Thoughts of Mira occupied her.

"Would you like me to make tarts?"

"That would be fine."

"I'll have them by suppertime if I start now."

She nodded and they continued toward the house. Then Madeline glanced back to Celia's house and stopped.

"Suddenly, Georgie, I seem to feel so very old. I never really accepted that before. But then I've never felt so alone before."

"You *are* old, Miz Abbott, that's a fact." Georgie offered his arm. "But you're not alone. On Sunday, I'll go back to services. Maybe you would want to come?"

Madeline smiled at him kindly. "Thank you, Georgie, I almost wish I could. But I am irredeemable. No, I am not meant for religion. When the time comes, Georgie, I shall rely on your intercession."

She took his arm as they continued up to the house. "Who knows, Georgie? Perhaps you're here to feed my soul as well as my stomach."

"*Both* be a humbling experience, Miz Abbott," Georgie replied.